KILLER
ON THE FENS

A gripping crime thriller with a huge twist

JOY ELLIS

Detective Nikki Galena Book 4

Revised edition 2024
Joffe Books, London
www.joffebooks.com

First published in Great Britain in 2016

This paperback edition was first published
in Great Britain in 2024

Cover art by Nick Castle

ISBN: 978-1-83526-605-2

This book is dedicated to Lynne Nicholson who delivered a swift wake-up call at exactly the right time. Thank you, Lynne, on behalf of myself and Nikki Galena.

CHAPTER ONE

Detective Inspector Nikki Galena's face was a mask of concentration as she accelerated her powerful car along the dangerous fenland lanes. Long shadows were forming as the evening drew in, and she was grateful that she'd actually paid attention during her advanced driving course.

This was the second time in a week that she had received a call from the nursing home about her father's failing health. 'Wicked bloody disease!' Nikki cursed as she eased the car around a deceptively sharp bend. The Alzheimer's had stolen most of his once astute brain years ago, but now he was in what the home called 'end stage,' and although she had been told this could go on for a long time, her gut feeling said otherwise.

As soon as she saw the smart, painted sign for the Glenfield Nursing Home, Nikki wondered what she would find when she got there. There had been something in the voice of the specialist nurse who had phoned her. Nothing was said, but she had detected an added anxiety in the tone and had begun to prepare herself.

All her visits to her father were harrowing. The mere fact that he didn't know her was bad enough, but when she remembered what a strong man he had been, it broke her heart. The airman, a fighter pilot who had flown Harrier jump jets in the Falklands War, now lay in bed or roamed the hallways of the home, with the memory circuits of his brain crashing and burning out.

Nikki pulled into a parking space and turned off the engine. His health wasn't the only thing that was worrying her. Recently she had been convinced that there was something he desperately wanted to tell her. Sadly it seemed that he had left it too long, and now she might never know what it was, other than that it concerned someone called Eve. In one scarily lucid moment, he had grabbed her wrist and begged her to "Find Eve!" For a second or two his eyes had cleared and shone with a frightening intensity. "For pity's sake, Nikki, you're a bloody detective! Find Eve!"

But what could Nikki say to him? She didn't know anyone by that name.

She locked the car and hurried up to the main doors, where to her concern she saw Molly Crane, her father's personal nurse, running towards her.

'DI Galena! Thank God you got here so quickly.' The nurse's face was etched with worry. 'The situation has altered since we rang you.' She turned and rushed Nikki towards the lift. 'I didn't ring again as I knew you'd be driving.'

'What's happened?' asked Nikki, not really wanting to know the answer.

'He's had a seizure.' Molly stabbed her finger on the button and the lift door sighed open.

'Were you with him?' asked Nikki, desperate to know that her dad had not been alone or frightened.

'Oh yes. I haven't left him for a minute. I was just checking his medication and, without any warning, he had a catastrophic reaction.' Molly Crane shook her head. 'It's not something we expect to see in the late stages, but nevertheless it happened.'

The lift juddered to a halt and, as they hurried out, the nurse explained what she meant. 'It's a moment of intense emotional pain. We think it's caused by a flash of realisation, of true awareness of their plight, and it triggers extreme

2

distress. It usually ends in the patient lashing out, either physically or verbally.' She looked at Nikki. 'Your father knocked over his bedside table and fought to get out of bed. By the time I raised the alarm, he had collapsed. The doctor is with him now and there's an ambulance on its way.'

Minutes later, Nikki watched dumbly as the doctor checked her father's vital signs, then lifted the lids and stared into his unfocussed eyes. She didn't have to ask how he was doing. The expression on the doctor's face said it all.

'He's not going to pull through this time, is he?' Nikki was no fool. She had spent more time than she would have liked in and around hospitals, and knew a lot about illness. 'I'm guessing he's had a cerebral haemorrhage?'

'Massive, I'd say, and he's weakening.'

Nikki looked at the man and whispered, 'Then please just let him go. He's been in hell for years. Don't try to bring him back now he has the chance of freedom.'

The doctor hesitated, then looked down at his patient. After a moment he said, 'I agree. He wouldn't survive the trip to hospital. We'll just make him as comfortable as possible.'

Molly went out of the room and Nikki could hear her speaking to someone. Then she returned, closed the door and softly said, 'I've cancelled the ambulance.'

Nikki took her father's hand and smiled at him, and suddenly the frail husk of a human being became her dad again, her lovely father, Wing Commander Frank Reed.

'Nikki . . .' Molly's hand was on her arm, and Nikki was vaguely aware that the nurse had never called her by her first name before. 'His breathing's changed.'

'Cheyne-Stokes respiration,' said the doctor solemnly. 'His heart is failing.'

For one moment, Nikki thought he would stop the awful irregular breathing and wake up, but instead the eyes flickered for a moment, then he let out a long sigh. She looked up at Molly, and saw a strange expression pass across the nurse's face. She'd heard it too. There had been one word hidden deep in that sigh.

3

Eve.

The doctor gently touched his neck. 'He's gone.'

Nikki didn't move. Then her mind began to race. There had been times when she had prayed for him to die. It hadn't been a selfish prayer, she just knew what an independent and proud man he was, and how having strangers attending to his every need would have utterly destroyed what was left of him. And now he had gone. Nikki felt terrible guilt at the relief that was flooding through her. And she also felt an irrational anger, because he had left her with an unanswered question, a stranger's name in his dying breath.

Then the anger disappeared as she looked at her father's ashen face. She remembered the good times, the fun they had had when she was a child, and the unconditional love that he had always given her.

'Bye, Dad.' She leaned across and kissed his forehead. 'And if it helps, I will find her for you. Somehow I will find Eve. I promise.'

CHAPTER TWO

The young man knew the treacherous marsh paths better than most. Especially at night.

He'd spent all his early years around Castor Fen and Flaxton Mere, but this evening was going to be the last time that he would tramp those boggy, uneven tracks.

As he loped along, his scrawny body casting a stick-thin shadow in the moonlight, he decided that it had all been worth it. All the lies, the deceit, the begging, borrowing and mainly stealing. All worth it. By tomorrow morning, he would be gone from here, and for the first time in his life, he would have some money in his pocket, some *real* money.

Prior to tonight, his whole existence had been one shitty mess, and although his problems were not quite over, he could at last allow himself a little smile. He was nearly there.

The moonlight made the desolate landscape appear weird and dreamlike. It reflected on dark pools of brackish water, making them look as wholesome as waste engine oil.

Finally he came to a narrow path that led away from the sea-bank; the long, high flood defence that formed a barrier between the salt-marsh and solid ground. He looked up and saw the strange, imposing silhouette of the old deserted air-field, RAF Flaxton Mere.

As he got closer, he could feel a nervousness steal over him. He'd been coming here for months, but it still gave him the creeps. Dark and brooding, the old buildings had been left to rot after World War II, but incredibly they had survived. Right now one of them was doing a great job providing a pretty clever hiding place for his big secret.

The clusters of shrubby trees were getting thicker and he felt more relaxed as he blended into the shadowy thickets. He'd never yet met anyone out here, but there had been nights when he had been certain that he wasn't alone. And it wasn't anything to do with Flaxton Mere's scary reputation, although it didn't help growing up with a grandmother who firmly believed in ghosts and ghouls.

He stopped in his tracks as a heavy curtain of night clouds blocked the moon. Then a shaft of moonlight escaped from the cloud, and like a spotlight to centre stage, he saw the rotting wooden door of the old storehouse. He moved stealthily across the stretch of open ground in front of the building, and slipped inside.

It took him just a few minutes to retrieve his prize, and with a wider smile, he pushed the large package into his rucksack and hurried back outside. Now all he had to do was lie low until morning, and not be late for his two prearranged meetings. He exhaled stale breath. After that, he would be gone, like the proverbial thief in the night.

He retraced his footsteps towards the perimeter fence of the airfield, then made his way towards one of several old concrete pillboxes that surrounded the place.

With one last look around, he ducked down and went inside.

As accommodation went, this would do very nicely for a night. Even the smell was not too bad. His own bedsit had smelt a lot worse after he'd had a skinful. Kicking some rubble and other rubbish to one side, he pulled a faded and tatty sleeping bag from his holdall and laid it on the floor. He crawled in, carefully taking the package with him, and felt almost comfortable.

He didn't expect to sleep. He didn't want to. He didn't dare. He just wanted to feel relatively safe. If he overslept and missed his meetings, then the consequences didn't bear thinking about. And not only for him, but his old gran too.

He curled up in a ball and congratulated himself. This place had been a stroke of bloody genius. No one ever came here. The locals, a rustic group of inbreds as far as he was concerned, never set foot on this desolate strip of land. According to them, it was the nerve centre of every ghostly and diabolical happening that folklore could come up with. He giggled at their stupidity. He'd lived in the town for long enough now to distance himself from his own rural background, and he loved his gran enough to forgive her anything, including her crackpot beliefs.

He shifted around and tried to find a flatter area to lie on.

No, there was nothing to fear out here, except perhaps him, and he was certainly not very nice to know.

A sound outside suddenly made him sit up. It was an odd noise. It was recognisable alright, yet surely it could not be!

With a grunt of concern, he scrambled out of the sleeping bag, stuffed his precious parcel into the loose waistband of his trousers, crouched down and hurried outside.

He searched the sky for the source of the noise. It was definitely a plane. The heavens were almost cloud-free and the moon much lower than it had been. He could see nothing, but the distinctive roar of an engine was getting louder.

In desperation, he clambered up onto the roof of the pillbox and stared around. It was not one of the jet fighters that, day and night, crashed through the Lincolnshire skies, and it sounded too powerful to be a light aircraft. Jesus! It was some kind of heavy-engined military plane and, shit, it was in trouble! The steady roar was suddenly irregular. A heart-stopping silence, then a stuttering choking as the engines struggled to cut in again.

He spun around full-circle on the concrete roof, and his heart jumped when he remembered the state of the runways.

Cracked, broken, non-existent in places. A death trap for anyone who thought they could bring a crippled plane down there.

The deafening noise was all around him, and for the second time that night, he sweated with fear. The terrible cacophony stopped. He heard the sound of a rushing wind, then only silence.

He stood, some seven or eight feet up in the air, like a great, stone jack-in-the-box. Then from a little way away, he heard a dull, earth-jarring thump, and he caught sight of flames flickering close to the remains of the old control tower.

His hand flew to his mouth and adrenalin pumped through him.

Everything that was important to him: the exchange, the pay-off, the threat to his gran, and the promised release from the stifling shithole that he had landed in, all screamed at him to run. But somewhere deep inside, in that under-used part of him that constituted his soul, he knew he had to go to the accident site. He wanted to help.

But if there was ever going to be a time to choose, he never found out. The next sound sent him clambering and falling from the pillbox, and running away with his hands clasped tightly to his ears and his addled mind almost at breaking point.

He was surrounded by the horrors of an air raid. The wailing sirens, urgent shouts and screaming, and all the horrible sounds of suffering that went with it. He didn't understand, and he wasn't waiting around for an explanation. He just ran.

A short way ahead he could dimly make out a gap in the wire. Not lessening his speed, he turned and headed for it, then caught his foot in a snare of barbed wire and pitched forward into a pile of rubble. Pain coursing through his lacerated ankle, and still struggling to find his footing, he was suddenly aware that loose rocks and small stones were sliding away from under his worn and slippery-soled sneakers. Then his gut turned over, as he found himself hurtling downwards, cracking his elbows, knees and head against solid stone.

Before his body crashed into the floor of the old ventilation shaft, he was vaguely aware that the only scream he could now hear was his own.

CHAPTER THREE

Nikki stared at Superintendent Greg Woodhall, and wondered how to tell him that she had no intention of taking the compassionate leave that he was offering her. The older man's face was full of sympathy, but Nikki knew that time to herself was the last thing she needed. Naturally there were the funeral arrangements to make, but her father had been typical old-school RAF, ordered and methodical. The family solicitor had already assured her that he had "put his house in order" the moment the Alzheimer's had reared its ugly head.

'I'm owed some time off anyway. I'll do what I have to do, but I *really* need to keep working, sir.'

Greg peered over his glasses at her and nodded. 'I've known you since you were a probationer, Nikki, so I expected that. But don't forget, it's a difficult time, and the grieving process takes everyone differently. When everything is arranged, by all means continue to work, but remember, if you need to take some time out, you can.'

'Funny thing is I don't actually *feel* anything right now — well, not in the same way I did when Hannah died.' Memories of her daughter flooded round her and Nikki sat back in her chair and sighed. 'Maybe it's this job. From the moment we join up, we learn to deal with death, don't we?'

'In a hundred different guises,' added the superintendent grimly. He smiled sadly at her. 'And in a way, because of his illness, your father died some time ago, didn't he? You've probably been grieving his loss for months, maybe years. Don't be too hard on yourself, Nikki. There's no rule book with sections and sub-sections that defines the exact method for grieving.'

'That's true, I guess,' said Nikki. 'It's just that when you spend years hardening yourself to death, you are always scared that you'll take it a step too far, and one day you'll wake up having lost the ability to feel anything at all.'

Greg snorted, then his smile widened. 'You'll never do that! You can be the hard-arsed Iron Lady of Greenborough nick when you need to be, but I promise you that you'll never lose the warmth in your heart.'

'That's good to hear.' Nikki straightened up. 'So, if it's alright with you, sir, and considering the fact that my sergeant has taken a few days' leave himself, I'll keep things ticking over here, and attend to my personal arrangements in tandem.'

Greg shrugged. 'I wouldn't say I'm exactly happy about it, but you do whatever you need to. Just don't burn out. I'm sure Joseph would come back in and cover for you under the circumstances.'

'That's exactly what I don't want, sir,' stated Nikki. 'Joseph has his daughter Tamsin staying with him. No way am I going to ruin that long-awaited reunion!'

Greg looked at her with interest. 'Rick Bainbridge told me something about that before he retired. The girl went with the mother when Joseph's marriage failed, isn't that it?'

Nikki nodded. 'That's right. This visit is a very big thing for Joseph.' Nikki knew more than anyone else about DS Joseph Easter's private life. Both she and Joseph had always been loners, private people with murky histories and secrets they had never shared. That was until they came together as an unwilling team in the Fenland Constabulary's Greenborough CID and found that, although they were total opposites, they shared a lot of common ground.

And one area was their daughters. She'd had Hannah, her only child, a beautiful teenager who'd died eighteen months ago. Joseph's girl, Tamsin, was intelligent and sparky, but lived halfway around the world, and had spent her early life hating him.

Nikki thought carefully about that. Actually Tamsin hated the man that Joseph used to be, a career soldier, a special services operative, highly skilled and trained to kill. But Nikki knew that man no longer existed, and she prayed that Tamsin would now see her father as he really was, a caring, brave and loyal police officer. A man who had never once given up on getting his daughter back.

'Does Joseph know about your father's death?' asked the superintendent.

'Yes, I rang him the night before last, sir, and it was my day off yesterday so he came over and we had a long heart-to-heart. He offered to help, but I'd already registered the death and seen the solicitor. Things are very straightforward. The family home is already in my name and due to the nature of his illness, I hold power of attorney.' She shrugged and threw her boss a weak smile. 'Plus, our solicitor said that my father left very clear instructions as to what he wants for the funeral, and it's exactly what I would have expected from him. He wanted to be cremated, very quiet, no fuss, no flowers, Elgar's *Nimrod* and donations to the Alzheimer's Society.'

'When will the funeral take place?'

'Around nine or ten days' time I think, sir. Some of the relatives are getting on a bit and they have travel arrangements to make, so I'm giving them as long as I can.'

She was about to tell the superintendent that she didn't want the whole station knowing about her father, when a uniformed officer knocked sharply on the door.

'Sorry to interrupt, but if it's convenient the duty sergeant needs you downstairs, ma'am.'

Greg raised his eyebrows and gave her a wry smile. 'Go. Rick also warned me that this station cannot function without your presence at every single incident.'

Nikki hurried after the man and, as they entered the front office, she found the place in uproar.

'WPC Collins! Go get PC Farrow, now!'

Nikki watched as the uniformed constable ran from the room. 'What the hell is going on, Sarge?'

'Kid down a well. Way out on Flaxton Mere marsh. Fire service has got him out and he's in Greenborough ITU.'

'And that's a reason for everyone to leap around like lunatics?'

'There's more to it than a simple "pussy down a well." Trumpton thinks we might like to take a look at him.'

Nikki noticed that the uniformed sergeant was smirking slightly.

'Oh, did I forget to mention the very large bag of white stuff and assorted other drugs stuffed down his trousers?' He raised his eyebrows innocently.

'Really! Now that is interesting.' She paused. 'Why didn't we get the shout straightaway? Why now, when the kid is already in hospital?'

The sergeant shrugged. 'The anonymous caller who reported it only asked for an ambulance. The paramedics radioed for the fire service to bring out their emergency gear for rescuing fallen climbers. We got missed out somewhere along the line. Oh, the injured man is touch and go by the way.'

'Do we know who he is?' Nikki asked.

'Not yet, and forgive me for cutting this short, but if I don't get Yvonne and Niall down to that hospital, someone else might get their sticky mitts on that bag of junk!'

'Too right,' said Nikki. 'But I'll attend. Tell them to meet me there.'

'I hoped you'd say that, ma'am.'

'No problem. I'm on it,' Nikki threw back as she hurried from the office.

* * *

She met the crew in the hospital foyer, and Nikki smiled at them as they hurried towards her.

WPC Yvonne Collins was one of the keystones on which Greenborough police station was built. She had a lot of years under her belt, an encyclopaedic knowledge of the lowlife of the fenland town, and a deep love of policing. She took no crap from anyone, villains and coppers alike, and although she could recite Butterworth's Police Law verbatim, she knew how to apply compassion and common sense to its complex legalities. In short, she was Nikki's kind of police officer. She glanced across to Yvonne's crew-mate, PC Niall Farrow. He, too, fitted the criteria, but in a very different way. Niall was young, good-looking and full of enthusiasm. He was bursting with old-fashioned zeal to catch the bad guys and save the world.

'Ah, the Old Bill has made it at last! Better late than never, guys.' A fireman, leaning casually against the side of a vending machine, threw them a smug smile.

'Oh great!' muttered Yvonne as they hurried down the corridor. 'Of all the crews that could have got this shout, it had to be Dice.'

Nikki grunted an agreement, then answered the fireman nicknamed Dice. 'Sorry. But as no one bothered to call us, and my crystal ball being in for a service, you know how it is.' She threw up her hands in mock desperation. 'You've got something for us?'

The big man flopped into a waiting-area chair, causing it to creak loudly. Nikki watched, half hoping that it would give way, but sadly it stayed firm beneath the broad buttocks. 'Sure have. And I think you may have an interesting little case here, DI Galena.'

The police officers grumbled, but the fireman continued undeterred. 'A lone man, about twenty plus years of age, out in the middle of nowhere, smashed out of his brains, with nothing on him other than a fortune in stuff?' He raised his eyebrows. 'Nice one, huh?'

Nikki bridled. Dice was famous for buttonholing police officers and bombarding them with his Sherlockian theories.

He might be a great firefighter, but he was a rubbish detective and most police officers avoided him like the plague.

'Maybe.' Her reply was terse. 'Now, hand it over!'

Dice reluctantly passed her the bag. 'Quite a haul! Apart from the heroin and the coke, there are bennies, dexies, poppers, E's, crystal meth, special K, and a whole load of stuff that I don't even recognise.' He leaned back, causing the chair to groan even more. 'Do you know what I think?'

'No, but *I* think you've just tampered with evidence, Dice.'

'All done properly, Inspector. We had to open the bag as the doc needed to know what the kid had taken.' The fireman held up a gloved hand. 'Now, as I was saying, I noted that although he was high as a kite when we got him out of that old ventilation shaft — oh, and that's what it was by the way, not a well as first reported, he wasn't a needle-man, because there were no tracks on his arms.'

'Thanks, Dice. It's great to know that your observational skills are working so well. But *we* need to see the doctor and I'm sure you've got a nice inferno somewhere to attend to.' Nikki gathered up Yvonne and Niall and they made a hurried exit.

They waited for about half an hour before the doctor who had admitted the unknown male could see them. Finally he turned up, looking bedraggled, tired and most un-doctor-like in scuffed trainers, a faded rugby top and equally faded jeans.

'I'm Dr Tim Bolton. Sorry to have kept you waiting.' He extended a hand and took them into the relatives' room. He was thin, lank-haired, sported a heavy five o'clock shadow and appeared to have existed without sleep for at least a month.

'What can you tell us about his injuries?' Nikki and Yvonne both had their notebooks open, while Niall remained standing by the door.

'He is suffering from exposure, hypothermia, a head injury, the extent of which we don't know although we doubt it is too serious, and a severely damaged leg. The leg is giving us more cause for concern than anything else. There is a possibility that he will lose it. *And* there is the tiny fact that he has taken an enormous quantity of drugs, which is why he hasn't regained consciousness. We know what he took, and it appears he was trying to kill the pain. Sadly there was no identification on him.'

Nikki frowned. 'Do you think he was stoned before he fell down the hole?'

'Doubtful. I think he was simply attempting his own form of analgesia, and if you saw the state of his leg, you'd know why.'

'How long do you think he'd been down there, Dr Bolton?'

'From the extent of the infection in the leg wound, and from his general condition, I'd say around two days.'

Yvonne looked up from her notes. 'What are his chances of recovery, doctor?'

The doctor puffed out his cheeks and shook his head. 'At a guess, seventy/thirty against. He's very weak. I reckon another hour underground and the fire crew would have brought up a dead body.'

'Has he been conscious at all?'

'For a while, in resus he was mumbling gibberish, but then he took a dive. They lost him for a few seconds but the crash team got him back.'

'Would we be able to take a look at him?' Yvonne asked hopefully.

'Certainly. Anything else I can help you with?'

Nikki frowned. 'You said he was mumbling. Anything coherent?'

'It sounded like he needed to be somewhere, somewhere important. We think he was saying, *"Must get there."* Then shortly afterwards, he crashed.'

'Does he have any distinguishing marks?' Yvonne asked. 'Tattoos? Scars?'

'Oh yes, a tiny tattoo on his left forearm. Nothing professional and it's well faded. A schoolkid thing with a blade and some ink probably.'

'What is it?'

The doctor shrugged. 'Hard to say. An amateur attempt at a dagger, maybe.'

Nikki added that to her notes. 'That will help.' She stood up. 'One last thing, was there anything to suggest that the fall was not accidental?'

'All I can say is that his injuries seemed to be consistent with a steep fall onto a solid surface. I saw nothing to make me believe it was anything other than an accident, but please, that's just my opinion, not a full medical assessment.'

'Don't worry, that's all I was asking for. Thanks for your time, Doctor.'

* * *

Nikki, Yvonne and Niall waited outside ITU until a nurse beckoned them in.

The sounds, the smells and the high-octane atmosphere in the intensive care unit were all too familiar to Nikki. She recognised perhaps sixty per cent of the staff and, as their work allowed, they all acknowledged her with either a wave or a word of greeting. Between them, they had kept her daughter alive for three years. And even though they had eventually lost her, she remained forever grateful for their efforts. Where there was life, there was hope, and until the very end, Nikki had never given up on a miracle for Hannah.

Nikki tried not to look around at the other patients, at their injuries or their distress, and instead stared down at the injured young man. His features were narrow, pointed, weasel-like, with bad skin and stained teeth, but he was no one that she recognised. 'Either of you know him?' she asked.

'Nope,' said Niall definitely, but Yvonne stared thoughtfully at the thin, pale face.

'I've never arrested him, that's for sure, but there's something about him that's familiar. I've certainly seen him around Greenborough.'

'There's this.' His nurse lifted the unconscious man's arm and pointed to the faded bluish tattoo.

'Prison tat?' asked Niall.

'No, the doc's right, it's kid's stuff. If he were older, I'd say it was blatant misuse of school ink.' Nikki frowned. 'And any self-respecting parent would have hung him out to dry for doing that to himself.'

Yvonne grimaced. 'I'd suggest that this bloke's parents wouldn't know self-respect if it bit their arse. Everything about this young man spells breadline.'

'So, if he's not known to us and he's skint, how come he's got a damn great bag of drugs on him?' Niall countered.

'I think you just answered your own question, my friend,' said Yvonne. 'I reckon he's had it with being broke and is trying to rectify the situation.'

Nikki turned to the nurse. 'Jan? How long before he wakes up?'

The nurse shrugged. 'It's more a case of *will* he wake up, I'm afraid. He took enough analgesic to see him to the other side of the Styx.' She gently touched his face. 'Poor guy was in agony. He must have thought that help would never get to him.' She pointed to the leg, carefully suspended in a frame and raised off the bed. 'Worst compound fracture I've seen in years. Two shards of what was left of his shin bone had ripped clear through his skin. And apparently he was found lying in several inches of dirty water. He must have spent two nights down there like that. Doesn't bear thinking about.'

'Can't exactly blame him for sampling his wares then, can you?' said Niall grimly.

'No.' Nikki exhaled. 'He may be a villain of one sort or another, but no one deserves that. Well, there's nothing more we can do here, but I'd like one of you to remain with him in case he wakes.'

'I'll stay, ma'am,' Yvonne offered. 'I certainly can't put a name to him right now, but maybe it will come back to me.'

Nikki nodded. 'Okay then, Niall, you come with me. We'd better turn this rather valuable packet in at the station, then get ourselves out to the spot where he was found.' She turned to Yvonne. 'Ring me direct if he says anything.'

'Wilco, ma'am.'

Nikki took a last look around the busy ward, then left the injured young man to the mercy of the machines, respirators and fluid-filled tubes that snaked around his corpse-like body.

* * *

As they drove from the hospital, Nikki suddenly had a picture in her head of a woman called Stephanie Taylor. She had been haunting the station for days now, asking for help in finding her missing brother, Anson. The problem was that Anson was not someone the police were particularly interested in finding. He was a twenty-three-year-old male, in good health, both physically and mentally, and could by no stretch of the imagination be referred to as vulnerable. And although they had never pinned anything on him, they were pretty certain that Anson was an up-and-coming drug dealer. The fact that he was apparently missing was, in their book, very good news. The best the police could offer Stephanie Taylor was the number for the Missing Person's Bureau.

Nikki tried to recall what Anson Taylor had looked like, but the only dealings she had ever had with him had been years ago when he was a spotty, gobby little kid, and she knew all too well that drugs could change a person, making them unrecognisable.

As soon as they were back at base, she'd ring Stephanie Taylor. She didn't think it was Anson, but the mystery man *had* been in possession of a large quantity of drugs, which would point to dealing, so there was a chance that they had inadvertently found her missing brother.

Nikki slowed down as a traffic light changed to red. 'Niall, where exactly did they say the ventilation shaft was?'

'Right out on the perimeters of the old World War II airfield at Flaxton Mere, ma'am. Quite close to the sea-bank and the marshes, I suspect.'

'You sound like you know the area.'

Niall tilted his head to one side. 'I guess I do. When I was a kid my dad and I used to bring his metal detector out here, and we'd walk around the old airfield looking for spent shell cases and bits of shrapnel.' He grinned at her. 'I found a WWII medal once, all battered. I decided that it had belonged to a fighter ace that had been blown out of the skies over the Mere. Great stuff!'

'And do you still read the *Eagle*?'

'I probably would if they still printed it, ma'am. As it is I have to make do with *X-men*.' Niall sighed a little wistfully. 'I really loved Dan Dare.'

'Why doesn't that surprise me?' Nikki smiled at the young policeman and accelerated away from the junction and back towards the station. As she drove, her thoughts went to what had happened. What the hell had a drug dealer been doing in such an out-of-the-way spot? It was miles from anywhere. She'd been out to Flaxton Mere herself as a young mum, taking little Hannah for picnics on the sea-bank. She recalled the strange place with a mixture of emotions. Feelings of melancholy, because it was a remote and lonely part of the fen, and exhilaration brought about by the huge skies and the unending vista of wetlands and silver water.

Nikki suddenly braked, then swung the car round. 'Sod getting the drugs back to base, they are safe enough with us. We're half way to the fen already, and there's no time like the present. Radio control and tell them what we're doing. We'll go renew your acquaintanceship with that desolate dump that was once RAF Flaxton Mere right now.' She grinned at him. 'You never know, you might find another medal.'

* * *

As it turned out, there was nothing to see, just a deep hole in the ground with some blue and white cordoning tape fixed around it.

A mud-splattered police car sat silently at the end of the track that led to the sea-bank, and two bored-looking uniformed officers stood close to the shaft, to protect the scene and make sure that no other poor sod fell down it. Not that anyone would, because no one in their right mind would go there in the first place.

'I'd forgotten just what a desolate bog this part of the fen is.' Nikki looked out over the dreary marshland. 'There are places along this stretch where you never hear a bird sing. Something to do with the air currents, they kind of swallow up sound. It can be quite disturbing if you happen to be out here alone.'

Niall kicked at some loose shingle and watched as it splashed into a deep puddle. 'It's a different world, isn't it, ma'am? Really weird.' He grimaced. 'And so are the locals. Half of them belong in the Middle Ages. They thrive on superstition.' He looked around. 'And who can blame them? Look at this place!'

'I used to think it was beautiful, all mysterious and otherworldly.' Nikki drew in a deep breath. 'Now, I'm not sure. Apart from the silent thing, the marsh along this stretch of the coast has always had a bad reputation.' She stared away from the lagoons of dark water and across to where the gloomy hulk of the old deserted control tower sat brooding over the bleak landscape. Even on a bright sunny day, the ruined building had a sinister feel to it. 'I'm amazed that so many of the old structures are still standing. I would have thought most of the old WWII watch offices had been demolished.'

'You're right, but this place is in pretty good nick, isn't it?' He looked around, eyes narrowed in the sunlight. 'There are still engine sheds and ammunition stores. Yvonne was telling me that the owner of Flaxton Mere has laid on water and electricity to some of the old hangars and he lets them out to small traders as business units.'

'For small, read dodgy,' added Nikki. 'No one with a reputable business would operate from a cesspit like this.' She frowned. 'Maybe we should pay them an unannounced visit. I'm willing to bet there won't be a legit man among them.'

'Yvonne would *really* like that, ma'am. She's been on about it for months, but as there have been no actual complaints about the place, the sergeant said it would be a waste of resources.'

'We'll see about that, shall we? Do you know who the owner is, Niall?'

'As far as I can recall, it's a bloke by the name of Shine. Karl Shine. He bought it from the military a few years ago.'

'With what intention?'

'Don't rightly know, ma'am, but I know a woman who will.' He grinned. 'I suggest you consult the oracle WPC Collins. If she knows as much as she usually does about the locals, then she'll tell you everything about Shine, from his taste in wine to his star sign.'

'I'll do that, although I'm not sure I care too much about his position in the zodiac. And right now, I see little point in hanging around here.' Nikki shook her head. 'What the hell was a guy, loaded with thousands of pounds' worth of drugs, doing out here in this wilderness?'

'Sorry, ma'am.' Niall shrugged. 'Ask me one on sport.'

CHAPTER FOUR

'What is it with you?' The desk sergeant looked at DI Joseph Easter and threw his hands in the air. 'If I got a chance to get out of here, I'd stay out. Aren't you off duty for a few days?'

Joseph grinned. 'I am, but my daughter has discovered the Greenborough shopping centre, so I thought I'd just check in, see if anything exciting is happening.'

The sergeant pointed to the door. 'Ask your boss.'

'Ma'am?' Joseph stepped forward as Nikki and Niall hurried into the foyer.

'Go home! You're on leave!' called out Nikki.

'And so are you, or you should be,' returned Joseph, so that only she could hear. 'Hell, Nikki, you've got a funeral to organise.' He looked at her with concern in his eyes. 'So what is so important that you are rushing around like a mad thing?'

'Nothing for you to worry about. You have a daughter and several years to catch up on. So go.'

He knew that, despite her dismissive tone, she was glad he was there. 'Tamsin's meeting me here when she's finished in town.' Joseph's face creased into a frown. 'So while I wait, tell me what's going on.'

Nikki gave him a brief rundown, and held up the fat bag of assorted drugs.

Joseph drew in a breath. 'Oh my! I don't think he'll get away with "for personal use only" as an excuse, do you? And you think the injured man is that missing dealer, Anson Taylor?'

'My gut says no, but I'm about to ring his sister and get her to take a look at him.' Nikki went into her office, found the woman's number and punched it into the phone.

'Are we still on for dinner at your place?' she asked as she waited for a reply.

'All prepared, and Tamsin's really looking forward to seeing you again. I think she's quite excited about tonight.'

'Really?' Nikki grinned suspiciously. 'Dinner with two old-fogey coppers? Are you sure about that?' Her smile faded as she turned her attention to the phone. 'Stephanie Taylor? Ah, it's DI Galena here, of Greenborough CID. I'm sorry to bother you, but I wonder if you might be able to help us?'

Joseph listened as Nikki explained what had happened, while keeping one eye on the office door for his daughter. He got the feeling that Tamsin had actually arranged to meet him here in order to "accidentally" bump into Niall Farrow again. Joseph knew that the two had kept in touch after getting thrown together in a dangerous situation a while back, and although Tamsin hotly denied it, Joseph smelt romance in the air. *And*, he had to admit that his daughter was really making an effort this time to heal the old wounds and the rift between them. It certainly wasn't plain sailing. In fact, for the last two days, from dawn to dusk, they had been tiptoeing around each other. The expression "walking on eggshells" had never sounded so right. But then this was a big thing. And Joseph knew that if he wanted to win back his daughter's love, he had to get it right this time, because there would be no second chances.

Nikki thanked the woman and promised to send a car round to take her to the hospital. Then she looked at Joseph incredulously. 'Well, that's a turn up for the books. I was wrong. It seems that Anson does have a home-made tattoo after all. I'm glad that WPC Yvonne Collins is already in

ITU. She'll escort Stephanie in, and we'll just have to take it from there.'

Joseph nodded. 'Can't do any more. So, how are the funeral arrangements going? Is there anything I can help with?'

'To be honest, Joseph, there's not much to do.' Nikki exhaled. 'My dad had everything sorted eons ago. He had even paid for the funeral. I've put an obituary in the *Telegraph* and the local papers, booked the Garden Restaurant in town for afterwards . . .' Nikki raised her eyebrows. 'And I spent hours last night chasing down relatives I've never even met, and his old RAF cronies. So much for a small, quiet service, I'm beginning to think he had more mates than a lottery winner!'

Joseph suddenly thought about his conversation with Nikki immediately after the old man had died. In his last coherent sentence he had told her to find someone called Eve. 'No mention of an Eve, I suppose?'

Nikki's face clouded. 'Funnily enough, there was one old guy, a man called Tug Owen, or Squadron Leader Anthony Blake-Owen to be absolutely correct. I seem to recall meeting him years ago. He was a great buddy of my father, and Dad had left a request that I pass on all his medals and RAF memorabilia to Tug. I mentioned the name Eve, and I swear he knew about her, but he clammed up tighter than a duck's backside.' Her frown deepened. 'I wish I had a bit more free time for all that, but I guess it'll have to wait.'

Joseph noticed Nikki's worried expression and decided to make a suggestion. 'I've been thinking. While you're busy here, perhaps Tamsin and I could do a bit of sleuthing for you? You said that your father had a lot of photo albums and letters stored in your attic? Perhaps, if you've no objection to us nosing through them, we might find a clue to Eve's identity.'

Nikki nodded vigorously. 'If you're sure? That would be great. I was going to ask you if you'd mind getting the boxes down for me.'

'No problem. How about after dinner tonight we all go back to your place for coffee? I'll do it then.' He looked at her and bit his lip. 'And to be honest, it would be doing me a favour too. It's pretty hard going, trying to put years of hurt behind you. It could just work as a bonding exercise, and at very least the distraction might help to fill some of the strained silences.'

'She's still a staunch pacifist, even now?'

'Nothing like she used to be. I think she's mellowing, but I don't think she'll ever forgive me for spending years clasping a Heckler and Koch HK417 rifle to my breast.'

'She was just a kid then, Joseph. If she's half the person you are, now that she's all grown up, she'll realise that the past doesn't exist anymore, and her father is, and always was, a good man.'

Joseph felt a jolt of wistfulness. It was his greatest wish, but even though things were going pretty well, he wasn't sure that it would happen. She had promised a year ago to spend some quality time with him, but it had never materialised. Now Tamsin was only staying with him because of a major hiccup in her travel plans with her mother. One call from Laura, and Tamsin would be jetting off again. He was on borrowed time, and he was horribly conscious of the ticking clock.

Nikki indicated towards the CID room door. 'Speaking of angels.'

Joseph's daughter, tall, willowy, with her father's light brown hair and thoughtful, expressive eyes, was deep in conversation with PC Niall Farrow.

The young constable looked across to Joseph and grinned. 'Hello, Sarge. I found this gorgeous young lady in the foyer, so thought I should escort her safely to you.'

Joseph looked at them together and decided that his suspicions were correct.

'Guess what, Dad. Niall's sister Ellie works for the Lincolnshire Wildlife Trust. And we were on a field course together after uni. How's that for a cool coincidence? Niall says she's studying the seals at Donna Nook, and if I'm still around, he'll take me up there on his free day.'

'That's a great idea,' said Joseph, and meant it. If nothing else, Niall could prove to be an ally and help keep Tamsin close to him.

After Niall left, Tamsin ran over to Nikki and gave her a hug. 'Dad told me about your father, Nikki. I'm so very sorry.'

Nikki looked mildly surprised but very pleased at the girl's thoughtfulness, and in no time they were chatting easily. Joseph watched them together and felt a stab of sadness as he thought of what Nikki was missing, with her own daughter so cruelly taken from her.

'We should get back,' said Joseph. 'We've got a car full of shopping, and as we have a guest tonight, I have culinary tasks to attend to.'

'And I have to get back to work.' Nikki sighed. 'I'll see you both later.'

* * *

Yvonne looked up to see one of her colleagues leading an anxious-looking woman down the hospital corridor towards her. She left the busy ITU and met them outside.

Stephanie Taylor was a homely woman, probably much younger than she appeared. Her clothes were far from new, but they were clean and neatly pressed. There was nothing about her appearance that would lead you to believe she might be connected with a drug dealer, and Yvonne, who prided herself on being a pretty shrewd judge of character, felt an immediate liking for her.

'Thank you so much for coming,' she said gently. 'I'm afraid he's very poorly, so please don't get your hopes up.'

They walked through the door and up to the bed. Yvonne placed her hand gently on Steph's shoulder, and jumped when the woman suddenly gave a bark of laughter.

'Pike!'

Yvonne led her quickly out of the room and went to get her a drink of water.

Stephanie sat, shaking and clasping her arms around herself. She took the glass and stared into it for a while before speaking. 'I'm so sorry. I guess I'd psyched myself up to see my brother,' she gave a little derisory snort, 'and I find *him* lying there instead.' She sipped the water, then took a deep breath. 'His name is William Pike. He's a friend of my brother and he was the first one I rang when Anson never came home. He swore he hadn't seen him.'

Yvonne wrote down his address. 'Have you any idea why he would have been out on the marsh at Flaxton Mere?'

'None at all. But then Pike isn't exactly the brightest light on the Christmas tree. He could have been up to any of a dozen hare-brained schemes.' Steph looked up at Yvonne. 'Do you have a brother, WPC Collins?'

'I do. Two younger brothers.'

'So can you appreciate how I feel? No matter how close to death Pike is, I'm still glad, because it's not my Anson in that bed.'

Yvonne nodded, pictured her own lovely brothers, Robin and Harry, and said that yes, she understood. 'But what about the tattoo?'

'They both had them. Blood brothers, would you believe? I nearly went mad when I saw Anson's arm. Naturally it had been Pike's stupid idea. As a child he used Anson as a crutch, always leant on him, copied his homework, leeched his pocket money *and* talked him into doing really stupid things. I detested him, but Anson acted like his big brother. I wouldn't like to tell you how many scrapes he got that little bastard out of. Pike is a parasite. Always has been.' Her eyes filled with tears. 'I'm sure he knows where my brother is, and if Anson's in trouble, it will have been Pike's fault. You can be sure of that.' She almost spat out the last sentence.

'Funny that he's not known to us, given his predilection for trouble.' Yvonne frowned. 'The name rings a few bells, but I'm certain he doesn't have a record.'

'He doesn't, but only because somehow Anson has always managed to save his skin for him.'

'Does he have any family that we can contact?'

'No. The mother ran off soon after he was born, and the father died a year or so ago. He does have a grandmother, from his dad's side of the family. She lives somewhere out on the marshes, I think.'

'And her name?'

Steph thought for a while. 'Sorry, but he just called her Granny Pike.'

Yvonne frowned. She remembered hearing the desk sergeant take a call the day before about a missing old lady. She could have sworn the name was Pike. But whatever, it wasn't this woman's problem. 'I'll get my colleague to take you home, Miss Taylor, and in the light of everything that's happened, I'm sure there *will* now be a search for your brother.'

Relief showed in her eyes, and Yvonne felt guilty. Stephanie Taylor was thinking they would be looking for her Anson out of concern for his safety. But Yvonne knew that they would most likely be looking for him as a suspect for attempted murder.

* * *

'Steph Taylor doesn't know the old lady's name, just said he called her Gran, but I'm certain the missing woman from the marsh was called Pike. Could you check it for me, ma'am?'

Nikki scrolled down the report on her computer. 'Got it. And you're right, Yvonne. It is Pike.' She sucked in air. 'This just gets better and better! We have one missing drug dealer, a half-dead junkie down a hole, and now his aged granny magicked away from her home. Great!'

'And the crew that checked out the old girl's home said that there was blood at the scene,' added Yvonne. 'Sounds pretty iffy, doesn't it, ma'am?'

'Let's just hope Pike wakes up pretty soon and gives us some answers. Has anyone arrived to take over from you? I'd like you back here. I need you to tell me all you know about the guy who owns Flaxton Mere, and then I suggest we go visit him.'

'Yes, ma'am, my relief is already here. I'll get on the road.'

'Good. Report to me when you arrive.' Nikki hung up, then saw the two other members of her team entering the CID room. 'Over here, guys!' she called out.

DC Cat Cullen threw her leather jacket over the back of her chair and moved quickly towards Nikki's office.

It was hard to believe that when Nikki had taken Cat under her wing, the girl had been an outsider, on the verge of being sent back to uniform. She was undoubtedly smart, but none of the teams had wanted a maverick with a timekeeping issue. None except for Nikki, who had not only recognised something of herself in the girl, but had seen untapped talents and decided to take a risk. Even after being seriously injured, and bearing scars to prove it, Cat had ploughed straight back in, never giving Nikki less than one hundred per cent.

As the young detective entered her office, and Nikki saw the excited expression on her face, she knew, not for the first time, that her gamble had paid off — with bonuses.

Cat grinned at her and ran a slender hand through her spiky, rough-cut hair. 'We've tied up that spate of fuel thefts out at Hawker's Drove, ma'am. Got the little bastards safely in the custody suite, *and* enough solid evidence to make even the CPS crack a smile.'

'Really good work. Well done both of you.' Nikki looked at the last member to join her team and saw him swell with pride.

DC Dave Harris had been another reject that she had gathered up, and found a diamond beneath the shabby exterior. She had seen through the facade that he put up to cover a painful home life, and discovered a true, old-style bobby, with all the right values. Dave didn't like technology. He came to his conclusions using a combination of long-term experience on the force, logic and simple intuition. He was in his fifties, heavier than he should be, and certainly no modern man, but he got results. And for some reason, he and the thoroughly modern, high-tech Cat Cullen gelled perfectly.

Nikki sat back and allowed herself to feel pretty pleased with her team. Okay, they weren't exactly classic cops. They had started out as a seriously dysfunctional group of misfits. Maybe that was their secret, because now they were hard to beat when it came to arrest and conviction rates.

'Close the door, Dave. I've something to tell you, and I'd prefer it stayed with us for the moment.'

Nikki told them about her father, and it wasn't easy, because Dave's wife, who also had Alzheimer's, had died only a year ago and she knew he was still hurting. 'So, I may be in and out a bit over the next few days tying up details, but I have decided I'd rather keep working.'

Both officers offered their condolences, then Dave added, 'I don't blame you, ma'am. I wish I'd done the same when my Lizzie passed away. It's a big mistake to take too much time out, especially when you are on your own.' He gave her a sad smile. 'But anything we can do to help, just ask, okay?'

'Definitely,' Cat added. 'Anything at all, ma'am.'

Nikki thanked them, but somehow felt that her words sounded hollow. She still felt no emotion welling up. No tears threatened to engulf her.

'Well, back to work.' She told them about Pike, the drugs, and the ventilation shaft, then passed them copies of a report that had just arrived from uniform as to the status of the search for his missing grandmother. 'According to the crew who dealt with it, Grandma Pike lives alone out on the marshes at Castor Fen. She's the local fenlanders' version of a vet by all accounts, and she takes in stray animals.' Nikki paused and thumbed through the report. 'A chap named Bourne called on her the night before last with a sick pup, but she wasn't there. He returned the next morning and she still wasn't around. As she never went out, and she always left the key under a flowerpot, he let himself in. Said the place was a tip, looked like there had been a struggle. There was

31

blood on the hearth, and he reckoned some of her animals had gone too.'

'It makes no sense,' said Dave, rubbing thoughtfully at his chin.

'I agree,' said Nikki, taking a large picture from an envelope in front of her. 'And neither does the fact that Pike was wearing *this* when they pulled him out of the shaft. Can you see any streetwise bloke going out like this?' She showed them a photo of the clothes that Pike had been wearing when he was found, in particular a multicoloured, homespun, woolly jumper. '*And* it's new.'

'That's gross,' said Cat flatly.

'It's the sort your gran knits you for Christmas and you never wear,' said Dave with a pained expression on his face. 'I suffered quite a few of those in my childhood.'

Nikki nodded. 'So we can only guess that he wore it to please her.'

'But where is she? How the hell can a little old lady disappear off the face of the fen?' grumbled Cat, staring at the printouts. 'I see that uniform have started a house to house, but in that desolate spot it could take a week.'

'Right, so have they checked the hospitals?' Nikki asked, 'Especially ones out of the area?'

'Yup.' Cat ran a finger down the list. 'Boston, Skeggie, Lincoln, Grantham, Peterborough, plus all the cottage hospitals. Apparently none of them have an unknown eighty-year-old female that they'd like claimed.'

'Well, unless she turns up living a secret life as a club rep in Ayia Napa, or William Pike wakes up, it looks like Granny Pike will be joining Amelia Earhart.'

'And the blood that was found on the hearth,' mused Dave, 'was definitely human, but the DNA report will take some time.'

'Any witness statements? Anyone noticed any recent visitors to the fen? Any strangers?'

'Says here that some kid saw a flashy car a few days back,' said Dave. 'It sounded like an Audi, but he never got a license number. The consensus is that it was most likely just lost. It happens all the time out there on those marsh lanes.'

'Mm, then we better concentrate on Pike. We need to confirm what Stephanie Taylor told WPC Collins, that the father is *brown bread* and the mother did a runner donkey's years ago.' Nikki sighed. 'And we still have Pike's buddy, the wannabe drug baron Anson Taylor missing.' Nikki frowned and rubbed at her temple thoughtfully. 'I wonder if Anson and Pike had a fight over those drugs, and Pike finished up down the shaft.' She suddenly felt frustrated by the whole thing. 'No, that doesn't ring true somehow. Why out there in such a remote and desolate area? I've got a distinctly funny feeling about all this.' She stood up. She never ignored instinct. 'Right, we'll take a closer look at that old airfield. Something drew William Pike to the place, so we can't afford to write it off as just some old deserted ruin. Maybe something is going on out there that shouldn't be.' She looked at Cat and Dave. 'Start with background. Find out all you can about RAF Flaxton Mere, past and present. Then we'll take a handful of uniforms and do a search. Okay, my friends, get digging, and keep me posted. As soon as Yvonne is back, I'm going to see the owner of that godforsaken place.'

'No problem, ma'am,' Cat gathered up the papers and walked to the door. 'We're on it.'

* * *

As the police officers discussed him, the young man called William Pike was staring at a bright white light. And even though it was very beautiful, he somehow found the strength to refuse to walk down that long tunnel. He was weak and close to death, but he refused to lose his tenuous grip on life.

His reason for turning down the generous offer of everlasting peace, and choosing to remain in a world of excruciating pain, was a simple one. In a moment of lucidity, at some point before he slipped into that deeper state of unconsciousness that they called coma, he had recognised someone in the big, bright room in which he lay.

CHAPTER FIVE

Karl Shine opened the door of his apartment to find two uniformed officers and a senior detective on his doorstep. His stomach lurched, threatening his recently digested dinner, and a feeling of dread surged through him, which was ridiculous considering he had done nothing wrong. Well, not yet. It was probably just a flashback to the old days — the bad old days.

He read their warrant cards, then held back the door and allowed them in.

As he indicated the matching leather sofas, he felt a tiny hint of satisfaction as their envious eyes swept around the beautifully furnished room.

'We traced a call from a mobile phone, sir. One that was requesting an ambulance to an incident at Flaxton Mere airfield? The call was anonymous, but it was made from a phone registered to you. Would that be correct, sir?'

Karl thought quickly. 'It was never meant to be anonymous, officers. I was so concerned for the young man down the shaft that as soon as I knew help was on the way, I simply rang off without leaving my details.' He threw them what he hoped was a convincing smile. 'How is he? Did he make it?'

'He's critical, sir,' said the detective named DI Galena. 'But if you hadn't found him, he would certainly be dead.'

The woman looked at him intently and he found her gaze disturbing. 'How *did* you come to find him?'

Karl took a deep breath. 'I was just checking the perimeter fences. The airfield is a dangerous place. I've put warning notices up all over, but people ignore them. Like the man down the shaft.'

'Did you know him?' asked the male constable, a young man with dark, piercing eyes.

'Never seen him before. And before you ask, I have no idea what he was doing. He certainly had no business to be there.'

'How long have you owned Flaxton Mere, sir?'

Karl's heart sank. He really did not want to talk about his investment. It should have changed his life and made him filthy rich, but now it hung around his neck like a rotting albatross and could see him in debt to the tune of hundreds of thousands of pounds. 'Three years, give or take a month or two.'

'And what are your intentions for it, sir?'

Fuck all, thought Karl bitterly, although of course that had not always been the case. First there was to be a small estate of prestige housing, then a sympathetic renovation job on the RAF buildings making them into a heritage museum, followed by more affordable dwellings that would attract southerners who were looking for a place in the country. Oh yes, it was the dream deal, the gilt-edged property investment that couldn't fail. *Until* he miscalculated the market, held back too long, and a storm of biblical proportions hit the coastline that edged Flaxton Mere, and turned a part of his prime building land into a lake of silt. 'To be frank, officers, I'm still considering my options.' He hoped he looked relaxed and at ease answering their damn fool questions. 'You can't really lose when you invest in land, can you? And I have several interesting schemes being considered by my people for viability.' Karl shifted uncomfortably. It had just occurred to him that this visit from the law regarding his 999 call really didn't warrant three officers. There must be something else bringing them to his door, something he wasn't yet aware of.

But then they were standing up, thanking him for his time, and preparing to leave. Karl's confusion increased. In a former life and a different location he'd had plenty of dealings with coppers, and this didn't feel right.

'By the way, sir,' the uniformed woman constable hung back. 'The business units in the old hangars? I assume they are all kosher? Rent books, proper tax declarations, all run correctly?'

Karl could have laughed out loud. Of course they weren't. They were strictly cash, no lease agreements and no questions asked about what the hell they were doing. He smiled reassuringly. 'Of course it's all above board. My secretary deals with it. She'll have all the relevant paperwork at the office. You are welcome to call by and check it. Naturally, due to the poor amenities and the distance from the town they pay very low rents with informal agreements, but when my plans come into operation, their units will be modernised and then new contracts will be drawn up and they will pay accordingly.'

The policewoman gave him a long stare, one that said, *I've got your number, sunshine, and if you think I believe that, then you're a fool.* But what she said was, 'Thanks for your time, sir. We'll probably be in touch.'

Karl held open the door, then casually asked, 'I suppose you've finished out at the airfield now?'

The detective inspector shook her head. 'Not yet, I'm afraid. We need to keep the crime scene secure, sir, and generally keep an eye on the whole area.'

'Crime scene?' There was an edge to his voice and he hoped the woman had not picked up on it.

'If he dies it could be murder, or manslaughter.'

'I thought he'd just fallen! Do you mean he was thrown?'

'Sorry, sir, but it's like you said yourself, we've no idea how he got there.'

Karl Shine's mouth went dry. Just how fucking naive could he be? He closed the door and headed straight to the cabinet that contained his scotch.

He poured himself three fingers and swilled back a good third of it in one hit. He noticed that his hand had a slight tremor, and he wasn't surprised. Just the thought of what was happening out at the airfield was enough to make him shake.

What he hadn't told them was that when half the coastline got washed away in the storm, the authorities decided it was cheaper to flood a large area close to Flaxton Mere, rather than try to build new sea defences. In ten years' time it would be a useless bog. And as the marsh was still encroaching into the land, planning permission would be out of the question. Everything he owned, and one hell of a lot of money that he didn't, was riding on him finding a way out of this shit, and fast.

He took another swallow of the whisky and let out a sigh. Because that wasn't the end of it, was it? When honesty had failed, he had approached someone from his past to help bail him out. And that someone would not be best pleased if he knew that his new project was being crawled all over by the Old Bill. Even the thought of the man's reaction to that scenario made Karl feel physically sick. He should never have allowed this to happen.

He drank the last of the scotch and poured another. Even losing everything and allowing his fabulous investment to be swallowed up by the North Sea was infinitely better than upsetting the infamous Freddie Carver, and now it looked as if he might have royally pissed him off.

Karl sat down on his very expensive leather sofa and allowed his head to sink into his hands. The day before he had made a deal with the devil, and now he had no idea how he could stop the chain of events that had already swung into action. With another sigh, which was almost a childish whimper, he curled up into a tight ball and closed his eyes.

He stayed like that for almost half an hour, then he slowly sat up and stretched his taut and strained neck muscles. He stood up, stretched again, then walked over to the huge full-length mirror that hung in the hallway.

In it he saw the reflection of a smart, well-groomed businessman. The short, stylishly cut dark hair, the casual, trendy clothes and the Tag Heuer watch all declared affluence, but he smiled bitterly and wondered how long he had before the bailiffs hauled away his home cinema system and his Beemer. He stared more deeply at his image, and didn't like what he saw. The man who looked out from behind his eyes was weak and scared.

It was all he had ever wanted. To make it big on Straight Street, and stick two fingers up at his shady beginnings and every single member of his stinking, lowlife family. And if the Flaxton Mere enterprise had come off, he would have been richer than any of them would have ever believed.

He straightened himself up, then walked back into the lounge and his unfinished single malt. This time he sipped it.

Maybe, just maybe, he could turn this around. He'd have to eat humble pie, but what did he have to lose? He set his empty glass down on the table. What did they say? Desperate times called for desperate measures. He gave a mirthless laugh. Well, they didn't come any more desperate than he was right now.

The laugh faded and he gritted his teeth. Then he picked up his car keys and made for the door to the integral garage.

CHAPTER SIX

That evening, Nikki stood in her bedroom at Cloud Cottage Farmhouse and looked out over the marsh. An evening mist had come down in a swirling, hazy mass, but it was far from depressing. In fact it was spellbinding. It seemed as if she were looking across to the silver grey waters of the Wash through a gently twisting veil of gossamer silk. And a quarter of a mile away, on the very edge of the marsh, she could see the familiar shape of Knot Cottage.

A wisp of smoke filtered from one of its two chimneys into the even wispier cloudy sky. Joseph had obviously decided that the evenings were still cool enough to warrant keeping the log burner alight.

She walked away from the window. It felt comfortable knowing that Joseph was living so close to her, and she thanked God that he had fallen in love with the airy beauty of the Fens, and not moved back to the town. She gazed through the almost hypnotic wispy strands of mist to Knot Cottage, and thought about Joseph.

He meant so much to her in so many ways. But it was complicated. Wasn't it always, she thought grimly. He was her only neighbour, her trusted work colleague and her closest friend. And what else? For a while she had believed

— well, unless she was completely mistaken, they had both believed that they had a future together, but fear had crept in and ruined the dream. They were too afraid to lose what they already had. She loved him, that was undeniable, but she knew what could happen to two career-minded people in such a volatile job. Best to keep the status quo.

As she pulled a sweater over her head she thought about the circumstances that had brought Joseph's daughter to Greenborough, and the more she considered it, the more she believed that Tamsin really did want some kind of relationship with her father.

Joseph's ex-wife had moved from Edinburgh to Chicago and was now a high flyer in the World Health Organisation. Her field was surgical safety and, according to Tamsin, they had been about to take a holiday in Switzerland when her mother had been called as an expert witness in a big court case in Southern Africa. It could take days, or weeks, Tamsin didn't know, but she had decided that she would prefer to be on hand in the UK, rather than try to rush out from the States when her mother was finally free.

Nikki pulled on some light socks and hunted in the bottom of her wardrobe for her soft leather loafers. Tamsin struck Nikki as the sort of girl who wouldn't think twice about grabbing a bucket seat and flying out at ten minutes' notice, so she was pretty sure the "impromptu" stay with her father had actually been carefully planned. As she ran down the stairs and grabbed her keys from the kitchen table, she sincerely hoped she was right.

* * *

It was just after nine when they finished the meal, and Nikki raised her glass in Joseph's direction. 'I admit to having been a trifle anxious when you reminded me that Tamsin was a vegetarian, but that supper was something else. Thank you.' Actually she had almost chickened out when she had heard the word "veggie." Nikki watched as Tamsin looked at her father with a mixture of irritation and interest.

'I told him not to fuss. I have no problem with other people eating whatever they want. Being vegetarian is my choice. I don't inflict my beliefs on anyone else.'

There was a haughty, almost defensive, tone to her voice, and Nikki realised that the girl was fighting with her feelings about her father. But Tamsin obviously didn't feel quite ready to make any decisions about him yet.

'Well,' said Nikki comfortably. 'If nothing else, I'll never knock vegetarian again, and believe me, that's saying something.'

'She *is* something of a philistine where food is concerned,' added Joseph. 'Although it's very satisfying to have someone clear their plate with such gusto.'

'I'm supposing that's a polite way of calling me a pig, is it?'

'Never. We get called that enough in our line of work, thank you. You just enjoy your food.' He raised an eyebrow in her direction. 'And speaking of appreciating things, if we have coffee over at yours, do you have any of that amazing brandy left?'

'My father's? Yes, I found another two bottles squirreled away at home. If you don't mind swinging around in my attic, I'll open one. Deal?'

* * *

An hour later, Tamsin and Nikki, with brandy glasses in their hands, sat on the floor of her lounge, surrounded by cardboard boxes and an assortment of cases.

'So what are we looking for?' asked Tamsin, carefully thumbing through a sheaf of military-looking papers.

Nikki stared at her father's things and wondered if she was up to this. But there would never be a better time. She looked fondly at Joseph and Tamsin. Now was probably as good as it got. 'Put anything that refers to the RAF to one side, and keep your eyes peeled for the name *Eve* on letters, backs of photos, notes, anything.'

Tamsin lifted out a packet of glossy pictures. 'Is this you?'

Nikki looked at the young woman with the eager, happy face, and the pretty blonde child on a brightly-coloured tricycle. 'Yes, that's me with Hannah. She must have been about two in that one.'

Tamsin looked through the other pictures. 'Dad told me what happened to Hannah.' The girl looked up. 'I'm so sorry. And now losing your father as well . . . it must be horrible for you. I don't know how you cope.'

'Some days I'm not too sure myself.' Nikki took a sip of her brandy. 'And then other days, well, you realise that life throws some pretty grim stuff at everyone at one time or another. You just have to get on with it. You're no good to anyone if you crack up.' She thought about her lovely girl, and the long, long time she had spent in the high dependency unit being cared for 24/7. Hannah had been in a persistent vegetative state, one step up from coma, until a simple cold had turned into pneumonia and she had nothing left to fight with.

Sadness swept over her. It was time to change the subject. She pulled the box towards her, and began to sift through her father's life. As she did, she told Tamsin all about his last request.

'Find Eve . . .' whispered Tamsin. 'Creepy. Stuff like that happens in scary movies, and it usually ends with the heroine up to her armpits in bodies.'

'Thanks for that, Tam. I have to sleep here tonight.'

Tamsin grinned at her. 'I can't imagine you being scared of anything.'

'Don't you believe it,' said Nikki grimly. 'I've seen things in this job that would scare the pants off anyone, me included.'

Joseph came back in, having washed off the dust from the loft. 'Don't you think it's rather soon to be doing all this?'

'I'm okay,' she said, and decided that she was. Her father had left her with a puzzle to solve, and who better to solve it than a detective? She smiled at them both, sipped her brandy and said, 'Okay, A-team, we have a missing woman to find. Let's do it.'

* * *

At four in the morning, an alarm went off in the intensive care unit.

Nurses dashed from their station to a woman's bedside, and the duty doctor and the crash team were called. They pronounced the time of death as four twenty-six, and the monitors were switched off and disconnected.

As the cover was respectfully pulled up over the closed lids of her dead eyes, another alarm sounded, and the team once again began resuscitation, this time on the comatose young man in the next bed.

CHAPTER SEVEN

Cat looked down at the heap of papers strewn across her desk, then back up to her boss. 'The internet has thrown up very little about the old RAF station.' She stared at some printouts. 'In fact I can find little more than that it was some kind of satellite station, which is pretty hard to believe, given its size and the number of buildings there. I looked up a few others of similar size and they were all major players in WWII, so why no info on Flaxton Mere?'

Dave walked across and joined them. 'Maybe it was finished too late and never used. I know they threw everything into these East Coast airfields when the threat of invasion became critical, then when it never happened a lot of places were abandoned.'

Nikki shrugged. 'Could be, I suppose. Perhaps our wealthy young entrepreneur, Mr Karl Shine, could tell us more.'

Cat gave a snort. 'I don't think Mr Shine wants to tell you anything. It doesn't sound as if he was too happy about your visit yesterday. Niall said, and I quote, "He was hair-spring taut and scared shitless, even if he did try to come over super-cool."'

'That lad has a nice way with words. It sums up Mr Shine a treat.' Nikki perched on the edge of Cat's desk. 'Have either of you managed to find anything out about him?'

'Next to nothing,' grumbled Dave. 'Karl Shine of Martin Park in Greenborough. He just seems to have arrived out of nowhere around three years back. He has no record, no past history, and bought a flashy house and that massive chunk of fenland with seemingly honestly earned cash.' He paused. 'And I believe that crock of shit about as much as I believe there are fairies at the bottom of my garden.'

Nikki grimaced. 'Anything else about the airfield?'

Cat turned over a sheet of paper and stared at what she had written. 'I noticed that most of the references regarding RAF Flaxton Mere were posted by a man called Joshua Flower. I googled him and found out that he's a professor of some kind, and the chairman of the local Greenborough Antiquarian Society. Reading his blog, it seems that there is a branch of the history society that is passionate about old airfields, Flaxton Mere in particular.'

'Then he sounds like the man to talk to, doesn't he?'

'He's out at present, but I've already rung and left a message on his answer machine.' Cat looked up. 'Dave and I will pay him a visit ASAP.'

'Good. And is that all we have?'

'Apart from the fact that we get more calls about unexplained disturbances in the Flaxton Fen and Castor Fen areas than anywhere else in the whole county,' said Dave.

'And most, I suppose, from our beloved Miss Quinney?' asked Nikki wryly.

'Ah yes. Mysterious lights on the marsh, unexplained sightings of men in dark clothes on the sea-bank in the dead of night, and weird noises that scare her chickens.' Cat rolled her eyes heavenward. 'Last time, as I recall, it was an alien landing in her raspberry canes.'

Nikki stood up. 'Well, apart from all that, I've asked uniform to keep up their presence at the airfield until either Pike wakes up, or we've managed to do a thorough search of the old buildings.' She looked down at Cat. 'If Mr Shine is not exactly forthcoming with us, I'd definitely try to involve your history professor. He might be prepared to be a tour guide if he knows so much about the place.'

Cat nodded. 'My thoughts precisely.'

'Good. Now I'm going to slip out for an hour. There are some things of my father's that I need to collect from the nursing home.'

Dave stood up. 'Want some company, guv?'

Nikki shook her head. 'Thanks for the offer, Dave. I do appreciate it, but I'm fine. You get on. And try to find some history on this Shine guy. Everyone has history, and if it's hard to find, then in my book, it's been purposely hidden and is bound to be shady.'

* * *

On the way to Glenfield, Nikki called into the local super-market and bought several bottles of wine and a 'thank you' card for the staff. When she arrived there she was met by Molly Crane, and she was glad that she'd made the effort.

'I know how busy you are, DI Galena, so I thought it might help if I packed his things up for you.' Molly ush-ered her into the manager's office, where she saw three boxes and an old leather case sitting together under the window. 'Everything is there as per the inventory of his belongings, plus a few things he accumulated.' She sat in one chair and indicated for Nikki to take the other. 'I need you to check and sign, if you wouldn't mind.' She smiled at Nikki. 'Can I make you a coffee, or a tea?'

'Black coffee, one sugar, would be great, thank you,' said Nikki. 'And I don't need to check his things, Molly. He had nothing of value here, and anyway, I trust you.'

Molly went out to the kitchen and returned a few min-utes later with two mugs of coffee. 'I'm glad you came in, DI Galena. I was going to call you.'

Nikki took her drink. 'Why was that?'

'Well, it may be nothing, but then again . . .' Molly Crane placed her mug on the desk and walked over to the boxes. She opened one and pulled out an old, well-thumbed book.

Nikki didn't recognise it as her father's, but took it from Molly and opened it.

Inside was an inscription, and there was no doubt in her mind that the writing belonged to her dad. *For my watcher in the night. May this while away the hours until dawn. F x.* Nikki stared at it and frowned. 'I've never seen it before. And I brought all his things in, so where did it come from?'

Molly shrugged. 'I have no idea, although he did have several old friends visit while he was here. It was at the back of his bedside cabinet. It was the title that caught my attention.'

'*The Eve of War.* Mm, Eve. I see what you mean,' Nikki said.

'As I said, it may be nothing at all, but there's something else. A picture fell out when I opened it. Look in the back.'

Between the last page and the cover of the old book, was a photograph. It was a 6x4 snap, the kind people took prior to the advent of digital cameras. Nikki held it closer. It was taken abroad and most likely on an air base. Four tanned men and two women sat and stood around a plastic table. Most had drinks in their hands, and two of the glasses were lifted in a salute to the photographer. Nikki wasn't sure, but she thought that one of the young men might be Tug Owen. The others meant nothing to her.

'I wondered if one of those women was his *watcher in the night?*' said Molly.

'I think I know this man here.' Nikki pointed to the handsome young airman. 'He's coming to the funeral, so I will certainly ask him.' She looked up at the nurse, and after a moment said, 'Molly? I didn't imagine it, did I?'

The woman shook her head. 'No, I heard it too. He said "Eve." I'm certain of it.'

Nikki nodded, but said no more.

* * *

47

Freddie Carver stepped from the Jacuzzi and, clutching the empty champagne flute in one pudgy hand, walked slowly along the length of his turquoise marble pool. He glanced at the row of exotic palms in huge ornate pottery containers and made a mental note to tell the gardener to clean them more regularly. He paused at the poolside bar and refilled his glass, then picked up the bottle and moved slowly towards the sauna.

He lowered his considerable bulk down onto the wooden slats and breathed in the hot, humid air. He was in a foul temper, which was not like him. Three things had upset him already, and he'd only been out of bed an hour.

First, the team of surveyors he had sent out to Flaxton Mere had returned with the news that they had only been on-site for a matter of hours when the perimeter road close to the sea-bank side of the Mere filled up with blue lights and uniforms. They had pulled out immediately using a different route, but they were far from happy at having had such a close call with the fuzz.

The second thing that had riled him was a visit from Karl Shine, babbling about an accident, some kid falling down a hole. Shine had repeated over and over that there was absolutely nothing to worry about. It had only been the emergency services getting the kid out, nothing else. He'd sworn that he would take care of everything and ring when the airfield was clear again.

Freddie sipped his drink and slowly shook his head. He knew from Shine's tone and body language that he was holding something back and Freddie didn't like that, not one bit. Because of old family ties and a liking for the boy's determination, he had sent out some top men and state-of-the-art equipment in order to discover exactly what they could do to salvage young Karl's innovative little project. And his men were special, highly experienced and highly paid, and they rarely worked on lawful assignments. If there were a way to make serious money out of Shine's pipe dream, then they would find it. But they did *not* work under the watchful gaze of the filth.

And then there was the third thing, equally as upsetting to Freddie. His clumsy cow of a wife had dropped a bottle of Bollinger. All in all, a great start to the day.

He sat back, thinking murderous thoughts and wondering what the hell had gone wrong with Karl Shine. Years ago the boy had shown great promise. He had been clear-minded and cunning. Freddie had liked that, and would have put money on the lad doing well. Then Karl had suddenly developed a yearning for the legitimate business world, and it seems that he did have a good try at it. But there you go, honesty never paid off, not if you wanted to be seriously and quickly rich.

Freddie emptied his glass and reached for the dark green bottle. He needed the drink to think clearly, and right now he was worried. Something odd had occurred when his men retreated from the airfield. His top man, an Irishman called Michael Finn, had not been with them. None of the others had seen him leave, but his truck had gone, and no one had heard from him since, including his wife. Now his phone was not answering, which gave Freddie grave cause for concern.

Michael was helping him out with Flaxton Mere as a favour, because of his expertise with maps and surveying. He was deeply involved in something far bigger than Karl Shine's miserable little enterprise. And that really worried Freddie. A key man in the biggest job he had ever undertaken had gone missing, and he was going to have to send out one of his very private investigators to find him, which would cost even more big money.

He swallowed a mouthful of champagne and decided to give Shine two days to get the pigs off his patch. If Karly Baby couldn't manage that, then he was on his own.

CHAPTER EIGHT

Karl got out to the airfield early. He hoped he had managed to placate Freddie but you could never tell with that slimy bastard. Whatever, he'd done his best, and right now he had other fish to fry. But first he had to visit the men who rented the units. He needed to play down the police presence and make sure that none of them did a runner without paying their rent. Money was getting scarce and he couldn't afford to throw it away.

The sky was heavy with cloud and it was difficult to see even as far as the creepy old ruin of a control tower. Karl shivered. He had walked through it once or twice when he first purchased the land and, unaccountably, it gave him the hee-bie-jeebies. Even so, he could see the potential of the place if it were restored and full of authentic RAF and wartime shit — sorry, *memorabilia*. Okay, Freddie had told him to shelve that idea and concentrate on housing, and he'd keep the old toad sweet. But if the old man could salvage Flaxton Mere for him, there were so many other possibilities.

He gave himself a mental shake. He was getting too far ahead of himself, and right now he had worries on a par with full thickness burns. Among them was the fact that one of Freddie's men had gone missing during his abbreviated visit to Flaxton Mere.

As Karl walked across to the old hangars he tried to put a face to Michael Finn. Only one man had stood out from the group of taciturn men that had arrived the day before. He was tall, with raven-black hair and strangely pale, blue eyes. He was certainly Irish, and had been the only one of Freddie's men to even acknowledge his presence. In fact he had seemed quite sociable, unlike his colleagues who had looked at Karl as if he was some kind of retard. They were not openly hostile, but they were far from friendly. And they told him nothing. They were in Freddie Carver's pay, and they clearly dealt only with him. Karl felt like the office junior and kept expecting them to send him out for coffee and doughnuts.

He pulled a face and thought miserably that if it hadn't been for the men's animosity towards him, he would never have left them and gone out to check the perimeter fences in the first place. And the shaft containing the injured man might have gone undiscovered for months.

He sighed. He wasn't a cruel person — he'd been on the wrong end of that particular trait in his childhood — but part of him wished that he'd never chanced across that man down the hole. More than anything, he regretted calling the emergency services. If he'd just thought about himself, and the fact that a crew of Freddie Carver's shady surveyors were working on his airfield, then maybe he could have found the courage to walk away.

Seeing one of his tenants unlocking their unit door brought him back to ground level. No use going over it all again, what was done was done. The best he could do now was pacify these guys and get the Old Bill off his land as quickly as possible.

* * *

An hour later he left the last of the disgruntled unit holders and made his way back to his Beemer. He'd have a "friendly" word with the resident police officer parked next to his car, just to see if there was any news on their departure, then he'd take himself into town for something to eat.

'Hello, Mr Shine! And how are we today?'

Karl's heart sank. That voice could only belong to the geek from the history society, Professor Joshua Bloody Flower. Karl looked across to the hardstanding close to the control tower and his heart sank even further. Another car was parked there. Great! He'd brought some of his cronies too. Just what Karl needed.

'Sorry, Professor, this is not a good time. We have the police here with us.'

'And that is exactly why we are here, sir. We have just heard about the dreadful accident, and we wondered if we could offer our assistance.'

'Thank you, but no, Professor.' The irritation in his voice was impossible to hide. This shower of weirdos was the last straw. 'I'm sure the police have everything in hand. Now, if you wouldn't mind leaving.'

'Wait!' The policeman walked towards them. 'And you are . . . ?'

Joshua Flower stepped forward. He was an imposing figure of around sixty, with a full head of wavy grey hair. He was wearing his usual old-style clothes, a tweed jacket with a moleskin waistcoat and ancient cord trousers in a strange ochre colour that made Karl feel mildly queasy.

Flower made a small bow, carefully enunciated his name and introduced the three others. 'Marcus Selby, Andrew Friar and Frank Kohler. My apologies, Constable, we are members of Greenborough history society and we have a particular interest in WWII airfields.'

'And what sort of assistance do you think you can offer, sir?'

Karl Shine was beginning to feel uncomfortable.

The tall bird-like chap called Selby, answered. 'We know this place better than anyone, officer.' He turned to Karl with an almost apologetic expression on his face. 'No offence to you, Mr Shine. It's partly because of your kindness in letting us research the airfield that we've spent years looking into its history, and we know that there is more to RAF Flaxton Mere than meets the eye.'

Karl's discomfort was becoming acute.

A different voice chimed in. 'And it's dangerous for those who don't know it. The man down the hole is proof of that.'

The policeman looked interested. 'At present we are only interested in what happened at the shaft, but if we need to investigate the old buildings, we may call on you.' He opened his notebook. 'I'll get your names, gentlemen, then I think perhaps you should do as Mr Shine says and leave.'

Karl watched helplessly as they gave their details. He'd only given them permission to spend time in the old buildings because he thought he could use their collective knowledge for free when he began his renovation project. Now the nosy bastards knew more about the place than he did. And what the hell did they mean by there being more to Flaxton Mere than met the eye? His brain began to go into overdrive. Hell, if there were secrets here he needed to know about them before Freddie Carver's men came back on-site! Part of him wanted to grab hold of Flower by his stupid tweed lapels and ask him what the hell they meant, but right now he wanted them gone.

He smiled with difficulty, and watched them walk away. All he could do was to wait until later, then go over the place with a fine-tooth comb. He had the keys. He owned the place, for heaven's sake. He'd have to check it out and pray that he discovered whatever he'd missed before. Freddie Carver wouldn't want any more nasty surprises, that was for sure.

* * *

Stephanie Taylor had taken to walking the streets of Greenborough. After the shock of having believed her brother to be dying, and then finding out that it was Pike lying in that hospital bed, she had begun once again to look for Anson.

She wasn't stupid enough to think the police would do much. And if they did, it would be because they wanted to question him regarding Pike's "accident." So it was down to her to find him.

She had started by going out at night, talking to the winos, the dossers and the kids who slept in shop doorways, but she'd soon realised that the dross of society were still there in the bright light of day, if you knew where to look. And close to noon, in a shadowy alley, wrapped tightly into a filthy sleeping bag and surrounded by cardboard boxes, she found someone that she was looking for.

A few nights ago, the girl had been on the verge of talking to her, then something had spooked her and she had taken off like a greyhound. This time the young woman didn't run away, although getting her to talk did not prove easy. Rather than mess around, Steph simply offered her money. Twenty pounds, if she knew anything that would help her find Anson. The woman had looked at Steph suspiciously.

'No catches? Just the money?'

Steph held the note out. 'It's all I've got, but it's yours if you help me.'

The woman extracted her gloved hand. 'I don't know much.'

'Whatever you know is a damned sight more than I do. Please?'

A small hand reached out, and Steph saw frightened eyes and a face that belonged to someone who was little more than a child. The girl could not have been more than fifteen. Horrified, Steph handed over the note and sat down on the filthy pavement next to her. 'My brother is Anson Taylor. He's missing and . . .' Her voice tailed off.

'You're not like him.' The voice was soft and surprisingly well-spoken. 'I used to buy from him sometimes, or from his scummy little friend.' She shivered a bit when she spoke of Pike. 'I hear he's had an accident.'

Steph ignored the remark. 'Have you seen Anson?'

The girl was busy pushing the twenty pound note deep into her baggy layers of clothing. 'Last Saturday night I needed a hit, but I couldn't find my usual supplier. I was getting really shaky, then I saw Pike. I called out to him but he never heard me. He was walking fast, head down, and then a few minutes later I saw Anson following him. Even though I needed a line, I didn't call out. There was something about him . . .' She paused. 'He looked mad as hell, and he was obviously tailing Pike.'

Steph whistled softly through her teeth, then half whispered, half growled, 'I knew it had to be something to do with that bastard, Pike. Where did they go?'

'I don't know, but I've seen Pike go off before, and always in the direction of the marsh.'

Steph thought about what she'd been told. Pike had been found in a shaft on Flaxton Mere. Had that been where her brother was going too?

She thanked the girl, almost wishing she had more to give her. After all, although she hated to admit it, it was the likes of Anson who kept kids like this high as kites and living rough.

As she approached her home in Mason Street, something deep inside told her that Anson was dead, and that he was somewhere on Flaxton Mere. But how would she convince the authorities of it? Even if they found her, the young addict would never repeat to the police what she had told Steph. Even though she knew in her heart it was true, who on earth would believe her?

As she slipped the key into the door, she thought that there was one person who might understand. With a glimmer of hope, Steph decided to contact WPC Yvonne Collins.

CHAPTER NINE

As Nikki walked into the reception area of the police station, she saw Stephanie Taylor talking to Yvonne Collins. Steph's face was almost grey, and Nikki suspected that the woman had neither eaten nor slept for days.

'Have you got a moment, ma'am?' asked Yvonne, looking worriedly at Nikki.

She nodded, then beckoned the two women in the direction of a spare interview room.

It didn't take long to realise that Steph had been far more successful in her investigations than they had. But then she was looking for someone she loved, and that gave her one hell of an incentive.

To begin with, Steph seemed reluctant to talk but after a while she seemed to come to a decision to trust Nikki. She told them all she knew, and filled them in on a few facts about Anson's childhood that had never found their way into a police file. And all through the conversation, Nikki kept feeling sharp stabs of recognition when the girl spoke of the way she felt about her wayward sibling. In Nikki's case it wasn't a sibling, but trying to keep a headstrong teenage daughter on the straight and narrow had been an exhausting task.

'I find it hard to describe how I feel.' Steph stared at the table in front of her. 'There's an emptiness, a coldness deep down that tells me he's dead. I hope you can understand that.' She sighed. 'What I can't expect you to understand is that I *know* he is out on Flaxton Mere. I can't explain it, but I know it's true.'

Nikki knew that the woman believed in what she was saying. But whether that was just because of what had happened to Pike, or simply because that had been the direction he was going in when he was seen for the last time, she didn't know. It certainly was not enough reason to send officers back out onto the fen. The super had already given her a breakdown of their budget for the month, and if it got any worse they would be doing high-speed chases on mountain bikes.

After a while she sent Yvonne out to get the woman a coffee. Then she thanked Steph for coming in and promised that they would do all they could, although she knew that might be limited. As the woman nodded sadly, Nikki leaned forward and touched her hand. 'I *do* understand, even though I don't have a brother. My daughter was a problem for a while. I know it's not the same thing, but sometimes the actions of people you love can tear your heart out, can't they?'

Steph smiled helplessly. 'I keep thinking about all the times we argued over Pike, and how Anson always took his side. I just hope he knew I only ever wanted the best for him.' Her voice tailed off, and Nikki saw a tear glistening in the corner of the woman's tired eyes. She's grieving already, thought Nikki, and felt something like envy. She wanted to grieve for her dad, but still there was just a void.

Yvonne brought in the coffees, and Nikki left the two women together. 'There's no rush, Steph. Stay with WPC Collins and take your time, okay?'

'Thank you, DI Galena. I appreciate it.' She paused. 'And thank you for not thinking I'm just some flaky airhead. One day you'll see I'm right about Anson.'

Nikki closed the door with the feeling that Stephanie Taylor was going to be proved correct on all counts.

* * *

The CID room was buzzing as Nikki walked in.

'Glad you're here, ma'am.' Dave waved to her. 'We've just heard from ITU that William Pike crashed last night, but they managed to get him back and he's regained partial consciousness.'

'Good. Is someone with him?'

'Yes, but Yvonne Collins has asked to be told when he's awake, because she'd like to talk to him herself.'

'She's downstairs in interview room two. Give her a few minutes to finish up, then tell her to get over to the hospital. What state is Pike in?'

'He's confused, but the doctors hope he'll be a little more coherent soon.' Dave stared down at some scribbled notes. 'We have had no luck with locating Granny Pike. Uniform haven't come up with a lead from the house to house, so I was rather wondering if we could give it to the media, see if they can help?'

Nikki nodded. 'I think we should. Little old ladies don't vanish, even on creepy Flaxton Fen.'

'It's the same with Anson Taylor, ma'am, nothing on him either, but I guess we won't mention him to the media, for obvious reasons.'

Nikki exhaled. 'Yvonne and I have just spoken to his sister.' She flopped down in a chair and told Dave everything Steph had said, including her feeling that he was dead somewhere on the fen.

'He could well be.' Dave looked a little sad, 'It's a bummer, isn't it? That woman adores her shitty brother, but unless we get something more concrete I can't see the budget allowing us to go back out there to search for him, can you, ma'am?'

Nikki grunted. 'No way, but go ahead and organise something about Granny Pike.'

'Guv?' Cat sat down opposite her. 'I've been thinking about the drugs that Pike was carrying. What were they exactly?'

Dave fished through a pile of reports, then listed a mixed bag of lethal goodies.

'Why?' asked Nikki.

'They just bother me. Quite a few officers have intimated that it was a simple deal that went wrong, in other words Pike making a collection from a supplier. Well, from what I've seen before, suppliers don't deal in odds and sods. A small bag of dexies? A handful of K? And although there was a heck of a lot of it, the white stuff wasn't even in one package, was it? I reckon he had been squirreling this stuff away, stealing from the dealer that we know he worked for,' she did an imaginary drum roll, 'da-da! Anson Taylor! So, if what that street addict told Stephanie Taylor was right, about Anson being mad as hell and following Pike, he could have discovered that fact for himself.'

Nikki nodded. 'I think you're right, Cat! It certainly makes sense. I think we'll give the fragrant Pike a chance to wake up and tell us something constructive, and if that doesn't happen we may have to take another walk around the airfield. In the meantime, Dave, gee up the media and keep your finger on the search for granny.' She frowned. 'I don't like the idea of old people going missing. Something about this really stinks.'

Dave nodded and rose to go. 'It's not just the old lady, is it? Her animals are missing too. So what the heck is that all about?'

'I wish I knew, Dave, I really do.'

* * *

By afternoon the police presence at Flaxton had dwindled to two bored officers, one pacing the area by the ventilator shaft, and one in the car reading a copy of the *Sun*. And that was perfect, as far as Karl Shine was concerned. No one would take any interest in him as he walked around, checking locks and conscientiously making sure the place was secure. The police didn't know that he was really trying to find out what the hell was going on, and what secrets this place harboured that he didn't know about.

As he methodically went from one spot to the next, he wished he'd had more time for the historians. They had offered to take him round on several occasions, but he'd always refused. Pushing aside a long strand of brambles, he thought perhaps he should ring one of them. It could save him a lot of time. Then he thought of Freddie Carver, and decided not to involve anyone else, unless he met with a dead end.

Which was just what he did an hour later, covered in cobwebs and with his shiny shoes scuffed and dusty. Standing on one leg at a time, he rubbed his shoes on the back of his trouser legs before climbing into his nice clean car.

He pulled a Mars bar from the glove compartment and chewed on it as he pondered on what to do. Should he ring one of the boring old sods and ask them outright? Or should he just forget about what Selby had said? The problem was that the man had said it to a copper, who had taken careful note of it. Ergo, *he* shouldn't be the one to stick his head in the sand and ignore it. And with Freddie in the background, he couldn't afford to. He needed to be on top of everything that was happening at the airfield. If anything else went wrong, he could really regret ever approaching Carver for help.

He screwed up the sweet wrapper, turned the key in the ignition, and listened to the gentle purr of the powerful engine. He'd better go home and find a phone number for one of them. It probably didn't matter which one he asked, half a dozen of them all professed to be experts on the place. He had no doubt that one of the "enthusiasts" would be absolutely delighted to introduce him to the secrets of Flaxton Mere.

* * *

Tamsin pulled yet another pile of old photographs from the shoebox, and looked up at her father. 'Are you sure you don't fancy your boss?'

Joseph raised his eyebrows. 'Oh Lord! How many more times? We just get on really well, that's all.' He stared at the large brown packing case that they had brought across from

Nikki's farmhouse the night before, and decided that they were never going to find the mysterious Eve. 'This doesn't feel right to me, rifling through other people's personal letters and memories.'

Tamsin looked surprised, and a little accusatory. 'I would have thought it was right up your street. Surely it's a job requirement for the police?'

'It's different when you're dealing with a crime. This is private stuff.'

'All the same, I think maybe it's better that we do it, don't you?' She looked at her father shrewdly. 'You may "get on really well," as you keep telling me, but I don't think you are aware that Nikki's struggling.'

Joseph sat down on the floor next to his daughter. 'I thought she was coping brilliantly.'

Tamsin gave a snort of derision. 'Men! You only see what's on the surface. Trust me, DI Nikki Galena may not know it herself, but she's holding it together by a shoestring.' She frowned, '*And* this Eve thing has really got to her.'

Joseph puffed out his cheeks. 'Then maybe you're right.' He pointed to the mass of papers, letters and photos. 'Perhaps it *is* better that we deal with it.'

'Ah, light dawns,' muttered Tamsin. 'And I suggest that when Nikki gets home, you collect the rest of her boxes and you and I put our collective brains into solving this.' A look of confusion passed swiftly across her face. It was as if she didn't want him to think that she might actually be enjoying working with him, so she added, 'Might as well do something constructive while I wait for my mother to call.'

Joseph chose not to comment, but looked instead at the open laptop that lay on the carpet next to Tamsin. 'What's that for?'

'As you do actually have a surprisingly half-decent broadband speed out here in the back of beyond, I'm tracing Nikki's father's military history from some of the details in these letters, and I'm trying to google some of the names mentioned.' She pointed to three neat piles of photographs.

'This is all forces stuff. This one is family, and this last pile,' she shrugged, 'could be anything. There are landscapes and civilians, but no indication of what, where, or who they are.'

'Anything interesting?'

'I've started with these.' Tamsin passed him nine or ten photos, all of smiling RAF personnel. 'These pictures have names and dates on the back. By a process of elimination, you can identify some of the people.' She jabbed her finger at one man. 'This porky bloke in fatigues, he's only in one shot, and the only name that isn't repeated on the other pictures is Lenny Courtney, so meet Fat Lenny.' She placed the picture to one side. 'The same with this woman with the tragic haircut, her name has to be Mary Fielding.'

'Have you ever considered a career in the police force? You've worked that out quicker than half of CID!'

'When hell freezes over!' Tamsin flung back. 'I want a job that promotes peace, helps needy people and saves lives.'

'Funnily enough,' said Joseph quietly, 'that's exactly what we strive for in the police force.'

Tamsin grunted and shifted further away from him. 'Oh, you know what I mean.'

Joseph did, and he also knew that the next few days with his emotionally mixed-up daughter were not going to be easy.

* * *

'Mr Carver, sir? Can we meet?'

Freddie recognised the rasp in the voice, and realised that his "private investigator" did not wish to talk on the phone.

'One hour, Monk. The usual place.'

Freddie pulled on a long, dark, and very expensive overcoat that he had purchased with the sole purpose of disguising his growing paunch, and called for his driver. He kissed his over-tanned young wife and said, 'I'll be out for lunch, angel. Try not to demolish the rest of the bubbly while I'm gone.'

The Front, a noisy and popular cocktail bar that attracted young wine-swilling and upwardly mobile locals, was a smart move on Freddie's part. It was his, of course, a nice little money-spinner, but heavily concealed with a shell company. And the two comfortable rooms upstairs were for his exclusive use, one as a private meeting place, and one as a bedroom — a bedroom that his darling wife knew nothing about.

Monk arrived minutes after him, and readily accepted the offer of a drink.

'It's to do with the airfield, sir. Michael Finn was definitely out there with the rest of the crew but, as you know, he never made it home to his digs. Michael's wife in Ireland hasn't heard from him, and what's even more worrying, neither has his contact on your other job. Now . . .' He paused for effect, but seeing his boss's face, seemed to think better of it and hurried on. 'I spoke to this kid who lives in a shitty little fen cottage on the edge of the marsh. He was playing there earlier in the day, and he saw a man who, from the boy's description, had to be Michael Finn. I then showed him a picture of Finn and he positively identified him. The kid said that he had some really fancy handheld computer and seemed to be measuring the land and taking notes and what I understood to be soil samples.'

'So he was certainly there, and working.'

'Oh yes, sir. But later on, the same kid saw a truck up on the path at the back of the airfield. The boy said he couldn't see the driver, but he said that the same dark-haired man was *asleep* in the passenger seat.'

'Asleep, huh?'

'That's what I thought.' Monk raised his eyebrows. 'And considering Michael had his own wheels and a lot of valuable equipment on board, he'd hardly be taking forty winks in a stranger's truck. I'm afraid that whatever happened to put Michael to "sleep" has made sure he won't be waking up again.'

Freddie swirled the vodka around in his glass and swore, cursing Karl-fucking-Shine and his property developing. He didn't know what the hell was going on in that marshy dump, but he did know that Karl was to blame. And that wasn't acceptable.

Monk placed his empty glass on the thick beechwood coffee table. 'So what's next, boss?'

Freddie didn't have to think for long. His anger at Karl was becoming hard to contain. He took an envelope from his pocket and passed it to Monk. 'It would appear that Shine has cost me a good man, a vital man where the other job is concerned. This is for what you've done so far. Now we need the services of Mr Fabian.'

Monk took the money, drew in a long breath, puffed out his cheeks, and nodded. 'I know where I can find him, Mr Carver. Shall I set up a meeting?'

'Not this time, Monk. You'll be the go-between. I have no wish to be connected in any way to this transaction, understand?' He jabbed his glass towards Monk. 'Do this discreetly and it'll be worth your while.'

Monk looked worried. 'Fabian likes to know who he's working for, Boss. That could be a problem.'

'Then fucking sort it. Or I'll find someone who will.' He saw the other man's Adam's apple move up and down in his skinny throat.

'Right, Mr Carver, I'll do it, don't worry. Is it the usual fee for Fabian?'

'Yes, the usual extortionate fee. Now, meet me here at seven tonight. I'll have all the information necessary for our friend to do a good job.'

Monk nodded and rose from his seat. 'Seven it is, boss.'

* * *

Monk hated working with Fabian. That weirdo's methods, although effective, made Monk sick to the stomach, but it would mean big money and he'd heard about a special shipment arriving next month. The purest of pure, with a massive street value. *If* he could raise enough to buy into it, he would never need the likes of Freddie Carver again.

As he walked back to his car, he considered how he could tackle the sinister Mr Fabian and set up the hit without involving Freddie. It wouldn't be easy, but he had a fair idea of how he could make it work.

Monk unlocked the car and eased himself behind the wheel. Carver might be a slimeball, but one thing was certain, if you did the job right he paid well, very well. And if he employed a man with Fabian's expertise, the rates were even higher.

Monk tapped thoughtfully on the leather steering wheel. Perhaps he should look at this situation differently. After all, there was more than one way to skin a cat, wasn't there?

CHAPTER TEN

Yvonne was getting used to the organised chaos in the ITU department. She sat close to the bed where William Pike lay, and while she kept one eye on the sleeping man, watched the professionals at work. It wasn't the kind of job that she would have wanted to do, but she had the highest regard for their expertise and their ability to work so calmly under such high-pressure conditions.

She stared at Pike and thought it a bit sad that there was no one to sit with him. No family and no loved ones. He might be a toerag of the first order, but for heaven's sake, the kid's heart had stopped the night before. Even when he woke up this time, there would only be a crusty old copper sitting beside his bed.

For a moment she almost laughed. Come to think of it, it wouldn't be that different if it were her in the bed. Certainly she had work colleagues and some of them were her closest friends, but both her parents were dead and her two brothers were married and had moved away. Robin had a Canadian wife and they lived in Alberta with their children, and Harry now lived and worked with his wife in Bali. Yvonne gave a little sigh. And as she had no partner, there would be no loved one to hold her hand and pray for her recovery.

She allowed her mind to wander. There had been some-one once, or there nearly had been. But that was a long while ago, and as Yvonne was far too practical to dwell on "could have beens", or "if onlys," she thought of the one soul who truly loved her. But even Holmes was nearing the end of his full and happy life. She smiled to herself.

She had rescued Holmes as a puppy, and now she "dog-shared" him with her next door neighbour, Ray. Yvonne exercised him, then dropped him off and collected him again after her shift had ended — a bit like a canine crèche. It was a very satisfactory arrangement, as her neighbour, an elderly, retired schoolteacher, was a great dog lover, but couldn't do long walks anymore. So it suited them both and Holmes got the best of both worlds, he was spoilt rotten and wanted for nothing. But Holmes was close to fifteen, a very good age for a field spaniel, and the thought of losing him made Yvonne go cold. She and Ray both lived alone in adjoining bunga-lows, and the dog, albeit deaf as a post and very wobbly, was a big part of both their lives.

Almost automatically, Yvonne checked her mobile. She dreaded finding a message from Ray, and she knew that one day soon it would happen, but . . . she smiled and pushed the phone back into her pocket. Not yet.

Yvonne glanced back to Pike and saw him stir. Then his eyes closed again and he snored softly, so she took the time to leaf through her notes on the young man's semi-conscious ramblings.

It was all rubbish of course. Air raids? Plane crashes? Lights on the fen? Fires? But one thing that probably wasn't rubbish was the constant mention of his grandmother.

Pike was now restless, moving painfully and moaning softly. His left temple was multicoloured with bruising, and decorated with a row of even stitches. The face, one that Yvonne suspected had always been thin, was partly covered with a week's growth of scraggy beard, and deeply etched with pain. His mutilated leg, suspended in some kind of metal cage, was thankfully covered by a light sheet. The very distinctive metallic smell of blood still hung around him.

'Gran . . . Gran, I'm so sorry.' It sounded like a child's voice and took Yvonne slightly by surprise.

'William? Can you hear me?'

The young man's eyes darted around, settling nowhere for long.

'William, we are trying to find your grandmother. Can you help us?'

Again the frightened eyes moved swiftly around the room.

'Do you know where you are, William?' Yvonne tried to make her voice sound soft and compassionate. She did not want to scare the little sod into clamming up on whatever treasures of information were swimming around in his addled brain. 'We really do need to find your gran. She's missing and we are worried for her safety.'

Pike made a strange gasping sigh, then said quite clearly, 'She's dead.'

Yvonne leaned closer. 'How do you know that?'

'I heard her die.'

Yvonne was confused. 'What do you mean, you *heard* her die?'

'The nurses and the doctors,' he swallowed noisily, 'they said she was dead.'

Yvonne thought for a moment or two, then stood up and went to the nurses' station. 'Sorry to bother you, but did anyone pass away in here recently?'

A nurse looked across to her colleague. 'Two in the last three days, isn't it, Tina?'

'Yes, old Mrs Hewitt, early hours of Saturday morning, and a young RTC victim, earlier today. Why, Officer?'

Yvonne nodded. 'It's all right. I think you've answered my question. William Pike must have thought the Hewitt lady was his grandmother. He's still very confused. Sorry to have bothered you.' She smiled her thanks and turned to walk away.

'Poor Mrs Hewitt. That was a real shame.'

Yvonne looked over her shoulder. 'Why?'

The nurse called Tina tilted her head to one side. 'Well, she had a massive heart attack, but instead of calling an ambulance, someone brought her into A&E in a car, then left her. All we knew was that her name was Hewitt and she lived in one of the marsh villages. Now she's dead, and we can't trace her relatives.'

Yvonne thought about it. 'What about social services? Can't they trace her?'

Tina shrugged. 'Not so far. Perhaps you can help?'

'We are pretty busy, but give the station a ring if you really can't track her down.'

'Okay, and the doctor says we will be moving your patient onto a ward tomorrow.'

Yvonne thanked her and returned to Pike. Slipping back into the chair, she said, 'Do you know where Anson Taylor is?'

'Anson will hate me.'

'Probably. Did you steal drugs from him?'

'He'll kill me when he finds me!' The voice had risen several decibels.

'I'll take that as a yes, shall I? And he won't kill you. We are here with you, and besides, Anson seems to have done a runner.'

Pike looked confused, then started whimpering. 'My leg! Oh, my leg! The pain! Give me something for the pain!'

A nurse appeared and checked his charts. 'Okay, William.' She turned to Yvonne.

'I think you'd better leave. We need to sort out some stronger pain relief.' She lowered her voice. 'His leg is still in a very bad way, if you understand? The surgeon will be doing another assessment shortly.' She stopped speaking and raised her eyebrows.

Yvonne gathered from the look that it was still possible that Pike would require an amputation. She nodded, but said, 'I'll wait outside.'

'The doctor will give him something to make him sleep until the morning. By tomorrow, if there are no more seizures and as long as he doesn't have to go back to theatre, he should be pretty alert.' The nurse accompanied her to the door. 'Why not leave your questions until then?'

'Okay, but our officers will have to keep watch tonight.'

As she walked back to the car park she was glad that Pike had started talking sense. No air raids or plane crashes this time, and to mistake a dying old lady for his gran was understandable given his condition. With any luck, by tomorrow he should be able to tell them more.

As Yvonne sat in her car and waited for DC Dave Harris to answer his phone, she began to wonder what had caused Pike's mind to hallucinate about air raids of all things. He was far too young to even recognise an air-raid siren. But deep in the recesses of her mind, the story was somehow familiar.

As she brought Dave Harris up to date, WPC Yvonne Collins started to worry that she was missing something vital.

* * *

At seven precisely, Monk entered the side door of the bar. In the room upstairs, Freddie was sitting on one of the two sofas. Monk wondered if that glass was soldered to his hand.

'Have you made contact?'

'Yes, Mr Carver.'

'And you told him what exactly?' The fat man got up and without asking, poured Monk a drink.

'That I've been contacted by a client who preferred to remain anonymous, boss.'

'And he accepted that?'

'Of course not, Mr Carver. So I told him, in the strictest confidence, that I suspected the client was actually the Dutchman.'

'Ah, clever. Fabian has been trying to find a way into that mob for years.' Carver nodded appreciatively. 'Very nice, Monk, very nice.' He picked up a large brown envelope from the table. 'Everything you need, my friend, is in here.

Photographs, full personal details and a down payment. And from now on, I want to know nothing until I read about his sad demise in the daily paper, and then you'll both be paid.' He threw the package across the table and Monk picked it up. It was appreciably heavier than previous "down payments." He swallowed his drink and left, his dream of working for himself just a little closer to fruition.

* * *

By nine that evening, Karl had decided that he could no longer put off ringing one of the history society members. He needed answers. It was rumoured that by morning the police would have moved off site, but he dare not invite Freddie's men back until he was one hundred per cent sure that they wouldn't be back for a full search if the need arose. And anyway, it wasn't right that a load of anoraks like Joshua Flower and his geeky friends knew more about his property than he did.

It took three attempts before one of them offered to meet him at the airfield early the next day and give him a tour. He was almost grateful that it wasn't Joshua but his brother Simon who had volunteered. At least the slightly younger man wasn't quite such a boring old fart.

'There really isn't an awful lot to show you, Mr Shine, just a couple of things that are not immediately apparent. The thing is, Flaxton Mere was meant to be special, and towards the end of 1944, when Britain . . .'

Karl realised that he'd been wrong about Simon. Immediately bored, he claimed another appointment, thanked the man for his help, verified the time and place of the meeting and hung up. Jesus! He'd only asked for an hour of the man's time, he didn't want a bloody history lesson! But at least it was all arranged, and afterwards, when he was certain that the Fenland Constabulary had left his land, he would ring Freddie and endeavour to keep him on side until he was sure they wouldn't be coming back.

71

He walked barefoot over the plush carpet of his lounge, and headed for the drinks cupboard. As he stretched out his arm to open it, he felt a slight draft on his back.

Forgetting the drink, he wandered back into the hall and looked around. There was no sound, and nothing was out of place. He checked the dining room and the study, but again, all was well. The quarry tiles of the kitchen floor felt cold to his feet, and he realised he had not closed the back door properly. He was not usually careless, but he had a lot on his mind at present.

Karl shut it and locked it, hearing the levers slip into place, and then went back for his drink. A long, hot bath and a single malt was what he needed right now, and nothing was going to stop him.

* * *

As Karl Shine wallowed in hot, steamy water, with the strains of Coldplay drifting around the house, a dark figure stood in his kitchen. The man, clad in black from ski-masked head to leather sports-shoed toe, was looking for a particular item. It took him two minutes to locate it, then he quietly slipped through the utility door, and into the darkness.

CHAPTER ELEVEN

Just after ten, Nikki decided that she really should go home, but Knot Cottage was so cosy and comfortable. She had not expected to have another meal cooked for her, but when she got in from work, Tamsin arrived on her doorstep asking her to join them for supper.

'I'm sorry to inflict the veggie bit on you again, but Dad's gone into overdrive.' Tamsin had tried to sound indifferent, but Nikki detected a note of pleasure in her voice. 'We have enough food to open a vegetarian restaurant.'

And she hadn't been far wrong. But Nikki knew something that Tamsin didn't.

Joseph only cooked on this grand scale when he was stressed. And by the look of the myriad of colourful bowls of food that he dished up, right now he was strung out.

Even so, the meal had been amazing, and although Tamsin occasionally found the need to make some mildly deprecating comment about her father, Nikki had picked up on a remarkable softening in the girl. *And* Tamsin seemed to have embraced the hunt for Eve with something bordering on fanaticism.

'Two things before you go?' Tamsin fished around in one of the old boxes. 'I thought you might like to keep this picture separate. It's really too beautiful to be stuffed in a cardboard box and left in an attic.'

Nikki looked at the photograph and smiled broadly. 'I wondered where that one had gone. It used to have pride of place on the mantelpiece when I was younger. It is stunning, isn't it?'

The picture was a studio shot, and showed a very attractive woman with a mane of auburn hair and the greenest of eyes. She was dressed in a simple cowl-neck sweater in a soft primrose colour. Her smile held just the slightest hint of amusement. 'That's my mother,' said Nikki softly. 'Kathy.'

Joseph took the photo from her and looked a little perplexed. 'Did the hair colour skip a generation?'

Nikki laughed softly. 'No. Kathy was my father's second wife. My biological mother was killed by a hit-and-run driver shortly after I was born.' She stared at the picture. 'They never caught the driver, and funnily enough that was one of the reasons why I decided to join the police force. I wanted to make things better. I didn't want other people to be left with unfinished business and unsolved cases.' She smiled at the woman in the picture. 'But hell, I'd love to have had that hair.'

Tamsin passed her a second photograph. 'And do you know this woman? Out of that one box of photos, she's the only puzzle.'

Nikki took the picture and felt a distinct shiver pass through her, though she had no idea why. She looked closely. 'I was going to say that I've never seen her before,' she paused, 'but I think maybe I have.' Nikki let out a long breath. 'I was given something today.' She still had the book from Glenfield in her handbag. She took it out and passed it to Tamsin. 'The writing inside is my father's, but how it came to be in his locker is a mystery. And there is a picture in the back. Take a look at it.'

Tamsin and Joseph gazed at it eagerly. 'It's the same woman!' breathed the girl. 'So who is she?'

'I suspect her name is Eve,' said Nikki quietly. 'And I'm not sure that I can wait for my father's friend Tug Owen to come up for the funeral.'

Tamsin stared at the picture. 'That man there! *He's* called Tug.' She picked out several of the RAF photos. 'Look, I identified him easily. He's in a lot of the shots.'

'And he's standing right next to the mystery woman in at least two of the photos, so he *must* know her,' said Joseph.

'Then why did he deny it?' mused Nikki. 'He was adamant about it.' She frowned, 'and I'm loath to challenge him again over the phone. I guess it will have to wait until we see him.'

Tamsin shrugged. 'Maybe she's not Eve. Perhaps we are jumping to conclusions.'

Nikki looked at them enquiringly. 'Would either of you like to place a bet on that?' She looked up. Two heads were slowly shaking from side to side. 'Thought not.'

* * *

PC Tinker and PC Jenkins sat in the car and took it in turns to cat nap. There was nothing to see on the dark fen, and boredom had set in hours ago.

As Bob Tinker snored softly, Reg Jenkins got out of the vehicle to stretch his legs.

The silence out on the marsh was complete. He heard no night birds, no rustling of small animals in the undergrowth, and no traffic noises drifting across from the road. There was no moon and no stars that he could see, just a cover of thick cloud and, not for the first time that night he wondered what the hell they were doing there.

It was obvious to him that this had been the clandestine meeting place of dealer and pusher, and after the transaction had taken place, Pike the plonker had fallen arse over elbow down the shaft. End of story.

He walked towards the cordoning that stood out dimly in the gloom, and stopped. Out towards the marsh, he had seen a light. Just a glimmer, then it was gone. He tried to keep his eyes trained on the spot. 'Bob! Come here, now!'

Bob Tinker woke up and ambled across. 'What's up?'

'I saw something.' Reg pointed in the direction of where the light had come from.'

'In this? How? It's black as hell.'

'A light. A small point of light. Look! There!' This time they both saw it. 'Jesus! Surely there isn't someone out on the marsh?'

'No one in their right mind would be out there. The tides cause all manner of bogs and deep water pockets in this part.' Bob peered, searching for another sign of life.

'What should we do?' Reg felt helpless. No way could they venture onto that soft, marshy terrain at night. 'Oh Lord, look!'

A tiny glimmer, no more than a soft lantern-like glow was dancing out towards the farthest point of Flaxton Mere fen. Then suddenly it was joined by another light.

Reg's mouth had gone dry. 'Poachers! It's their torch beams!'

'Talk sense, mate. No local would be daft enough to go out on the marsh with no moonlight to guide them.'

'But they've lived here all their lives, they know these treacherous spots.'

'And that's why you won't find a poacher out there. Think about it! The tide is about to turn and the ground gets waterlogged quicker than you can run! Believe me, if anyone is out there, they are in big trouble!' Bob gathered himself. 'I'll get the loudhailer. We'll try to warn them.' He ran back to the car, threw open the boot and returned, already shouting a warning across the dark fenland.

As his shouts died away, the lights returned. Again Bob's voice bellowed into the night, but the strange lights still danced across the watery land.

'Stop.' Reg's voice was shaky. 'You ever heard of the will-o'-the-wisp?'

'The jack-o'-lantern. Yes, it's methane gas. Is that what we're looking at?' Bob stared again at the flickering lights.

'Dunno. Some say they are corpse candles, heralding a death. Then others recko—'

'Oh fuck, what's that?'

'What's what?' Reg gulped, having just frightened himself with talk of corpses. Then he heard it, and there was no denying it was the sound of a laugh. Not a hearty guffaw, but more of a low, throaty chuckle.

This time both men retreated to a position close by the car, where they stood rooted to the spot. 'Any ideas, Reg? And I mean sensible ones?' Bob's voice held a distinct tremor.

Reg opened the driver's door and looked at his crewmate. 'Answer me this. Has this weird shit anything to do with why we're stuck out here?'

'No.'

'Will anyone believe us?'

'Absolutely not. We'll get told we're no better than old Miss Quinney. A pair of prats who've been spooked by scary stories.'

'Then get in the car and lock your door! Shift change is in half an hour and then we are out of here. This never happened, right?'

CHAPTER TWELVE

Karl picked up his bunch of keys from the hall table, and pulled on a thick sweater, knowing it would be chilly in the bowels of the derelict buildings. He pushed his cell phone into the pocket of his slacks and quickly looked around before leaving. Finding the back door open the night before had unnerved him. He had even done a recce of his home before he turned in, to check that there was no one concealed in his wardrobe or under his bed, ready to nick his plasma screen as he slept.

Now, in the light of day, he laughed at himself. Tiptoeing around, opening cupboard doors and peering under beds. What a plank!

He looked at his watch and saw it was time to go. The old wallet of Flaxton Mere keys was still in the glove compartment of the car, so, with a last glance around, Shine went out through the utility door and into the gloom of the double integral garage.

He pressed the remote button on his car key, and saw the BMW's lights flash. He opened the driver's door and slipped in comfortably behind the leather steering wheel.

Although he would never admit it, the latent schoolboy in him was quite looking forward to this adventure, even if it had to be in the company of a zealot!

He reached forward to activate the electronic garage door system, and gagged loudly as a terrible force squeezed his windpipe. Both his hands flew up to his oxygen-starved throat and ineffectually tore at whatever was exerting that bone-crushing pressure. Apart from the fear at the realisation that air passages and blood vessels were closing down on him, there was a roaring noise in his ears that filled his whole pain-wracked world. His ability to move was failing, although in his final attempt to free his airway, he was still just about able to register a fingernail tearing from its bed. His body was rigid, but his legs thrashed against the car. Then, as his protruding tongue seemed to swell to an impossible size, a welcome blackness descended over him.

* * *

Monk stood in his backyard and hoped the smoke from the incinerator would not draw attention to what he was doing. If his plan went well he would soon be moving from this grim part of town, and into something more suited to his tastes. His rent was paid up for another three months. By the time it was due again, he would have invested his money from Freddie, sold on his share of the shipment, and be ready, willing and able to change his lifestyle. Not that he wanted too much change — he liked living alone. In his line of work you didn't need someone watching your every move, and if he were honest with himself, he didn't like sharing his money. Women were a drain on resources, so when he needed a bit of carnal satisfaction, it was easier to buy it. It was worth it not to have a woman nagging him to decorate or to take her shopping.

As the fire died down, he threw in the information and photographs that Freddie Carver had given him. Karl Shine's smiling face blackened and bubbled, then curled into strange tortured shapes before succumbing to the heat. He prodded the glowing ashes with an old hoe, mixing and turning until nothing recognisable was left.

It had been so easy! Just a little bit of careful thought, and job done. And he had Fabian's cut as well as his own! Freddie would be well pleased. That fat git had no time for procrastinators. Speed and efficiency was what he liked and you only got one chance with Freddie. One mistake and you were off the payroll, one way or another.

Monk placed the lid on the galvanised bin and walked away. Depending on how long it took for Shine to be discovered, he would soon be making one last visit to Freddie to collect those well-earned wages.

* * *

Nikki flopped down at her desk and switched on her computer. She had checked with uniform and there was no word on the streets about Anson Taylor and with Pike still sedated, she was at an impasse. She had just begun reading through the reports from the night before, when the phone rang and she heard Joseph's voice.

'Tam and I have just uncovered a pretty weird coincidence in one of these boxes of your father's, Nikki.'

'But we don't believe in coincidences, do we?'

'We don't, but it can't be anything else.'

Nikki heard the rustling of paper, then Joseph said, 'Your father has some papers in a leather folder. They look a bit official, but as you'd said it was okay . . .'

'Get on with it, Joseph.'

'They refer to RAF Flaxton Mere.'

Nikki sat bolt upright. 'What! He was never based locally, and Flaxton is a Second World War station. Dad flew Harrier jump jets for heavens' sake, and I can't see too many of them taking off from that dump!'

'We can't make sense of it, Nikki, but there is also a memo. It's some kind of contact details, and there's a name at the bottom, someone called Eve Anderson.'

'Eve,' whispered Nikki. 'Now why do I feel so uncomfortable that she's connected in some way to that scary bloody airfield?'

There was a pause. 'We feel the same. I get the feeling that there is more to that place than we know about. Tamsin is going to start checking the internet. Luckily she's shit-hot with a keyboard.'

Nikki's eyes narrowed. 'That's great, but as soon as I've sorted things out here, I'm going to get hold of that history society, and we'll go there ourselves. Uniform said they were happy to help and that they know the place better than anyone including the owner, so I want the full tour with nothing held back. Want to come?'

Joseph spoke softly to his daughter, then said, 'Okay, what time?'

'I'll collar one of the historians and get back to you.'

* * *

Nikki saw Joseph's car already parked on an area of concrete hard standing close to the old watchtower. Next to him was a small battered Renault Clio and a flashy vintage motorbike.

As she locked the car, she saw that Joseph and his daughter were in conversation with a grey-haired eccentric-looking man, and that there were three other men beside the little Clio, all chatting animatedly. 'Great,' she murmured to herself. 'A bloody coach party.'

As she walked towards them one of the men stepped forward. He seemed familiar in some way. He could have been anything from forty to fifty plus, his dress was sporty-casual and his greying hair was thick and wavy, although neatly cut with a floppy fringe and a side parting. And there was a twinkle in his eye that made him look quite boyish, whatever his true age.

'I know you,' she said bluntly.

The man stuck out a hand and grinned at her. 'And I know you, DI Galena. We've been on more than one shout together, from different sides of the emergency services, of course.'

Nikki concentrated her thoughts for a moment, then said, 'Ah, Blue Watch. You're a firefighter.'

'Spot on. Simon Flower, brother to that old windbag over there.' He pointed fondly towards the grey-haired man who Nikki now knew to be Joshua Flower. 'But although I'm still with the fire department, I'm an investigator now.'

'And an aficionado of desolate and dreary derelict airfields?'

'No, you're referring to my brother.' He laughed and the eyes sparkled. 'And generally this place would not interest me one iota, but it does have a fascinating history and a few surprises too.'

Nikki frowned. 'Like what?'

Simon Flower's smile broadened and Nikki couldn't help but notice that he was extremely attractive, considering his probable age and the dangerous kind of work that he'd done. 'I'd better leave that to my brother to explain. This place is his baby.' He pointed in Joshua's direction. 'Come on. Let me introduce you to the History Boys.'

Simon did the honours, and Nikki found herself surrounded by eager faces and names that she recognised from the list provided earlier by uniform.

'Before we go into the buildings, Professor Flower, what can you tell us briefly about this particular station?'

Joshua took a deep breath, then said, 'Well, it was originally a fighter station with grass landing strips, but it was brought up to date in the 1940s with the typical A-plan concrete runways and dispersal pans for heavier bombers. As you can see, they scattered the hangars, sheds, stores and defences well away from the main control room, which was damned sensible, because if one got hit, at least the others wouldn't go up with it.'

Nikki noticed that Joseph was staring at Joshua Flower and listening with real interest. Even she realised that he was not the crumbly old bore they had expected, and although the man was passionate about WWII history, he explained everything in a manner that held their attention. He was certainly eccentric, but compared with some of the dry-as-dust academic speakers that Nikki had suffered in the past Flower could almost be considered a ray of sunshine. He had a kind of charisma that drew you in and held you there.

'Well, other than the stuff that you posted yourself, there is nothing much about it on the internet,' said Tamsin. 'Unlike some of the other stations, where there are pages of information.'

'Just so, young lady, and that's because this place is something of an enigma.' He tapped the side of his nose conspiratorially. 'It has secrets.' Flower smiled cryptically. 'Oh yes. It has a long history, but I'll make it simple. Originally the RAF decided to turn it from a small fighter station into what was called a decoy site, to protect some of the larger fields. It was to have dummy planes and landing lights, and they even planned to spray the ground to make it look like an A-plan runway. But when they looked closely at the location and the land available, they changed their minds. Initially they had believed the land to be too low and silty, and too close to the marsh to be safe, but ground studies showed that the site was higher and far more stable than first thought. So they allowed the "dummy" rumour to spread, but in reality they began to construct a major airfield.' He glanced around at his entranced audience. 'And there is a wonderfully preserved area beneath the main control room. We discovered it when we began researching and mapping the place for historical reference. It is almost as it was during the war, only the paraphernalia that would have been there is gone.'

'It's one of the reasons that we want to preserve it,' chipped in a man named Selby. 'There are very few places left in such incredibly good order. It would be absolute sacrilege to destroy it.'

'And the owner wants to do that?' asked Joseph.

'He *says* he wants to restore it, Detective, but we believe otherwise. We know he already has plans to build prestige housing, and we also know that once he begins, he'll want more and more, and our old historical military buildings will go under the wrecker's ball.'

'Can he do that?' asked Tamsin.

'He owns the land. He can do whatever he wants. There is no protection order at Flaxton Mere. He could rip it to shreds any time he wanted.'

Joseph nodded. 'And what do you know about him?'

'Karl Shine? Not a lot, although we try to keep him sweet, because he allows us access. He has no objection to us researching the place, and he lets us come and go pretty much as we wish. He's even given us keys for the padlocks.' Flower shrugged. 'But that could change very quickly when he starts his project.'

'That's why our group is fighting to get something legal in place, to protect the watch office, the control room and the bunker,' added Selby vehemently. 'And fast.'

'By the way, as you've just mentioned Shine,' Simon interjected. 'He was on the blower last night ringing round some of the club members to try and get a "guided tour." He insisted that it had to be this morning, so as I was free, I came out on the bike, but the silly sod didn't turn up.'

'Did you ring him?'

'There was no answer. Just a recorded message.'

'Funny,' murmured Nikki to Joseph. 'Uniform said that Shine's red BMW has been out here from dawn till dusk since Pike's accident, but the car's certainly not here now, is it?'

'Something must have cropped up, or maybe he just forgot,' said Joseph doubtfully.

Nikki felt a niggle of concern and decided to try to contact the man herself as soon as their trip was over.

'Don't be surprised if some more of the society turn up, Detective Inspector. As soon as any of the guys know we're coming out here, they usually tag along. It's such a fascinating place it attracts them like moths to a flame.'

Joshua's smile and obvious fervour for his "subject," made it difficult to be angry, and Nikki decided that perhaps it wouldn't be a bad thing to know who else had an interest in this godforsaken junkyard. 'So, where do we start?'

'Right here in the watchtower. But first, hard hats and battery lanterns for everyone.' He opened his boot and took out a large cardboard box. Then he turned to Nikki. 'We do have a certain amount of lighting down there, in the form of big Calor lamps, but there are unlit passages and we need to keep you safe.' He looked around at his troop, and smiled. 'All kitted out? Then follow me!'

Prior to going inside, Nikki had no idea of what an old air base would look like. Sure, they littered the Lincolnshire countryside, but their numbers were declining fast, and they were either being demolished or just disintegrating. So she was not prepared for the size of the place or what existed beneath the ground.

'Simply amazing, isn't it?' Joshua's excited voice echoed around them. 'The idea was that they would command the skies from below the earth.' He waved a hand towards the massive underground room that stretched out ahead of them. 'Walk with me and I'll tell you about Flaxton Mere's well-kept secret.'

He moved through the big room in the direction of a wide passageway. 'During the war, it was believed that a German invasion was very much on the cards. RAF Flaxton Mere, because of its location and numerous other considerations, was chosen to be what we would now call a super-airfield.' The professor cleared his throat, then continued. 'Considerable work was started to construct four separate strike-proof bunkers, one for high-ranking personnel, one to house a state-of-the-art communication centre, one for the servicemen and women, and one massive area that would serve as a depot for vehicles, armoured cars and the like. Apart from the bunkers, there would have been storerooms, bomb stores and a multitude of other installations. Flaxton Mere was to have been the nerve centre that would control all the surrounding airfields, from Lincoln to Cambridge.'

Joseph let out a long, low whistle. 'That's some installation! Especially considering there are very few underground facilities of any kind in this county because of the soft fenland soil.'

'This site is very rare, a complete anomaly. The soils are complex in their structure. It seems that there was once a monastery here, built on what was then a ridge, an area of high ground some way from the marshes. The wetlands have now encroached, and the terrible storms have altered the coastline completely.' Joshua shook his head. 'And one day soon, I'm sure it will surrender to the flood.' He exhaled, 'But I digress. Back to the war! It soon became clear that the invasion would never happen, and this super-station would not be required. Work stopped. The private contractors that had been brought in from far and wide were sworn to secrecy, then disbanded. So, as the RAF had taken great pains to keep everything very much under wraps, it didn't take too long for people to forget it ever existed. If it hadn't been for the collective memories of the history society, we would never have uncovered all this.'

The professor explained that sadly little was left. 'This is the only intact bunker, the one designed as a control room, although there are numerous underground stores and passages. We've been mapping them for years.'

'And is it all structurally safe?' asked Joseph.

'The tunnels and chambers that we use are fine. You met my brother Simon, and as you know he is a fire investigation and safety officer. He has checked the underground areas personally. We have no wish to lose anyone through negligence, I assure you.'

As they continued into a wide tunnel, Nikki walked along beside Joshua, Selby and Joseph, and she began to feel the atmosphere of RAF Flaxton Mere at a time of war. She saw in her mind's eye uniformed men and women hurrying down the long corridors, opening heavy metal-framed doors, papers tucked beneath their arms and gas masks slung over one shoulder. She saw pallets stacked high with great gleaming shell cases, being carefully moved from stores to loading bays. And she imagined the awareness that at any moment enemy bombers could make a lucky strike, and this bunker would become a sealed tomb.

Nikki was usually not fanciful, but this odd place and the sound of Joshua's hypnotic voice explaining what had gone on so many years ago, made her feel strange, as if she had slipped out of her own time zone and fallen back into the 1940s.

As they walked through the main control room and down a long straight corridor to what was left of a massive underground storeroom, Nikki felt certain that this was not the only part left undamaged. Yes, some of it would have succumbed to the passing of time, but she was convinced that there was more than this. 'You said that you have been mapping the area, Professor Flower. Do you have those maps with you?'

'They are on our computer, Inspector, but I've asked Andrew Friar, another of our number, to print them off for you. They are by no means conclusive, but they are an indication of the original infrastructure. And we do have some old plans on record, although they bear little resemblance to what is left today.' He looked at his watch. 'With any luck, Andrew will be here by the time we surface.'

'Where's Tamsin?' asked Nikki, looking around.

'She's taken a different route, with Simon and Frank Kohler.' Joshua smiled reassuringly. 'And she's in safe hands. Those two know every inch of this place.'

'To see what?'

'Storage cellars, map rooms, all much smaller than the main bunker, but interesting nevertheless.' He paused. 'Oh, and there is one little surprise.' He nodded to himself. 'Simon is probably showing Miss Easter the "secret tunnel" he found last year.'

Before Joshua could continue, Nikki heard the sound of running footsteps. She looked around and was surprised to see a familiar figure racing up behind them. 'Dave?'

'Ma'am!' Dave Harris, out of breath and wide-eyed at the strange location in which he had found himself, caught them up. 'I need a word. It's urgent.'

She led him away from the others, noting his worried expression.

'I've been asked to get you all out of here. To evacuate these premises and get everyone to the main car park.'

Nikki stiffened. 'What's happened?'

'We need to seal off the entire area, ma'am. The body of Karl Shine has just been found, and he didn't croak through natural causes. So, considering all the other factors, like the guy down the shaft, and the drugs and so on . . .' Dave left the sentence unfinished.

Nikki nodded. 'Then we need to get everyone out. We could be trampling vital evidence underfoot.' She turned back to Joshua. 'I'm sorry, sir, but you need to get your friends out of here. There has been an incident that we believe is connected to this place. We need to clear the area to protect any evidence. Where are the others?'

The two historians looked at each other with troubled expressions, then Joshua grabbed Selby's arm and said, 'You take the officers to the passage where Simon will be and I'll make sure none of the others have followed us down here.'

Selby nodded. Nikki added, 'Dave, go with the professor and make sure no one else comes in.'

Selby beckoned to them. 'Come with me.' He turned, and with an unusual loping gait went back down the corridor and opened a small door.

His large battery-powered lantern showed a shadowy passage stretching off in front of them. Their footsteps sounded strangely muffled as they half ran through what seemed an endless corridor linking storage rooms and cellars. Nikki tried to remember the route, but as they circumnavigated old shelving units and benches, piles of broken furniture and in one place a stack of what looked like empty fuel drums, she knew that she was hopelessly lost.

'Not much further.' Selby sounded out of breath. 'We'll go through the east chamber.' He indicated an opening that led down a long, wide passageway.

'This place is a maze!'

'You haven't seen the half of it, Inspector.' Selby's eyes glittered in the torchlight.

'Then why did the professor just tell us that there was little left other than the main bunker, a few stores and the corridors?' asked Joseph edgily.

'We don't generally tell *anyone* about this place. We need to get our preservation order on it before the size and importance of Flaxton Mere is made public.'

They were entering a small empty chamber with one rotting wooden door that was wedged open. The damp smell that oozed from the tunnel made Nikki think of ancient crypts and abandoned cellars.

'Simon! Frank! Come back! It's urgent!' Selby's voice echoed down the tunnel.

'Damn! This passage goes on for miles. They're obviously out of earshot.'

'Does it have another exit?' asked Joseph, clearly anxious that two strange men had taken his daughter off into the middle of nowhere.

'No.' Selby shone his torch along shiny, moss-covered walls. 'It did once. It was an escape route in case the enemy infiltrated the bunkers, or if there was a fire or an emergency. The exits were sealed up at some point, which with the marsh water rising much higher now, is a blessing.'

'Then why the hell has Simon Flower taken my daughter down a dark, stinking tunnel that goes nowhere?' Joseph's anger was filled with concern.

'Because it is a bit of an enigma, and please don't worry. Simon and Frank know this place as well as I do. Tamsin will be quite safe with them, I assure you.'

'Sir, we have a job to do,' butted in Nikki. 'Could we just locate Tamsin and the others and get everyone out of here?'

From behind them, Nikki heard more footsteps, and in the torchlight, Nikki saw Joshua Flower hurrying towards them. 'Everyone is out and accounted for, with the exception of those three.'

'Then let's go,' said Joseph impatiently, moving towards the damp passageway.

'Let me.' Marcus Selby spoke up. 'It's pointless us all trooping down there. It's narrow, and I know it well, so I'll be quicker.' In seconds the beam of his flashlight could be seen disappearing into the tunnel.

'What did Selby mean by an "enigma?"' Joseph remained staring along the tunnel.

Joshua Flower did not answer immediately. Then he switched off his own torch to save the batteries. 'I suppose if we are to have half the Fenland Constabulary down here poking about, you will need to know our secrets.'

'Every last one of them, Professor,' said Nikki coldly.

'I was afraid that might be the case.'

'Forgive me for asking, but why should this ghastly and probably very dangerous wreck hold secrets that you wish to guard so jealously?' Nikki squatted down on her haunches, her back to the cold wall.

'History. Precious history.' He sighed. 'This place is unique. It could have meant the difference between keeping our war planes flying or losing them to the *Luftwaffe*. Our group has spent *years* trying to uncover the true history of this amazing piece of our heritage, and suddenly it is being threatened by man and nature simultaneously.'

'And the enigma of this particular tunnel?'

'Ah, yes. We are unsure as to whether this route was constructed by luck or design, but it follows a much older system that was in existence long before the war. Remember I mentioned the monastery? This ground belonged to the church. Records show not only a monastery but a very ancient place of worship even prior to that.' He drew in a deep breath. 'And the monks, it seems, were not averse to a spot of smuggling. This tunnel led from the monastery out into the marsh, where they had constructed a series of bolt-holes, man-made caves where contraband was stored, to be either moved on for sale or brought in from boats out in the Wash, and up to the church.'

Joshua's voice worked its magic and Nikki found she was interested, despite her concern for Tamsin.

'At intervals along this tunnel, there are small circular chambers. Some were used as storerooms for the monks' booty. Others were portals that led up to the caves, and one was actually a tiny chapel. We believe that for all their illegal doings, they did not want to miss their devotions, so if a couple of the brothers were working in the tunnel and the bell rang, they would still have somewhere to worship.'

'And the chapel is still there?' asked Joseph, not taking his eyes from the tunnel.

Flower said, 'Yes, although it's little more than a six-by-six hole, with a small semi-circular recess in the wall with an ancient crucifix standing in it.'

Nikki whistled softly, then dragged her mind back to the investigation. 'Can we rely on your help to search this place properly?'

'We have already offered, when that unfortunate boy fell down the shaft.'

'I know, but I get the feeling we would only have been shown the parts that you wanted us to see. In fact,' she threw the man a knowing glance, 'I suspect your intentions were to keep us *away* from your precious tunnels.'

Joshua let out a small sigh. 'I confess, Inspector. That is the truth of it.'

'Where the hell is Selby?' Joseph moved forward and shone his light down the passageway. 'He's been gone for ages.'

'He's coming. Listen.'

A moment later Selby emerged into the dancing light of their torch beams. 'I don't understand it! They're not there. The tunnel is empty.'

* * *

Half an hour later, surrounded by police cars, vans and assorted personnel, Nikki, Joseph and Dave Harris stood with four grim-faced members of the history group.

'Mr Brewer, you and your wife arrived just after we went down into the bunker. You spoke to Simon Flower and Frank Kohler?'

Bill Brewer was in his sixties and looked like one of the "experts" from *Bargain Hunt*. He wore an old, but well-cared-for three-piece suit, complete with gold watch chain, a fresh flower in his lapel and polished black boots. He nodded vigorously. 'Yes. Simon asked if we wanted to go into the marsh tunnel.'

'That's right, officer,' added Margaret Brewer, his rotund wife. 'But we've been mapping one of the old stores and we wanted to get on with that.'

'Okay, then no more messing around. It's time to get a full search underway.' Nikki gritted her teeth. 'Have you guys got *any* idea where else they might have gone?'

The Brewers, Selby and Flower shook their heads. 'There is nowhere else of interest that is safe, and Simon would not risk anything happening to anyone.'

Nikki had a sinking feeling in her stomach about the truth of that statement. She covered her concern with a slightly accusatory belligerence. 'You people should never have been allowed on this site. It is a bloody death trap.' She was going to say more when she caught a warning glance from Joseph. Better not to antagonise the one group of people who could prove useful in a proper search. 'Right, well, I have to ask you all to stay here until I can get an officer to take your details.'

A uniformed officer and a couple of anxious-looking constables approached her.

'Get the teams ready, Sergeant. We have a big area to cover before twilight.'

Before he could reply, Dave's voice rang out. 'Hey, ma'am! Look!'

From the far edge of the marsh, three figures were making their way towards them.

'Thank God! It's Tamsin!' The relief in Joseph's voice was palpable.

'And Simon and Frank,' added Joshua Flower. 'But where on earth . . . ?'

'Hi, Dad. What's all this about?' Tamsin looked puzzled.

Joseph was ashen. 'It was nearly a major manhunt for the three of you.'

Nikki interrupted. 'We were told you were in a bloody tunnel, so what the hell were you doing out there?'

'We *were* in a tunnel,' Simon said excitedly, 'but there had been a small landslip, and it revealed another way out to the fen. We've been looking for it for years!'

'Simon thinks it was used by smugglers,' added Tamsin, clearly unfazed by her adventure. Then she looked around and took in the flashing blue lights and uniformed officers. 'Oh shit! Dad? Please tell me all this is not because we went exploring?'

Nikki drew in a deep breath and said, 'Relax, Tamsin. At least you're safe. Now I can turn this over to uniform to secure the area.' She beckoned to Joseph and lowered her voice. 'Get Tamsin out of here. I have to go back to the station and set up a murder room, but I'll ring you later with an update.'

Joseph nodded, then whispered, 'I'm going to cancel my leave. You'll need me.'

'Wait until we know the facts about Karl Shine's death. Don't forget you have Tamsin to consider. You can't leave her stuck out on Cloud Fen, it's too bloody dangerous.' Nikki touched his arm lightly. 'In the meantime, work on that link between Eve, my father, and this hellhole. It's really worrying me. Now, go. I'll ring you later.'

CHAPTER THIRTEEN

'Oh my!' Professor Rory Wilkinson, the home office pathologist, leant over his latest acquisition and exclaimed, 'Whoever wanted you dead, my friend, certainly made sure of it.' He pushed his wire frame glasses further up the bridge of his nose and looked more closely at the mortal remains of Karl Shine.

'Looks pretty straightforward to me.' One of the mortuary technicians was carefully removing Karl's clothing.

'Well now, Matthew, you say that, but there are *such* secrets within this treasure chest of a body. What we see on the surface makes your assumption *seem* correct, but beneath the skin,' he waved a slender hand in the air, 'who knows?'

Matt shrugged as he carefully laid out the clothes on another table. 'Whatever you say, Prof, but I still think it's an open and shut case.'

Rory gave his assistant a withering look. 'Very droll. Now, if you'd be kind enough to measure and weigh this gentleman, we can get the external examination out of the way, and then the master will do what the master does best.'

'I don't know how you can be so passionate about slicing up dead people,' said Matt flatly.

'Sometimes I despair of you, young man. Now, come here.' The tall forensic scientist pointed to the body on the steel table. 'Behold! All the complexities of the universe are contained within the intricate composition of this human body and you, Matthew, are one of the privileged few who get to see that miracle with your own eyes.'

'All that's as may be, but at the end of the day it's still slicing up dead people.'

Rory raised his eyes heavenwards. 'Dear Lord, forgive me for asking, but if it's not too much trouble, could my next technician have a soul, please?'

Matthew, well used to the pathologist waxing lyrical over his cadavers, adjusted the microphone above the table and stood back. 'If I were you, I'd just settle for one with a strong stomach.'

Rory knew when he was beaten. 'Beggars can't be choosers, I suppose. Let's begin. File number 4725. Karl Daniel Shine. Here we have the body of a well-nourished, thirty-five-year-old white male. His weight is . . .'

Later, as Matt began cleaning up and preparing for their next silent guest, Rory Wilkinson checked over the detailed description of the injuries sustained by the deceased. It was well known that a killer who chose strangulation as his method of dispatch usually used far more force than was actually necessary. In this case, having studied the body in situ, it was clear that the assailant had been concealed in the back of the car, and when Shine was seated, had thrown a length of nylon tow rope over his head, and yanked it backwards with more than considerable force. 'Enough to practically behead the poor sod', muttered Rory. The killer had crossed the rope behind the driver's headrest, and simply hung on until his victim was asphyxiated. Amazing, thought the pathologist. The murderer strangled him most effectively, but never once touched him.

'Can I take a break now, Prof?'

'Certainly. Bring me back a Kit Kat when you come, will you?'

'Sure. Oh, and congratulations on your discovery, boss. I now see your point about not assuming too much.'

Rory laughed. 'Even I did not expect that little gem, Matthew.'

The young man left, leaving Rory to mull over the paradox. Someone had gone to great lengths to kill Karl Shine. They had risked being convicted of murder and incarcerated for life, when, if they had allowed the apparently fit and healthy Mr Shine to live, he would have died of natural causes in a matter of weeks.

At the base of Karl Shine's brain, in an area called the Circle of Willis, Rory had found a berry-like swelling. The aneurysm was at the branching point of an artery, and the weakness was such that it could have ruptured at any moment. The sub-arachnoid haemorrhage that would have followed would doubtless have proved fatal. It was indeed remarkable that it had not burst during his death throes.

This would make jolly good reading in the case file. He hoped DI Galena would appreciate the irony as she hunted for the perpetrator of such a pointless killing. 'Funny old world,' thought Rory, as he checked to see who was next.

* * *

In the newly instated murder room, Nikki stared at the whiteboard that covered a large part of the far wall. There was not much on it yet, but in a matter of hours it would depict a full-blown case. There would be names, locations, victims, suspects and photographs. A few days ago she had found the blank surface irritating. She liked to be busy and had wanted a case to work on. Well, now she had one.

At the top of the board was an A4 size photograph of Karl Shine. Next to it was one of Shine in his car that the police photographer had taken. It was difficult to believe that they were the same person. In the first, he was looking directly into the camera, slightly tanned with smartly cut hair and a satisfied grin on his face. In the second, his face and neck were swollen, the skin a purplish colour, with pinpoint haemorrhages around the eyes. His throat was badly damaged, with an almost horizontal ligature mark cut deep into the flesh. Even without the forensic report, bright blue fibres from the tow rope could clearly be seen protruding from the scorched skin.

Nikki stood up and looked at the room full of officers. 'Sorry. I know it's getting towards the end of the day, but I want to make sure we all know what we're dealing with.' She pointed to the photograph. 'This is Karl Daniel Shine. Thirty-five years old, single, lived alone in Martin Park, Greenborough. Murdered in his car, a red BMW, which was parked in his integral garage, at around eight thirty this morning. We obviously haven't got the pathologist's report yet, but as you can see, he was strangled, apparently by a person concealed in the back of the car. A set of spare keys were left on the back seat, so we assume the killer stole them earlier and locked himself in the car to wait for Shine.' She paused and looked across to where Cat sat. 'What have you and Dave dug up on this man?'

Cat flipped through her notebook. 'Not a lot more than we had before, ma'am. Seems to have been a bit of a loner. The house is mortgaged to the hilt, but it's worth a lot on the market. I've yet to discover how he made his money, there is no visible source of income, but his lifestyle was pretty comfortable. He purchased the old Flaxton Mere airfield from the RAF about three years ago, but has pretty well sat on it ever since. I've got hold of his solicitor, who I have to say is not a happy man. If he mentioned the word, "procrastination" once, he mentioned it a dozen times. I'm seeing him at six tonight to talk to him about what intentions Shine had for the airfield. Other than that, I've hit a big fat zero.'

'Parents?'

'Sorry, but they are part of that zero I just mentioned.'

'And you, Dave? Anything else?'

'Nothing specific, ma'am. I've found nothing under Karl Shine on the police computer. In fact all his business dealings look clean. But,' Dave rubbed at his forehead, 'I was on a case about five or six years ago, and we had our eye on a bloke called Daniel *Shire*. We never actually nailed him for anything, but he kept turning up in our investigations. I reckon it's the same man.'

'What sort of investigations?' Nikki asked with interest.

'Fraud, deception and money laundering.'

'Then check this Daniel Shire out, Dave, and while Cat is investigating his finances, see what else you can find out about our victim's private life. Yvonne and Niall? You two stay with the William Pike and Anson Taylor area of the enquiry. I want to know if there was any connection, no matter how tenuous, between either of them and Karl Shine. Now,' Nikki stared at them, her face hard, 'I'm certain that Flaxton Mere is the key to everything. Shine *owned* it. Pike was found with a bagful of drugs *on* it. Taylor went missing presumably on his way *to* it. Pike's missing grandmother lives *close to* it. Are we all agreed so far?'

There was a murmur of assent and Nikki continued. 'With that in mind, I've already got a team out at the airfield, but the super is very concerned about safety issues. Flaxton Mere is hazardous in the extreme.'

Dave wholeheartedly agreed. 'Especially if you aren't familiar with it, ma'am. Can I suggest we involve the history society and their maps and plans right from the word go?'

Nikki nodded. 'I agree we need them, but the uniforms must do a sweep first. Then at first light, we'll engage our *History Boys* and go in ourselves. Right now, go home and get your beauty sleep. We have an early start in the morning.'

* * *

Karl Shine's murder made the ten o'clock news, making Monk a very happy man. He rang his boss's mobile number and asked if he could meet with him the next day. As he had hoped, it was to be the usual place at eleven, and Freddie sounded in very good spirits. And so he should. It had been an efficient and professional hit, just the kind fat-man Carver liked.

CHAPTER FOURTEEN

A thin mist was still burning off the marsh, giving the watery landscape the unreal quality of a film set. Nikki half expected to see men in jeans and T-shirts moving the dry ice machine around.

'Our mates found sod all, then?' Dave looked weary and he stifled a yawn. 'I was half hoping they'd find something so we could skip this early morning jaunt.'

'No such luck. I see the others are already here, and our historical helpers are on their way.' Nikki watched as two cars and a motorcycle pulled into the parking area.

Cat ambled across to them. 'Morning, ma'am. Morning, Dave.' She looked back to where the history society people were getting out of their cars, and sighed. 'Oh boy! This should be fun.'

Nikki agreed. She hated using members of the public, no matter how well-meaning they were. In general they were as useful as a chocolate poker. But as the police knew sod all about the airfield, she was forced to admit that this time they might actually be helpful.

She nodded politely to the five men, then began allotting areas to be searched.

For hours they trudged through the debris and wreckage of the main buildings and storerooms. The dust and grime stuck to their shoes and the depressing atmosphere clung to their spirits.

Peering into a shallow recess off a long corridor beneath the watchtower, Nikki was haunted by the thought that her father might have walked this very route, alongside a woman called Eve.

When her radio crackled into life, her father's mysterious life was temporarily forgotten. The reception was poor and she knew that the further underground she went, the worse it would get. She listened carefully, and realised that Cat Cullen's group had made some kind of discovery. They had located an exterior storehouse with footprints leading to it, and as it was nowhere near the area visited by the historians, Cat suspected they might have discovered Pike's reason for being on the fen. A residue of white powder found on a shelf indicated a possible hiding place for a stash of drugs.

Nice one, thought Nikki. Forensics would get a match on the sole markings in the dust on the floor, and it was highly unlikely that the deposits were icing sugar.

For another hour they combed the buildings, and then Nikki decided to call everyone back to the rendezvous point. Apart from the footprints, they had found nothing.

'Seems that's it.' Nikki stared down at the line of ticks on her search list.

'Should we check the pillboxes around the perimeter?' asked Niall.

'Don't see much point.' Dave brushed a smudge of limey whitewash from his jacket. 'If there's nothing of import in the main buildings, I doubt we'll find anything out there.'

Nikki wanted to agree, but said, 'We're here now, and as we have the help of these good people,' she indicated the group of civilians, 'let's do it properly.'

Marcus Selby took a tentative step forward. 'I think your sergeant is probably right, Inspector. Those pillboxes are just smelly little concrete huts.'

Nikki thought about this, then said, 'No, they need checking. Niall and Yvonne, see to that before you return to the station.'

Joshua Flower raised a hand. 'I'll go with them. I'm in no hurry to get away. Even though I'm sure Marcus is perfectly correct.'

Nikki thanked their guides, and said that she was satisfied that Flaxton Mere held nothing that was of use to them in the hunt for Karl Shine's killer. Then, as they walked away, she wondered if that were true.

* * *

As she picked her way through the rubble of a collapsed wall, Yvonne decided that, sunny day or not, this miserable place was giving her the shivers and she would be very glad to be back in her police car and speeding towards the nick.

The first pillbox was some way off and Joshua Flower fell into step beside her.

'I get the feeling that you'd rather be somewhere else, officer?'

'Make that *anywhere* else, sir,' answered Yvonne grimly. She looked at the older man with interest. 'Unlike you, I think?'

'We are all different, aren't we? Under normal circumstances, I couldn't be happier out here.'

'I know that you're local, sir, but what's your profession?' enquired Yvonne.

'I retired early, my dear. My time is my own, which I admit is something of a relief. I was an architect. I did not like working to deadlines, so I started lecturing on the subject, but I couldn't take to university life either. Now the peace and quiet of being able to do as I please is most agreeable to me.'

'And is there a Mrs Flower?'

'No, sadly there isn't.' Flower shrugged. 'Married life isn't for everyone I suppose.'

Yvonne silently agreed, then said, 'I'm sorry, Professor. I think it's the job. I'm too nosy for my own good.' She changed the subject. 'I'm not surprised you were a lecturer, sir. You have a wonderful way of speaking. So where does the interest in airfields come from?'

The professor held back a bramble. 'This county is jam-packed full of them, and with my love of architecture and history, it just happened organically.'

'And Simon? He's with the fire service, isn't he? What got him into all this?'

'He drifted along after me, and he loves the place because he's a born explorer.' He looked up at the clear blue sky, an almost wistful look on his face. 'He was studying history, but gave up and helped our father for a while, then he went into the army. He was in the Royal Engineers, and abroad most of the time, but I think he missed home. When he came out, he joined the fire service. That suited him much better.'

'I don't think our paths ever crossed. Was he a full-time fire officer?'

'Oh yes, he was with Boston's Blue Watch up until about five years ago, and then the poor blighter developed a severe chest condition. He's still with the service, but as you already know, he's involved with fire investigations and safety issues now.'

Yvonne was just about to ask more when she saw Niall beckoning to them.

'I see what your mate meant about stinky, Professor!'

The older man nodded. 'I doubt we'll find any useful clues around here.'

They moved on, walking carefully around the perimeter, checking the uneven ground as they went, parting tufts of thick, coarse grass and holding back vicious blackberry branches with sticks in order to peer into shadowy clumps of overgrowth.

'Last one.' Yvonne looked at the ugly structure in front of her.

'Allow me to spare your dainty nostrils,' said Niall gallantly. 'I'll go it alone!' He bent down and ducked under the concrete lintel.

'Oh, smashing!' His voice echoed. 'You two don't know what you're missing!'

'I know only too well, and I doubt you'll need to spend too long in there, PC Farrow. Once you've seen one, you've seen them all.' The professor was peering into the opening.

Niall asked, 'Why has this one got a great lump of concrete in the middle?'

'They sometimes put a solid structure like a brick or stone wall in the centre. The idea was that if a grenade or a shot entered via the loophole, it wouldn't ricochet around inside and wipe out the entire garrison. That other heavy mount near the front gun port was the mounting for the main gun, probably a Hotchkiss six-pounder. Those other smaller lintels by the remaining loopholes were for light machine guns.'

Yvonne noticed that the man's voice still had a professorial tone. He couldn't help delivering a lecture.

'Doesn't matter how far off the beaten track you go,' Niall was still muttering, 'the bleeding lager louts will still find somewhere like this to use as a toilet. Ouch, bugger!' The exclamation was followed by a clatter, and another oath.

Yvonne stifled a laugh. 'Are you all right in there?'

'Banged my bloody head, dropped my bloody torch, and now I've cracked my bloody elbow on one of your bloody machine gun ports.' Niall struggled out of the low entrance and brushed himself down. 'Sorry about that.' This was to Joshua. 'But I pity the poor sods that had to get in there to protect the realm.'

Yvonne reached across and rubbed at a dusty patch on her partner's shoulder. 'But nothing of interest?'

Niall was quiet for a moment, then shook his head. 'Nah, nothing except some general crud and something sticky that I would prefer not to talk about.' He looked across to the lone police car keeping watch on the sea-bank. 'Time to give up, I guess.'

* * *

103

At ten o'clock, Monk called into a local estate agent and browsed their "properties for sale" boards. He didn't know exactly how well he would do on this deal, but he enjoyed the window shopping. There was a smart, two-bedroom bachelor apartment, ready in two months, in a new build on Greenborough's Granary Wharf. Very modern, very private, very nice indeed. Monk had had it up to his eyebrows with what his landlord had called a "bijou terraced character cottage." He'd seen holding cells with more character than 14A, Cannon Place.

He asked for the details and a wispy blonde girl with impossibly scarlet, high-gloss lips, removed a glossy brochure from a filing cabinet and offered it to him. 'You would have to move fast on this property, sir. They are going like hotcakes.'

He smiled at her and said that he would be checking his investments and would ring back later. He folded the brochure in half and slipped it into his inside pocket. Granary Wharf had a swanky sound to it. It would do very nicely, thank you.

As always, Freddie was there ahead of him. He sat like a great over-dressed Buddha, the usual glass glued to his hand. On the table in front of him were two packages, one for him and one for Fabian, and Monk's heart raced at the sight.

Freddie waved a hand towards the other sofa. 'So, there were no problems?'

Monk sat. 'None at all. Smooth as silk, Mr Carver.'

'And quickly done, Monk. I am impressed.' He nodded, smiling serenely. 'And Fabian still believes that he was working for the Dutchman?'

Monk nodded furiously and accepted the scotch that Freddie was passing him.

'Good, good. An excellent job. I'll have no hesitation in using Mr Fabian again.'

Monk took a swallow, and nodded. 'Absolutely, Mr Carver. He's first class.' He looked longingly at the packages, his deposit on Granary Wharf.

'Ah, yes, here we are.' A sweaty hand pushed the brown envelopes towards him.

'Thank you, boss.' He picked them up, noting their very reassuring weight. He pushed one packet deep into an inside pocket and waved the other one at Freddie. 'I'll take this to Fabian.' He glanced at his watch. 'I'm meeting him shortly.'

'Really?' The familiar soft, sibilant voice came from behind.

Monk spun round. 'Fa—!' The rest of the name was cut short, because the hollow-point bullet had torn away most of his bottom jaw.

A second bullet smashed through his left elbow. If he had been a medical man, Monk would have marvelled that the marksman had managed to destroy his humerus, his radius and his ulna, along with various blood vessels, tendons, ligaments, bursa and cartilage, all with a single accurate shot. As it was, Monk was no longer capable of registering anything other than intense pain, although in some tiny compartment of his mind that still sparked with consciousness he did recall why he hated Fabian. It was because Fabian loved his work so very much.

Through a hazy, bloody mist he saw the bloated figure of Freddie Carver. It was laughing.

'Silly boy, Monk. Surely you knew that no one rips off Freddie and gets away with it? Whatever were you thinking? But credit where credit's due. Well done for taking care of Karly Baby. If you hadn't tried to deceive me, I would have been happy to give you this.' He bent over and pulled the package from Monk's stained and torn jacket. 'As it is, well . . .'

In his last few seconds, Monk thought of the girl with the ruby lips. She was handing him the key to his brand new flat in Granary Wharf.

CHAPTER FIFTEEN

It had taken Steph almost an hour to sneak onto the airfield. The two police officers in the car up on the sea-bank seemed to be watching one particular area, and she had finally managed to creep past the old pillboxes and into the comparative safety of the overgrown ground around the control tower.

The place did not frighten her, although she felt that it should, considering what had happened to Pike. But she knew in her heart that it was the temporary resting place of her brother, and somehow that managed to calm her, give her peace. She thought that maybe he was watching over her. She had no idea why she had come here. The notion had entered her head earlier in the day, and she seemed to have had no option but to obey.

She concealed herself in a small hollowed-out space between a partially collapsed red brick wall and some tall reedy grass. From this spot she calculated that she could see most of the deserted buildings and the police car, but remain pretty well hidden.

She nestled down, the spiky grass and thistles scratching her legs through her thin black jeans, pulled her fleece jacket around her and considered her situation. There had been no master plan. She was certainly no avenging angel, rescuing her luckless brother where all others had failed. The reason for her journey across miles of farmland, marsh and fen was simple. She wanted to be with Anson.

Most people wouldn't understand how she felt about her brother, and why should they? Most people hadn't had to endure their childhood. Steph never allowed herself to wallow in the miseries of the past. She couldn't afford to. It had taken all her strength and all her resolve, but she had finally built a new life for herself and Anson, and it was as far from their tainted upbringing as she could possibly make it.

'What goes around comes around,' Steph murmured softly into the breeze off the marsh, then she gave a harsh little laugh. Her father's constant abuse had to end somewhere, and it did on the day that he lifted his hand to Anson. And on that day Steph went to the police.

From then on it was the two of them, but Anson wasn't easy. As he grew up, she forgave him for as many of his misdemeanours as she could, and chose to shut her eyes to the others.

She leant back against the remains of the wall. That had been her biggest mistake.

So here she was, with a shoulder bag containing several small bottles of water, a large bar of chocolate and a family pack of digestive biscuits. Her meagre rations wouldn't last long, but she was going to stay until they found her brother, and if they didn't, she couldn't even contemplate living without knowing what had happened to him, so it really didn't matter, did it?

She pushed the bag beneath the leafy branches of an elder bush and looked around. She wanted to wander about, to see if Anson called her to any one particular spot, but she knew she would have to be very careful not to be seen. The last thing she wanted was to be loaded into the back of a police car and taken home again. Not now she had come this far.

Steph sat on the ground, hugged her knees and rocked slowly backwards and forwards. Home, she supposed, was now here, this sad and lonely spot inhabited only by ghosts of the past — and her brother.

* * *

Tamsin sat at Joseph's home computer, with her own laptop to one side of her. One screen was full of archive material that she was using as a point of reference, and the other moved frenetically up and down as she scrolled through different sites.

'We need Nikki,' muttered Tamsin. 'And some background on her father.'

'I think the murder enquiry might put a lid on that idea.'

'Damn.' Tamsin hit the keys aggressively. Then she thumbed through some of the old letters from Frank Reed's boxes. 'Well, I've managed to identify another link in the chain.' She turned round and looked at Joseph. 'According to letters from friends and colleagues, Nikki's father had a desk job with the MOD until,' she leafed through the letters, 'eight years ago.'

Joseph nodded. 'Sounds about right. Nikki said he only gave up work when the first signs of Alzheimer's began to manifest.'

'There's mention in one of Tug's letters that Frank must be "*Very pleased to be working with one of the old crew again. Especially her!*" Eve, maybe?'

'Maybe, and if that's the case, Nikki is right. Tug does know about Eve, even if he's denying it. Where does he live?'

'Up until the last letter, a place called Fenton Magna, in Dorset.'

Joseph grunted. 'Bit too far away for a quick visit and a quiet word.'

'Then phone him. And ask him about this as well.' Tamsin pointed to some papers. 'There are two more memos here from Eve Anderson, and both have the reference RAF FM.'

'Mm.' Joseph walked over to the window and looked out across the marsh. They were getting into murky waters.

They needed to find what the MOD's post-war interest in Flaxton Mere was. Which would be an impossible job for a civilian, and difficult for a police officer. No one in their right mind took on the MOD. At best it was a waste of time, and at worst, you could find yourself in deep shit. He turned back to his daughter. 'Right, Tug Owen seems like our only option right now. But do me a favour, and check out the phone listings for his number. I don't want to bother Nikki when she's a man down and has a murder to solve.'

Tamsin gave him a searching look. 'You can't wait to get back to work, can you?'

'I'd be lying if said no. We're a team, and a good one. A murder case needs a full complement, but,' he looked at her with love in his eyes, 'and this is a very big "but," there is nothing, and I mean *nothing*, that I'd rather be doing right now, other than spending time with my lovely daughter.'

He was a little sad that Tamsin didn't reply. But then she didn't say anything negative either, so he took it as another baby step forward.

He went to the kitchen. He needed a strong coffee before ringing Wing Commander Frank Reed's best buddy. When he returned to Tamsin, she had started on yet another box.

'I've got Tug Owen's number from an online directory site. It's on the table.'

Joseph thanked her, placed a mug of coffee beside her and picked up the number. This could be tricky. He didn't want to put the man's back up, and if he was protecting some dark secret, there was no telling how he would react.

'Dad?'

Joseph looked at his daughter. Her expression was both thoughtful and worried. 'What have you found?'

'Something I wish I hadn't.' Tamsin passed him a scuffed, leather-bound notebook.

He took it and leafed through it. It wasn't a diary, but each page was crammed with a mass of notes and dates and little scribbled pictures. Joseph sighed. It didn't take long to understand what had upset Tam. The dates spanned two decades, and the repeated references to EA made Joseph's heart sink.

'Nikki's dad was involved with Eve, wasn't he?' Tamsin had stood up and was looking over Joseph's shoulder at the book. 'Look, *"EA's appointment today, worried sick."* And, *"EA late for rendezvous. Getting difficult for her. Wish it was over."* I don't think we need an interpreter to get the gist of that, do we?' She touched her father's arm. 'What the heck are we going to tell Nikki?'

'Nothing. Well, nothing until I've spoken to this Tug.'

'If he really was such a solid mate, he'll certainly know if Frank was having an affair.' Tamsin frowned. 'Bastard!'

'It happens, Tam. I'm not defending him, but he never left his wife or Nikki. Maybe he saw sense before it was too late.'

'At least you never cheated on Mum,' Tamsin said quietly. She added, 'You were just in love with your precious career.'

Joseph lowered his head. 'There was more to it than that, Tam. It was complicated.'

'Mum said the same thing.'

For a moment Joseph thought his daughter was going to open up about why she had chosen to cut him out of her life, but she just picked up her coffee, sipped it, then said, 'You'd better phone Tug Owen.'

* * *

'Excuse me, Niall. That's the second time you've gone all moody on me since I got back to the station. What's the matter?'

Niall looked at Yvonne anxiously. 'Would you be prepared to go along with one of Constable Niall Farrow's *amazing and mind-blowing hunches*?'

Yvonne frowned. 'You mean the kind that has no connection to logic or reason?'

'That's the one.'

'Fine. Spill the beans.'

'Ah, now here we have the problem. I'm not sure that I have any beans to spill, but I need to go back to Flaxton Mere.'

'Right.' Yvonne looked him full in the face. 'And this is something that is really, truly bothering you?' He didn't have to speak. One look at his tight lips and his definite nod told her everything. 'Then we should tell DI Galena.'

'What if I'm wrong? I've nothing concrete to tell her.'

'If anyone understands the importance of hunches, it's the inspector.' Yvonne picked up her hat from the table. 'So if you won't tell her, I will.'

* * *

As Yvonne and Niall arrived at Flaxton Mere, they saw two white-suited SOCOs moving in and out of the store where the footprints had been found.

'Have we got time to see what they've come up with?' Yvonne asked.

Niall nodded miserably. 'Sure. DI Galena's not here yet, and my big hunch could be a crock of shit anyway.'

'Ah, Batman and Robin! Welcome to the Cocaine Kid's hidey-hole.' The SOCO on duty grinned as they approached. 'And guess what? There were *two* sets of prints on the floor. We've lifted them both, and one is a much bigger shoe size than the light trainers you lot noticed. We've photographed them and from the difference in stride, we reckon your second visitor is much taller than the first.'

'Two people?'

'Yup, and there were a lot of prints. This was no one-off visit. We'll get this stuff back to the lab and see what the experts can tell us.' The SOCO placed the sealed evidence bags into a plastic case and loaded it into the back of his car before stripping off his protective suit. 'Right. Well I'm through here. See you!'

As he drove off, Yvonne looked at her partner and said, 'Okay, let's hear what's bugging you about this dreary place.'

Niall strode off in the direction of one of the pillboxes. 'It's something to do with these things.' He stood outside the first one, took a deep breath and ducked inside.

This time Yvonne followed, and was immediately confronted by a wall of graffiti. She smiled, understanding that *Wayne* may well be a *Wanker*, but what *Shaz* had had to do to become a *Yum-Yum Girl*, left her wondering.

Niall was stamping around, kicking piles of debris from one side of the pillbox to the other. 'There's nothing here. How many of these things were there?'

'Five. The last one we looked at, the one where you bumped your head, that was bigger and it had that wall inside.'

Niall smacked the side of his forehead. 'You've got it, Vonnie!'

'I have?'

'Yes! I bumped my head, I dropped my torch, and I thought I'd bust the glass. Considering the thickness of the concrete it was lucky it didn't shatter.' Niall was almost running across the waste ground. 'Come on!'

'And your point being?' Yvonne trotted after him.

'There's a smaller one, near the boundary fence. And it's got a different kind of floor! Okay, it might be nothing, but there are enough passages and underground places in this dump to warrant checking it out. It could be another tunnel.'

As they approached the old wartime defence, Yvonne felt a shiver course through her body, and she instinctively reached out and stopped Niall from charging inside. 'Be careful. This doesn't feel right somehow.'

They went in with caution, not speaking, but each trusted the others' instincts. Yvonne stamped on the floor with her regulation black shoe heel. It felt pretty solid to her.

'Over here, Von!' Niall dropped to his knees and began scraping at the ground. 'I bloody well knew it! Look!'

As she watched, he lifted a large sheet of something that looked like a plaster-covered loft hatch, and revealed a heavy wooden trapdoor beneath.

'Hold it, Niall! Not without the guv'nor. And we should call for back-up.' Her shivers had turned into full-blown tremors. 'I'll ring her mobile and get her ETA, and I'll go and get Bob and Reg from the squad car. Don't lift that hatch until I get back! Understand?'

Niall knew there was no arguing with her.

* * *

Nikki had been parking her car beneath the watch office when she got the call, and within ten minutes five officers were staring down a steep flight of stone steps.

As their torch beams met in a small, empty room, Niall began lowering himself down. 'Hey! Someone has been using this place, there's a lantern. Come down, the stairs are safe.' Niall pulled on gloves and tried the lantern. Instantly the whitewashed room sprang into life. 'There's no dust or dirt here. What do you make of it?'

'It's more a case of what do we make of *that*.' Nikki pointed to the only other thing in the room. A solid wooden door, with freshly oiled hinges and lock.

PC Bob Tinker moved across to it and tried to turn the handle. 'Locked. And I wouldn't like to put my shoulder to that. We'll need an enforcer.'

Yvonne eyed it up and down, then looked at their beefy colleague, Reg. 'There is a shovel in the boot of our vehicle. Do you think you can smash that lock?'

A big smile spread across Reg's face. 'Oh yes, I should think so. I'll go fetch it. And, ma'am, should I radio in while I'm above ground?'

Nikki paused. 'Let's find out what we've got first. Just get the shovel for starters.'

The lock flew halfway across the room and to the screeching sound of splintering wood, the door ceased to be a problem. Niall moved forward with the three others close behind him, and slowly pulled it open. 'More steps.'

'What the f . . . ?' Reg's whispered enquiry tailed away.

'What in heaven's name is this place?' Niall was making his way down the steps, shining his torch from one side to the other.

Moving closely together, Nikki, Yvonne and the others followed him. When they reached the bottom step, they stopped and looked around.

'It's a crypt, isn't it? An underground chapel.' Nikki could hear Niall swallowing.

'Look at that ceiling! It's vaulted like a church, and there are candles all over.'

'Which means it's being used.' Yvonne's voice had a slight tremor.

'Black magic?' Reg offered. 'So where's the altar?'

'More like a religious cult. The candles are cream, not black.' Niall sounded dazed.

They slowly moved away from the steps, beams of light bouncing off the pale stone of the ancient walls.

'Oh God! What is that?' Yvonne's powerful light was glinting on something distinctly un-churchlike — high-tech, and made of steel. Four other beams met hers, and there, centre stage, stood a mortuary table.

'I think we've just found your altar, Reg,' said Nikki.

'Some bloody altar! This is like something out of Frankenstein!'

'Yeah, all we need is some creepy freak playing the organ!' Bob said with bravado.

Niall had moved away from the small group, past the table up on its raised stone pedestal, and was looking through a massive archway.

'Ma'am?' His voice sounded hollow and his tone immediately stopped the banter. 'I think it's time to get back up.'

Nikki and Yvonne moved to his side and stared at the scene in front of them.

'It's . . .' whispered Yvonne. 'My God, it's a cemetery.'

Through the archway, and several feet lower than the area in which they stood, was another vaulted chamber.

Nikki didn't need her torch to see, as four huge candles were already burning, one in each corner of the crypt.

Nikki's hand flew to her mouth as she gazed at the coffins. Lines of them, stacked on stone ledges, one above the other, from the dusty stone floor to the shadowy roof. Some, the higher ones, were old rotting caskets that belonged to a bygone age, in heavy dark wood with ornate brass fittings.

And below those, row upon row of identical plain wooden coffins.

Niall slowly moved towards the nearest wooden box, but Yvonne grasped his shoulder. 'This is not for us, Niall. We need forensics down here.'

'I think,' said Nikki haltingly, 'I think that we do need to see for ourselves what we are dealing with.' She took a deep breath and pulled on her gloves. 'These newer ones are not even nailed down. I'll hold the torch, Bob, you put your gloves on and carefully open it, but don't touch a thing.'

Together they lifted the first lid, and then the second, and the third. Each coffin contained a body.

Nikki felt as if her brain had stopped functioning. Then she looked up and saw Niall. He was staring slack-mouthed, directly into an open casket. 'This one looks like it's sleeping.' He lowered the lid and asked blankly, 'Why? Why is that?'

'Because they've all been embalmed, that's why.' A shiver shot like an icy arrow between Nikki's shoulders. 'Can't you smell the chemicals?'

She moved on to the next coffin and pushed up the lid. A face looked up at her. A young dead face surrounded by a halo of corn-blonde curls. The naked body was covered with a thin white sheet and seemed unblemished, other than the neat stitching running from ear to ear.

Suddenly, she'd seen enough. 'Come on, let's get out of here. Yvonne was right. This is a major crime scene and we're wrecking it! We shouldn't be here.'

'And I suppose that goes for her, too?' Bob Tinker pointed in the direction of the thin, saucer-eyed woman who stood, like a wraith herself, immediately behind them.

'Anson?'

CHAPTER SIXTEEN

The innocuous-looking pillbox, the kind that no one looked twice at, was lit up like Southend Pier. Every available officer had been brought in to contain the site, and Professor Rory Wilkinson had conjured up forensic science officers from across five counties.

Yvonne sat on a grass-covered mound with Steph Taylor, and watched the white suits move in and out of the pillbox like worker bees at a hive. Steph had refused to leave the area, and nothing anyone could say would budge her. And Yvonne, whose two lovely brothers were safe in the bosom of their families, understood completely. If Robin or Harry had been lying dead in that awful place, she would have done the same.

From the moment she had seen the strange space with its rows of coffins, Yvonne had known that Anson Taylor would be found there. So did his sister. And so they sat together in silence, watching and waiting for the inevitable.

* * *

'Well, this certainly beats the Paris catacombs.' Rory looked with something like admiration at the niches cut out of the walls in order to store the great collection of coffins. 'It's a burial chamber like no other I've ever seen.'

'Thank God for that!' Nikki growled. 'I'd hate to think this sort of thing was commonplace. What the hell has been going on here, Rory?'

The pathologist pushed his glasses higher up his nose and said, 'Apart from the obvious? That is, the lair of the mother of all serial killers, and the resting place of nineteen of his victims.'

Nikki bit hard on her thumbnail. 'It's *that* thing that gives me the bloody creeps! What the hell is it? And how did it get down here?' Her gaze was directed at the steel table, raised up on its podium, and lit from all angles by their halogen lights.

'Ah, now I can tell you *exactly* what that is, dear Detective Inspector. Let me show you.' He stepped up onto the raised area, Nikki following reluctantly. 'This is a relocatable mortuary facility. Look.' He pointed down to a recessed area just behind the table and a few steps lower. 'See, it's not just the table, it's the whole shebang.'

'Good God!' Nikki looked down into a small, purpose-built modular panelled room. She put her hands on her hips, jutted her chin forward and asked, 'Okay, what am I looking at?'

'Everything you require for your post-mortem and body storage, including instrument and organ sink, dissecting area, scales, low-level tray sluice, an excellent stacking trolley, a stainless steel three bay by five tier refrigerated body storage cabinet, oh, and an air extraction unit which I happen to know is capable of more than twenty air changes p/h on a negative pressure . . .'

'Hold it right there! So this is high-tech stuff? How does it operate in a bloody crypt?'

'I should think that the large generator in the adjoining cellar has quite a lot to do with it.' Rory smiled benignly. 'But all this equipment most definitely did not come in the way we did, and since we aren't in Narnia, it certainly didn't arrive through the back of a wardrobe. I think you need to start looking for another entrance. Now, I have to go back to the victims. It's going to take for ever to get them all DNA tested and into a proper storage facility for post-mortem examination.' He stopped and shook his head. 'And right now our county facility at Fenchester Hospital, the one that's kitted out to cope with epidemics and major disasters, is undergoing a refit. So, unless we use refrigerated lorries, I'm seriously considering keeping them here.'

'Really? Or is that one of your famous, ever so slightly dubious jokes?'

'I'm deadly serious. The conditions down here are exceptional. Some of those bodies are beautifully preserved, a credit to the mortician — well, except that he probably murdered them in the first place.'

'I suppose he's hardly likely to come back when he sees this circus. What are you proposing?'

'That I do the initial work in situ. Not the full post-mortems, but I can catalogue them, take samples and bag up any evidence right here. That can go straight to the lab, then we can seal the coffins. It will help to avoid cross-contamination.'

It was possible. In the circumstances, Nikki could afford a full team to mount security and protection for the technicians, and they would certainly get men drafted in from other divisions.

She looked around her and shivered. The obvious horrors of the strange, cavernous scene of crime had overshadowed other more subtle aspects. Apart from the beautifully preserved victims, there were dozens of carefully-trimmed candles, big oil burners for sweet-scented oils, and a huge glass bowl full of fresh flowers and grasses. Nikki drew in a long breath. There was going to be one very unhappy bunny out there somewhere, and a very nasty one at that. How the killer would react now was beyond her imagination.

'Let's talk about this later, Rory. I agree you are going to be here for an eternity anyway, the workload is phenomenal. The final decision will be for higher ranks than I, but for what it's worth, I think you have a point.'

She walked with him back to the chamber where the bodies were stored. 'Any idea how long this has been going on?'

'Not yet. We need to open up all the coffins. I noticed the ones on the near wall are open, and most of the others are sealed, so they may be older. The preservation effects of embalming are only temporary, so we may get some choice surprises as we open our boxes. Ah, and I have to tell you that just before we began our conversation, Matthew discovered two recent ones. One has only been dead for a day or two.'

'That could be that poor girl's brother, Anson Taylor.'

'Do you want to see them? They are both male, and one is quite gorgeous!'

Nikki grimaced. 'Rory! But, yes, I'd better, I suppose.'

Rory led her over to the centre of the facing wall. 'I'm afraid you'll have to stand on this.' He placed a kick-step in front of the coffin, and Nikki stepped onto it.

'Oh my! You would never know he was dead! His colour! And the condition of his hair! You're right, he looks beautiful!' Nikki had been expecting a pallid corpse but as she looked at the raven-haired young man, she felt the urge to touch his smooth skin to check for warmth.

'I told you he was gorgeous. Our man is an expert, Inspector. I don't think it will be hard for you to track him down. Not many people possess such skill.'

'A professional?'

'Well, I know for a fact that Greenborough adult education doesn't offer evening classes in Embalming for Beginners, and it's not something that is wildly popular as a hobby.' He gave her an angelic smile. 'So, is it your missing Mr Taylor?'

'No. No, it's not him. But you said there was another one?'

'One bunk higher, I'm afraid. I'll get a stepladder.'

Nikki waited and wondered if she would recognise Anson Taylor.

'Here we are. Up you go.' Rory held the ladder and she began to climb past the immaculate body of the handsome mystery man.

'From Steph's description and my vague recollection, I'd say that's him.' Nikki looked at the dead man's arm. 'And yes, he has a home-inked tattoo. It's Anson, I've no doubt. Although as his sister is outside, I suppose she could verify it.'

'As she has already been in here, I don't think another visit is appropriate. My assistants and I will bring the coffin down, put him on a trolley and take him out to her. Once we've checked this spot for evidence, and since we have a chance to positively identify him, he can go directly back to the mortuary for a post-mortem. Then she can visit him in the chapel of rest.'

'Thanks, Rory. That's very thoughtful of you.'

'No trouble, Inspector. Now forgive me, but I must get on.'

Nikki went back out onto the shadowy fen and pulled out her mobile. It was time to explain as much as she could to Joseph. And this time she would not say no when he offered to cancel his leave.

* * *

Later that evening, Stephanie Taylor identified her brother, and finally agreed to be taken home. She declined to break the news to their father, and let the police do it. Her father had been the cause of all the heartbreak in her and Anson's life. He was a drinker, an abuser and a bully. If she hadn't found the courage to blow the whistle on him, she had no doubt at all that she and her brother would have died years ago. She hoped the bastard would not come to the funeral, but if he did, at least it would be the last time she'd ever have to see him.

* * *

That night, as Fabian and his new go-between disposed of Monk's carefully wrapped and weighted body, Carver set about shredding and burning every paper, document and file that Karl Shine had given him on his blasted airfield project.

By midnight, one man's dream, the fantastic property development and renovation scheme that was RAF Flaxton Mere, had ceased to exist. But sadly, with the disappearance and probable demise of Freddie's top man, Michael Finn, so had the biggest job that Carver had ever planned. It had been a once-in-a-lifetime scam, carefully crafted onto a tight timeline around a major London event, and Michael had been the key player. He had no understudy, no one of equal expertise was waiting in the wings, ready to run on at a moment's notice. And there was no time to find one. Freddie's life-changing, money-spinning scheme was dead in the water, a bit like Monk, the DIY killer who had erroneously believed that he could double-cross him by taking his own generous cut *and* the fat wad of money that should have been Fabian's.

As the last document reduced to ashes, Freddie decided that he had never hated anyone as much as he hated Karl Shine. Even knowing that he was now lying on a mortuary slab gave him little satisfaction. He had tried to do the boy a favour for old times' sake, and in return, Shine had managed to sabotage Carver's whole world.

He sighed and closed the heavy doors of the wood-burning stove. On careful examination of his present position, Freddie had decided that he had little option but to close up business and take a very long holiday, preferably somewhere hot.

CHAPTER SEVENTEEN

Overnight, Greenborough police station had transformed from a moderately quiet market town cop-shop, into the hub of the universe.

Officers from surrounding divisions poured in, and although the place heaved with men and women, there was an odd feeling of quiet disbelief and shock hanging over the rooms and corridors.

Superintendent Greg Woodhall called an early morning meeting. 'First, I'd like to thank the teams from Nottingham and Humberside for joining us, and we also have the assistance of the force psychologist, Richard Foley.' He nodded towards a smart, fair-haired man who leant casually against the back wall. 'He will remain on-site for the duration of this major enquiry.'

Greg stood with his hands behind his back and rocked back and forth. 'I cannot emphasise strongly enough how important it is that we find the person who has killed so many victims. Whatever you are working on, if it can be put on hold, do so. I want every available officer working this case. Now, I'll pass you over to DI Galena and she'll bring you up to speed on what was found at Flaxton Mere.'

Nikki spoke for around ten minutes. She felt that her words were ill-chosen and inadequate. How could she briefly describe what she had seen — the results of a lifetime devoted to murder? The things in that crypt had been the stuff of Edgar Allen Poe, and were quite beyond a simple detective with the Fenland Constabulary.

'So, we will need to question *everyone* who has any connection to, or knowledge of, Flaxton Mere. That will include the owners and the employees of the industrial units in the hangars, the history society members, and anyone who had dealings with Karl Shine. We've been told there were surveyors on the airfield a few days ago, but we have no idea where they came from, or what company they worked for.'

She ended by saying that the forensic evidence would be vital and that, while every effort was being made to speed things up, the investigation was on such a massive scale that it would take time. Before she drew the meeting to a close, Nikki added, 'This monster has been living among us. He, or she, will most likely be someone we have come across, maybe even had a drink with or met through work. And if we hadn't made this terrible discovery, the killer would have gone on killing, right under our noses. We cannot let him get away. Let's get to work! Let's find him before he murders anyone else.'

* * *

Yvonne replaced the phone and walked quickly to the boss's office. 'Pike's awake and wants to talk to someone. As I saw him before, would you mind if I went, ma'am?'

Nikki looked about as grey and drawn as Yvonne had ever seen her. 'He's not high on my list of priorities but as his gran is still missing, I suppose we must. Yes, off you go.'

When she arrived at the room into which Pike had been moved, Yvonne found the ferret-like creature trying to eat a bowl of something resembling wallpaper paste. His skinny form barely made a shape under the covers.

Pike was fully conscious, and now he was hidden in the quiet room just off the main ward, he seemed considerably less flaky.

'Ready to talk about your adventure, Mr Pike?' She kept her voice friendly.

After trying to look at her balefully, he suddenly gave up, leant back into his pillows and began to explain how he came to fall down the shaft.

'I ain't no smackhead, so you can forget telling me I was high, but I swear to God that I heard a plane coming down. Heard the engines cutting out, and I heard it hit the ground. No shit, officer, I heard it crash, then I saw flames and heard this 'orrible screaming. I wanted to help, but then it all got too much for me and I ran, and went straight down that bloody hole.'

Yvonne looked at him carefully. She'd had enough experience with liars over the years, and she could tell that whatever he was describing had actually happened in some way. 'But there has certainly been no report of an air crash, civil or military. Have you ever heard anything like it before? You'd been out there plenty of times, hadn't you?'

'Never. It was really 'orrible.' He spooned in another mouthful of milk pudding and glared at the bowl suspiciously. 'Do you think this is porridge?'

'I'd say it looks more like Artex, but back to the Mere. It's a spooky spot, isn't it?'

'That's why I chose it to hide me stuff.' He tried to ease his shattered leg and winced with pain. 'I'd been skimming drugs from Anson Taylor for months and stashing them in one of the old buildings on the airfield.'

'And Anson found out?'

Pike shrugged. 'Not that I know of. I 'aven't seen Anson for days.' He bit his lip and stared at Yvonne. 'Me old gran's really dead, you know. They say I imagined it, but I didn't. She was brought into that place I was in before I came here.'

'What, ITU?'

'Yeah, that's it. But she died. And I killed her.'

'No, William, you didn't. You couldn't have lifted a finger to hurt her. You had more wires coming out of you than a national grid pylon. And the nurse told me her name was . . .' Yvonne struggled to remember. 'Something else, but nothing like Pike.'

'I don't care what you say, Constable Smartass, I saw her wheeled past me. The doctors thought I was out of it, but I could hear them, and I *saw* me gran.'

'You *thought* you saw her, but okay, say it was her, how did you manage to kill her? You were a mess of drips, drains, monitors and,' she pointed to his injured leg, 'oh yes, and don't forget the half ton of scaffolding wrapped around your leg.'

Pike was silent.

'Come on. You're going to be here for a very long time. Why not just talk to me?' Yvonne smiled as the youth eyed her up surreptitiously.

He sighed and hung his head. 'I gamble. I owed money to some seriously bad men. A dealer was going to buy the stash of drugs that I stole from Anson, then I was going to settle the debt, and bugger off, but I missed the meeting.'

'And they had threatened you with what?'

'They said they'd kill gran.'

'Well, I know she's missing, but that old lady on the next trolley died of a heart condition, plain and simple. And after what you've just told me, we really need to find your gran, so how about you stop telling me she was here and help us find her.'

Pike stuck out his chin and closed his eyes. 'I know what I know.'

Yvonne changed tack. 'So tell me about Flaxton Mere.'

Pike muttered. 'Well, there are often odd lights, out on the marsh.'

'What sort of lights?' A deep voice came from the doorway. 'Come on, Pike! Spit it out. What sort of bloody lights?'

Yvonne looked up to see the troubled face of PC Bob Tinker, and he looked as if he'd seen a ghost.

'Dunno really. Lots of the fen dwellers have seen them. Me gran says it's the hobby lantern leading lost travellers to their watery graves.'

'Yeah, right. And anything else?' Bob sounded wary.

'A friend of gran's said she heard strange noises out there once. She was collecting samphire and she heard whispering and laughing. She might have been on the parsnip wine, but I dunno.' He shrugged. 'It's a weird place. Scary.'

Yvonne frowned. 'Bob? What's rattling you? We've all heard about the lights. Anyone who's ever taken a call from old Miss Quinney knows about them.'

'Reg and I heard noises, a sort of creepy laughter, and we saw moving lights when we were on duty up on the sea-bank the other night. Perhaps we should have reported it, but . . .' His voice faded into silence.

'But you were afraid of being called a big girl's blouse?' Yvonne knew all about male coppers' egos.

'Something like that.' He looked at Yvonne. 'But I think I'll mention it now.'

Pike had given up on the porridge and was staring at Yvonne. 'So what did they say the old woman's name was?'

Yvonne thought hard. 'Howitt? Howlett, no Hewitt. That's it, Hetty Hewitt.'

Pike went even paler. He stared straight ahead. 'You wouldn't listen, would you? I friggin' told you she was dead! Me gran's maiden name is Hewitt, Hester Hewitt.'

* * *

An hour later, Nikki joined Yvonne and Bob at the hospital.

'We've arranged for a DNA test from the late Mrs Hewitt, Mr Pike. If it is a match with samples we've taken from your grandmother's home, then we'll know for certain. Now, can you give me the names of your grandmother's closest female friends? If she really is Mrs Pike, then we need to know what happened, who brought her here, and where her animals are.'

A very subdued Pike gave them three names, then said, 'I'd try Miss Quinney first.' He looked at Yvonne. 'She's the one you mentioned earlier, the old girl who complains about the lights. She went to school with gran, always calls her Hetty.'

He looked miserably at her. 'Do you promise me that gran wasn't hurt?'

Yvonne could tell that Pike's concern was genuine. She said, 'ITU said it was a massive coronary, and examination showed scarring on her heart, maybe from rheumatic fever as a child, but whatever, William, no one helped her on her way, I promise you. Okay?'

'Thanks. Listen, if I help you, would it make things better for me, when I finally get out of here? I mean, I know you'll be nicking me for dealing,' the voice had lost its former aggression, 'but I spent a lot of time hanging around with Anson when he was making deals, so I can tell you a lot about drug suppliers, and maybe other things too.'

'We'll talk when you are stronger. And naturally, if you assist us, there will be a certain amount that we can do to make things easier for you.' Nikki turned to go, then said. 'We'll let you know about your grandmother.'

'No need.' Pike looked like a little lost kid. 'I know what I saw.'

Outside, Bob told Nikki about the things he and his crew-mate had heard while on watch on the fen. 'Now I'm beginning to wonder if there isn't more to all this than just the superstitious crap.'

'Me too,' Nikki puffed out her cheeks, 'but I have to get back to the station. Perhaps one of you would go check out Mrs Quinney? We need to tie this mess up before we can concentrate fully on the serial killer.'

'I'll do it,' said Yvonne. 'I'll pick up Niall, and we'll go directly.'

* * *

A vast expanse of fields stretched out on either side of the long fen drove. Apart from a tiny dot that Yvonne knew to be a tractor way up ahead, the police car was the only vehicle for miles.

'I wouldn't like to say how many times I've got lumbered with Miss Quinney.' She grinned as she accelerated past the tractor. 'Last time I saw her she told me that the local RSPB group were actually a foreign spy-ring. If it isn't alien spacecraft over the marsh, it's sightings of Johnny Foreigner landing on the beaches. I'm never too sure if she's barking or just lonely.'

'What if she isn't so daft after all?' murmured Niall thoughtfully. 'Okay, the bit about "ET" and "the men in black" is rubbish, but too many people, including two police officers, have seen lights, so maybe there is something in it.'

'I agree. But what?'

They drove the last few miles in silence.

Miss Quinney came to the door wearing a threadbare knitted cardigan, faded corduroys and a bobble hat, and declared that she was far too busy to talk to them.

Yvonne and Niall immediately saw why, as behind her in the sitting room, sprawled out on her settee, were two elderly lurchers, a moth-eaten spaniel, a ragged-looking German shepherd and an even more decrepit Jack Russell. One of several cats wound itself around their ankles, and the Strange Case of the Missing Animals was solved.

'You picked the animals up after you took your friend, Hetty Hewitt, or Hester Pike as we know her, to the hospital, didn't you, Miss Quinney?'

'Well, I could hardly leave them to fend for themselves, could I?'

'So, tell us what happened, and why did you give her name as Hewitt?'

'I've known Hetty since I was three. She'll always be Hetty Hewitt to me. And I don't know what happened.' Her arms were firmly crossed in front of her twig-like frame. 'She came knocking on my door saying that she'd had a funny turn. She doesn't have a car, so I gave her a cup of tea and then we went off to see the doctor in Caster Fen village. Half way there she started gasping, said she had terrible pains in her chest, so I drove her to Greenborough Hospital. What else could I have done?'

'Miss Quinney, I'm not criticising you. We are just wondering why you left her there and never went back to see her?'

'I had to get the animals, didn't I? And one of her old cats led me a right song and dance, nearly wrecked the place trying to catch it. Look!' She proffered a scrawny arm for Yvonne's inspection. Three wounds, now scabbing over, ran from her elbow to her wrist. 'Bleeding like a stuck pig I was! Still, I knew Hetty were right poorly so I couldn't leave them, and I never go near the marsh after dark.' The voice was fast becoming a wail. 'And now I can't leave them at all, can I?'

Yvonne smiled at her gently. 'Miss Quinney, can we come in? We'd like to talk to you about your friend, and if you're up to it, we really will listen to you this time.' She paused. 'It's about the lights.'

* * *

As Niall drove off the fen, Yvonne leafed through a dog-eared old exercise book.

'Well! For such a funny old bird, this is the most concise record of the comings and goings on the marsh that you could wish to see! She could show you a thing or two about taking notes, lad! Listen to this . . . *8.30 Friday 14. Lights commenced. Moved in an easterly direction, flicked for ten minutes, then faded. Recommenced at 9.45 p.m. and repeated above pattern.*' Yvonne stabbed her finger on the page. 'Now that *is* interesting, because Reg and Bob saw lights at around that time, and it was a Friday! What do you make of that?'

'Well, if we are talking about something really simple, I'd say a time switch.' Niall turned and grinned at her. 'They turn lights on and off at allotted times, don't they?'

'I think maybe we should take a look down on that marsh, don't you?'

CHAPTER EIGHTEEN

Joseph hurried along the corridor to the interview rooms, then halted abruptly as his phone rang. He glanced at it and saw a number he didn't recognise. He flipped it open and heard a voice say, 'I got your message, Sergeant Easter. Sorry I missed you. My name is Tug Owen.'

Joseph ducked into an empty room and closed the door. 'Thank you for returning the call, Mr Owen.' Joseph desperately tried to think of what to say to the man.

'It's about Frank Reed, I assume,' Owen prompted. 'I've been expecting this, although I thought it would be Nikki Galena ringing. I didn't fool her, did I?'

'No sir. But it takes a lot to fool the inspector.' Joseph felt relief at the way the conversation was going.

'What do you already know, Sergeant?'

'I know about Eve Anderson.' Then he added with a slight shiver, 'And about Flaxton Mere.'

'I very much doubt that you do.' There was a soft humourless laugh. 'You know that Eve exists. You know she is somehow connected to Frank, and you've seen the name RAF Flaxton Mere on documents, but apart from that, Sergeant, you know nothing.'

Joseph swore to himself. The easy conversation had taken a distinct downward turn. 'So what can you tell me, sir?'

There was the sound of a sigh. 'Whatever I tell you will cause Nikki a great deal of pain. Do you really want to know?'

'Sorry, but painful or not, I think you know the answer to that.'

'Then first understand that Frank Reed loved Kathy. He would never have left her, but he and Eve . . .' The man hesitated. 'Years before, they went through a terrible ordeal together and they formed a special sort of bond.'

'What kind of a bond?'

'Do I have to spell it out?' He sighed, then said, 'It was complicated.'

Joseph remembered saying those very words to Tamsin, and wondered if all break-ups and breakdowns came under that heading when you scratched beneath the surface.

'Frank was in pieces, Sergeant. He admitted to me that Eve meant the world to him, but she was a career RAF officer, and at the time she would not give up her career to settle down. Because of that, Frank moved on, and he met Kathy.'

'How long ago was this?'

'Eons. He was a young man, and despite still caring deeply for Eve, he fell desperately in love with Kathy.' Tug made a little huffing sound. 'The incident that happened, when he and Eve were thrown together under horrific conditions, left a permanent imprint on both of them, and neither could truly let the other go. Frank became living proof that you *can* love two people.'

'What happened? What was the incident?'

'I'm sorry, it was classified. Still is. But suffice to say there was an accident aboard an aircraft carrier and they were trapped for days.'

Joseph knew from experience the kind of bonds that formed with your military brothers, and he knew first-hand what trauma could do. He decided to move on.

'But they met again, years later, at Flaxton Mere airfield.'

'They tried to work together, but the past got in the way. It was a disaster.'

'What was happening at Flaxton Mere, sir? Why the interest in that old place?'

'All I can tell you is that Frank was asked to take a team out there and do a detailed report for the MOD, post decommissioning, prior to selling off the land. He was to work in conjunction with a government department, and when he made contact, he found that his opposite number was none other than Eve Anderson.'

Joseph did a few calculations in his head. 'But surely his wife Kathy was dead by then?'

'She was, but Frank was an honourable man and he possessed a conscience, plus he loved Nikki to distraction. It tore him to shreds.'

'You said working together was a disaster.'

'It was. As the years passed, Eve had discovered that she had made a terrible mistake. Without Frank, she was lost. She never married, even though she knew Frank had a new life with Kathy. But then when they met again at Flaxton Mere, and she realised that he was finally free, or so she believed, he wouldn't be with her.' Tug Owen made a little tutting sound. 'Frank tried to explain, but in the end she walked off, and he never saw her again. Much later, he realised that Nikki would probably have understood, or at least accepted the situation, and Kathy would never have wanted him to live alone. He had thrown away his last chance of happiness.'

'Did he go after her?'

There was a long silence, then Tug Owen said, 'Yes, he did, but he never found her. That, I believe, is why he wanted Nikki to look for her. Something happened years ago, something Frank should have told Nikki about, but he never did. He said it was never the right time.'

'But if he was as orderly as Nikki says, why didn't he write it in a letter for her to read after he'd died?'

'He told me it was something that had to be spoken about face to face. He wasn't a hard man, and he didn't want

Nikki hurt by an impersonal note.' Tug sighed. 'I guess his mind gave out before he got around to it.'

'And do you know what it is?' Joseph asked.

'Sorry, no, although I do have a suspicion.'

Joseph glanced at his watch. He had interviews piling up, and he'd promised to meet Tamsin, but there were still things he needed to know. 'Mr Owen? Did Frank ever tell you about his first wife?'

'He did, of course he did. After all, we were close friends. She died in a tragic accident, I believe, when Nikki was a baby.' The line went quiet for a moment. 'I'm sorry, but try as I might I can't recall her name.'

'No matter.' He thanked the man for his help, and promised to ring him before the funeral to let him know how much of the information, if any, he'd passed on to Nikki.

As he left the room, he wished with all his heart that they had never agreed to look for Eve. No matter what they discovered now, it was going to wreck Nikki's image of her father forever.

* * *

Yvonne and Niall drove back out to the marsh, but not to the crime scene. They were more interested in the sea-bank path that led across the edge of the marsh. The tide was still going out, which gave them plenty of time to get out to where Bob and Reg said they had seen the lights.

'Have you been out here before, Vonnie?'

She nodded. 'I came here when I was young, and I know it's the tide that we have to be wary of, not the mud. We won't get sucked under, just keep to the firmer ground, okay?'

Carefully they picked their way across the boggy, wet ground, slipping on the damp grassy hillocks and cursing at the shallow greasy-looking water pools that turned out to be deeper than they looked.

'This godforsaken place goes on for miles! We'll never find anything out here. We need half the station with us.' Niall stared sadly at his mud-caked boots.

'Well, I think we both know that that isn't going to happen, my cherub, so quit moaning and keep looking.'

They stood together, staring around the lonely marsh, and wondering what they were doing there, with wet socks and mud-splattered uniforms.

Yvonne looked at her wristwatch. 'We've got another fifteen minutes before we have to start back. There's a breeze getting up, which usually means that the tide's on the turn. Killer or no killer, we are not getting caught out here!'

'Agreed.' Niall kicked at the lush green leaves of some kind of marsh plant. 'I'm not sure what I thought we'd find anyway.'

'Something like this, maybe?'

Niall moved across to where his crew-mate half knelt in a patch of coarse marsh grass, then let out a long whistle.

Attached to a wooden stake that had been driven deep into the soft soil, was what looked at first glance to be a lamp of some kind. Closer examination showed it to be three triangular mirrors forming a prism. A reflector.

'Here's another one!' Niall moved several metres away. 'But this has foil strips hanging from it.'

They found six reflectors in total.

'So, all we need now is to find out where the original light source comes from and when night falls, we'll try it out for ourselves.' Niall looked back towards the sea-bank and just beyond, to the old ruined building that had once been the watchtower for RAF Flaxton Mere. 'Job done, my friend! Now let's get off this bloody bog.'

* * *

Nikki took one look at Rory Wilkinson and hoped that she looked better than he did. For all his jokes and black humour, the enormity of this discovery had even got to him. He had been in the crypt all night and was now heading into his second day without sleep. He seemed to have taken on the role of guardian of the Flaxton Mere necropolis.

'Rory, I have to point out that a practically comatose forensic scientist is not a lot of use. Plus the lack of sleep is doing absolutely nothing for your dashing good looks.'

'Yes, I'm desperately glad that this place doesn't have mirrors. The shock of seeing my ravaged physiognomy could bring me out in hives.'

'So you'll take a break? We do have a rota in place.'

'I'd love to, but there is only one of *me*, and whereas I would normally savour that unique position, until Dr Bass gets here from Cambridge, this is it.' He pointed to a folding camp bed and a sleeping bag, pushed into a small niche next to the burial chamber. 'And no comments regarding the *camp* bit, if you don't mind. Half of Greenborough got there before you.'

'You're staying down here? For heavens' sake, man! You can't sleep here!'

'You are right! SOCOs are *so* noisy! Chatter like magpies, can't get a wink.'

'Rory, please! You are *not* staying here. I know you feel a responsibility to get these poor souls identified, but not at the expense of your health, and possibly your sanity.' Nikki was emphatic. The thought of having to spend one minute longer than necessary in this chamber of horrors made her shudder.

'Sorry, Inspector, but it's only until my colleague arrives. He's an expert in archaeological forensics, and I think he is going to find a few very unusual surprises at this little dig.'

'Like what?'

The pathologist ran a slender hand through his floppy fringe, and pushed it unsuccessfully away from his forehead. 'I've just opened one of the older boxes and I thought it strange that I wasn't overpowered by the stench. I found a body that had been, well, almost mummified. The air quality down here is exceptional, but the fact that the body didn't stink was because the internal organs had been removed. The body cavities had then been packed with herbs, spices and some sort of linen material soaked in oils, including cedarwood if I'm not mistaken. It's bizarre, the trouble this man has gone to.' He raised his hands in amazement.

'Why?'

'Now, there is a question! And I can't answer it, Inspector, but I can tell you one thing. This killer, and I am only assuming that he does his killing himself, spends an inordinate amount of time cleaning and preparing his victims' bodies.'

'In preparation for something sexual? I mean, is he a fastidious necrophiliac?'

'Absolutely not. Not one of them, man or woman, has been assaulted or abused in any way by their friendly mortician. Frankly, guessing that a lot of these persons were tramps or runaways, they are probably more hygienic now than they've ever been. Which is a refreshing thought . . . But I digress. You remember the dark-haired, blue-eyed male that I showed you?'

'His eyes were closed, but I assume you mean the gorgeous one?'

'Exactly. He was the last to die. Well, he has been expertly embalmed, using up-to-date chemicals — glutaraldehyde, I suspect, as the skin tone is very natural. But not only that, his hair has been washed and trimmed, and the skin has been treated with some kind of sweet-smelling moisturising cream.' He indicated a large plastic toolbox. 'That there is full of cosmetics, make-up, oils, shampoos, soaps — you name it. Anyway, as we've progressed through opening the boxes, we can see how his methods have improved over the years. It seems that he keeps them "on view" until they start to lose their looks, then he seals them up. As I said, he took care of these people. Your psychologist should have a field day with this lot.'

'I'll pass it on. Now I have to get back and report all this to the super, but before I go, any clue about the coffins themselves? I mean, they are all identical, aren't they?

'Yes, mass produced and they are certainly old. I'm making no guesses about them, but I think my friend Doc Bass will be able to help you with that little conundrum. Hopefully he will be here by tomorrow morning.'

Nikki climbed up the stone steps, glancing back at the scene below her, where ghostly hooded and white-suited figures moved purposefully backwards and forwards. Although she had been in the force for many years and had dealt with more than her fair share of murders, even she was finding the sheer scale of this crime hard to get her head around.

Above ground, it was an enormous relief to see the massive uniformed presence. The airfield was virtually sealed off, although at the main gates and all around the perimeter fencing, the media gathered, baying for news about the gruesome discovery. Today they would make a statement, but it would be short on detail. For once the actual truth was more chilling than the rumours.

She smiled bitterly as she drove through the sea of faces and cameras. This was just the beginning. She had thought they had problems with one dead property owner, a missing drug dealer, a disappearing old lady and a handful of animals. No way could their proposed statement mention the finding of some nineteen bodies. It would make Greenborough the Mecca for every poor soul who had ever made an enquiry to the police or the missing persons bureau. They would be inundated with calls, and the town would be flooded with grieving partners and relatives, all desperate for closure.

As she pulled out into the main road she cursed under her breath. The assignment was tough enough, but before long the curious would start drifting into town, and not only would that hamper their enquiries, they would have the added concern of trying to protect them. Like it or not, Greenborough had a serial killer on the loose, a man who had been prevented from returning to his refuge, which would make him dangerous beyond all imagining. How the hell could they be expected to protect a town full of visitors from a psychotic murderer?

She moved the gear lever up into fifth, and decided that it was a problem for those higher up in the ranks to ponder over. Nikki had the killer to catch.

* * *

'Professor Wilkinson! Can we close this one, please? We've taken our samples and the photographer has finished with her.'

Rory nodded to the technician. As soon as their preliminary tests had been done, the bodies were being numbered and the lids temporarily sealed, to await full post-mortem. The first victims had been easier to process, in spite of each coffin being scrutinised minutely for evidence of the person who had put them there in the first place, but the older ones were taking considerably more time.

The pathologist grimly wished that Stuart Bass would get here. He could do with some expert help right now. And Stuart was an expert all right. It was just unfortunate that he had a prior commitment that he needed a few days to extricate himself from — the small matter of his honeymoon. Rory yawned again and decided that he was not entirely sure how long he was going to be able to keep up the pace.

The sound of a hammer sealing up a coffin brought him back to reality. 'Matthew? Are we fully staffed for cataloguing these poor souls?'

'We will be by this afternoon, sir. Your request for assistance has been granted.'

'Good, good. Right, better press on then. It helps having the tower in situ, doesn't it?' He looked at their latest acquisition, a painter and decorator's scaffolding tower that allowed easier and safer access to the stone shelves and their deceased residents.

'You're not kidding, Prof. Oh, by the way, the police sergeant wants to know if they can start the search for the other entrance. They've had no luck from outside.'

Rory nodded. He took off his glasses and wiped the lens absent-mindedly on the sleeve of his white suit. 'It's an amazing structure, Matthew.'

'What was it, Prof? I mean, was it an underground church?'

'Undoubtedly it was religious in nature. One of the historians told the DI that this was once the site of a monastery, and some other religious edifice before that. I expect you have visited many grand churches that have magnificent crypts beneath their chancels, full of shrines and tombs and saints' relics.' He sat back on a stone ledge. 'I could be wrong, but I think that the smaller chamber was an undercroft. They were often found beneath a monastery, mainly used for storage and administration purposes.'

'And this big chamber with the coffins?'

'That's where my theories get fuzzy, Matthew. This place is full of contradictions. It is clearly a burial vault. I mean, it's holding exactly what it was meant to hold, dead bodies in coffins. But why so many?'

Matthew shrugged. 'Pass.'

Rory patted his younger helper on the shoulder. 'Go tell the sergeant that he can send in the cavalry. The only place I don't want them is the burial vault, because of the bodies.'

As Matthew went off to give the uniformed officer the go-ahead for the search for the other entrance, Rory returned to his work. He gazed across the sea of wooden boxes with their silent occupants. It was going to be a very long day.

'Excuse me, sir? May I take a short break?' It was one of the on-loan SOCOs.

'Had enough already?'

'No, sir, not at all, just need a . . . a . . .'

'Toilet break might be the expression that you're looking for?'

'Exactly.'

'Well, hurry back. We have an awful lot of guests here that we need to take care of, and I'm sure they will miss you if you are gone too long, eh, Mr . . . ?' Rory tried to read the official identity pass around the man's neck.

'Sean Fowler, sir. I'm on loan from Nottingham.' He gave the pathologist an odd look. 'You talk like the victims are still alive.'

'Until we can provide them with legal death certificates, they are not technically dead, Sean Fowler from Nottingham. Well, the older ones may have been declared as such, but until I can give them a name and recognise their passing properly, I prefer to think of them in a sort of cryogenic state, just waiting, if you know what I mean?'

Again the odd look and Rory realised that yet another underling had decided his temporary boss was as mad as a box of frogs.

'You'll be telling me you like this place next.'

Rory considered his reply carefully. 'I have attended sites of intense pain and suffering, with bodies devastated and torn asunder. I have seen too many victims of someone else's rage and evil desires, and compared to those scenes, Mr Fowler, this is indeed a peaceful place.'

'It contains nineteen murder victims and heaven knows how many dead monks!'

'Nineteen beautifully prepared and looked-after bodies, placed among flowers and candles. The dead here are better cared for than most people care for their deceased relatives, let me tell you. They tend their graves regularly for a while, then it's once a week, then once a month, then every year at Christmas the guilt sets in and they try to clean it up a bit, until they gravel it over . . .' He shrugged. 'Ring any bells? Have you noticed the state of most cemeteries? Then look at this vault. It is clean, it is tidy, the flowers were changed recently, even the water in the vases doesn't smell. And when do we think all this began? How many years ago?'

The SOCO shrugged. 'I'm sorry, sir, but I haven't seen the earlier victims, but a long while back, I'd guess. I do take your point, but whoever did this, you can't condone it, surely?'

Rory looked patiently at the technician. 'Many people agree, myself included, that I am a little eccentric, but apart from extreme cases of euthanasia in the terminally ill, I would *never* condone the taking of a precious life. I would, however, like to try to understand the psychology of this killer. At least he has shown respect for the human body. He hasn't left his victims like some I have seen, violated and mutilated.'

'It takes all sorts, I suppose, even in the world of murderers, but if you'll excuse me, Professor, I really have to go, er, literally.'

140

The SOCO hurried off towards the stairs, brushing past Matt as he went.

'The sarge says they'll start the search immediately. And he says thanks, Prof. He owes you one.'

* * *

As Nikki walked through the front doors, she was met by Joseph.

'I've hired Tamsin a car, now I can't be with her 24/7. She just drove in and we grabbed a quick lunch together.'

'Good idea, but don't leave her on her own for too long.' Images of what lay beneath the ground in rows of wooden coffins returned to her. 'In fact, why not bring her in here? She could help out in a civilian capacity,' Nikki lowered her voice, 'until we get our killer in a secure cell.'

'I thought of that too, but she's so bloody stubborn,' Joseph grumbled. 'Just like her mother.'

'Then pull rank. She's young and pretty and we have a madman right here in Greenborough. I'll clear it with the super. I know she can't be involved in anything sensitive, but she could help the office manager out. Tell her I've specifically asked for her. I'm willing to bet she agrees.'

They had reached the CID room, and Nikki could barely see the floor for policemen's feet. For once she had more officers at her disposal than she could ever have dreamed of, but she was still up to her neck in unanswered questions. She looked at Joseph. 'Seems like the perfect moment for an update.'

She walked to the front of the room and rapped on a desk with a stapler. 'Okay, everyone! Just a brief overview, if you could listen up.'

A hush came over the crowded room.

'The main thing we need to remember is that although the burial chamber has been "operational" for many years, the last victim was only killed three days ago, which is very worrying indeed. Now,' she looked across the sea of faces, 'has anyone got any news on that relocatable mortuary system?'

'Yes, ma'am. I've traced several manufacturers, and most just hire them out.' A young DC flipped over the page of a notepad.

'Why? Hardly a bouncy castle, is it?'

'They are meant as a means of keeping businesses going during refurbishments of the workplace, ma'am. So far I haven't found anyone in this area who has rented or bought one, and although they've emailed all the specs, complete with photographs, I haven't found the exact same model yet.'

'Right, then as soon as you get pictures of ours, email them to all the makers. Maybe someone can identify who made them. Now, how about the chemicals? The formaldehyde or whatever it is?'

'Nothing yet, guv. I've contacted the people who supply the local funeral directors and embalmers, but you can order the stuff off the internet.' The detective sighed. 'Like every other bloody thing these days.'

'Right, but stick with that if you would. How about the candles?'

'Could have got them anywhere, guv. The discount stores, supermarkets and garden centres are all selling church candles. He's not using any particular brand either, so . . .'

The DI nodded. 'Okay, ditch that, and we'll all concentrate on suspects. Joseph, how did you get on this morning?'

'We've seen the owners of the businesses that operate out of the hangars, ma'am, and although most of them are wetting themselves because of our presence there, no one has stood out as a possible suspect.' He smiled. 'Although we've stashed away a fair bit of knowledge about their dodgy activities, and we'll be more than happy to follow that up at a later date.'

'Okay. Cat, have you got the lists and those pictures I asked for of our main suspects, our trusty history society?'

The detective stood and passed her an envelope. 'Yes, ma'am. Full membership list, plus photos of the six members of the group who are interested in airfields.'

She attached the six photos to the whiteboard.

'Right. Here we have Professor Joshua Flower and his brother Simon Flower, Bill Brewer, Marcus Selby, Frank Kohler and Andrew Friar. They are all local to Caster Village, and are the ones we are interested in.' Nikki looked at the team earnestly. 'I don't need to tell you how fast we have to work. We have a ruthless killer out there who will be seriously pissed off with us. So, watch your backs. No matter how beautifully he treats his victims, I don't want any of you to finish up as number twenty. Now, I need three pairs to go out and have a nice long chat with our historians. I don't want them brought in, I want it done in their own homes, and check out everything you can while you're there. Keep your eyes peeled. I want everything you can dig up on these guys, and more. So, Joseph and I will talk to Joshua Flower and his brother Simon. Cat, I suggest that you take Niall with you and visit Marcus Selby and Andrew Friar. Dave, you take Yvonne and speak to Bill Brewer and Frank Kohler. I want full reports ready for the morning briefing. The rest of you get on with your enquiries and report any findings directly.' She paused. 'Yes, Constable?'

A WPC had entered the room. 'Ma'am? Professor Wilkinson wants to speak to you urgently. Can you go back to the scene?'

'Can't I speak to him on the phone?'

'He reckons the phones and the radios are both playing up down there, ma'am, and it's most important that he doesn't leave the crypt.'

'Did he say why, Constable?' She had interviews to carry out and really wasn't in the mood for Rory's jokes.

'Well, to use his words, ma'am, he thinks he might have just had a jolly chat with the killer.'

CHAPTER NINETEEN

'We were about to let uniform in to look for the *hidden door to the lost world.*' Nikki noted that Rory was far from being his usual self. 'Matt went off to see the sergeant, and I was left talking to a SOCO — or so I thought.' He ran his hand through his hair and shook his head. 'He'd asked to go for a break, and when he didn't return I got to thinking that something wasn't quite right about him. It was his ID. It *was* an official ID, but different from ours, so I got one of your men to check the names of the Nottingham team, and there was no Sean Fowler.'

'How the hell did he get in?' Nikki almost shook with anger. 'We have men at every damned point, and *no one* gets down here without a valid pass.'

'Respectfully, Inspector, I don't think he came in by the front door. I believe he used the entrance that you are so desperately seeking. There are fresh white suits in a convenient pile over there. Simple. Put one on, pull the hood over your head, and voila! We all look the same.'

'I gathered that from your remarkable description,' she said testily.

'Yes, rather good, wasn't it? A man of medium/slightly taller than average height, wearing a white all-in-one disposable suit, hair colour unknown, eye colour distorted by artificial lights, no distinguishing marks or features and no discernible accent.' He grinned hopelessly. 'Not much to go on, but I swear I'd know him again.'

Nikki threw up her hands in despair. 'And how the hell would you do that? You said it yourself, we all look the same in these bloody suits.'

'There was something about him. It was as if he were searching, probing your mind for something, and sadly I think he may have found something in mine.' Rory pushed his glasses up and massaged the bridge of his nose with his thumb and forefinger. 'I have a strong and rather disconcerting feeling that we will meet again.'

* * *

Nikki drove back to the station, worried because Rory had dug his heels in about not leaving the crypt. She had increased security, but still feared for his safety. She just hoped that his colleague would get a move on and give him a break, before he either cracked or met up with his friendly scene of crime officer again.

Joseph had waited for her to return before interviewing the Flower brothers, and she told him about Rory's encounter as they drove to Castor Fen Village.

'Shit! So he returned to his killing ground,' breathed Joseph.

'With considerable ease. He strolled in through his "other" entrance, the one he knows about and we bloody well don't.'

'I wonder why?' Joseph stared out across acres of freshly ploughed fields.

'Because they do. It's well documented that killers feel the need to return to the scene. And maybe he just needed to see for himself what was going on.' Nikki eased her car around a winding bend, and then accelerated onto the straight road. She glanced hopefully across to Joseph. 'Any further forward with finding Eve?'

'All this has caused something of a hold-up, although Tam is still hard at it.'

Nikki thought he sounded mildly evasive, but perhaps she was just tired.

'I rang her with your proposition, and you were right. She'll be coming in with me tomorrow.' He shook his head. 'Which, believe me, feels sincerely weird.'

'A good kind of weird?'

'Very good, ma'am. Next left and we're into Castor Fen Village.'

* * *

Half an hour later they sat outside the Flowers' home. The meeting with Joshua Flower had brought up nothing that they could use, and as his brother was at work they had promised to return later that evening to interview Simon. 'Any thoughts?' Nikki chewed on the end of her pen.

'Intelligent, academic, well-off, an interesting chap to listen to, made a change to hear someone stringing a full sentence together without a swear word . . . or am I spending too much time in the mess room?'

'Probably. I admit he's interesting, but after a while he begins to get up my nose. I don't like the way he lectures you rather than just answering the questions.'

'Force of habit. It was his job, wasn't it? And he knows that airfield very well.'

'Too well?'

Joseph turned and looked at her. 'Surely you don't think he's our man? He's charming. I thought serial killers were without social graces, you know, emotionless. That's how come they can do the dreadful things that they do.'

'Depends how clever they are. Some blend in with society by being cunning mimics.'

'Yes, but,' Joseph seemed honestly shocked that Nikki was so suspicious about Joshua, 'he's too . . . what do I mean?

He *interacts* too well, and he's honestly passionate about history. I just can't buy into the murderer bit.'

'You're probably right.' Nikki massaged the back of her neck to ease the tense muscles. 'What's getting to me is the fact that our history society, with all their maps and books and historical tomes, and knowing *all* they do about that place, have completely missed that bloody great underground chapel. It's huge, damn it!'

'Well, someone certainly knew about it, didn't they?'

'And has done for decades. I'll be glad when we start to get some solid forensic results. Dates and stuff. Like when he first killed.'

'That's going to take time. I don't envy our pathologist right now, do you?'

'You do know he's got a sleeping bag down there, *and* a camp bed?'

'You're kidding! God! I'd never have put our Rory down as having balls. You wouldn't get me staying down there for all the tea in China!'

'He seems quite at home.'

'Now you're really worrying me!' He pulled a horrified face.

Nikki smiled. 'The poor sod looks like a ghost himself. I've warned him, but he refuses to budge until his forensic mate gets there.' Nikki started the car. 'Time to get back. I'll be interested to hear what the others have turned up.'

* * *

Dave pulled into the curb, parked under a massive horse chestnut tree and tried to picture the man they were going to interview. He remembered a slight accent that he couldn't quite place, and that Kohler had been very polite, even if he did possess piercing sharp eyes that looked unnervingly straight into yours. When he had seen him at the airfield, Dave had noticed that the man was wearing one blue and one green sock, which led him to believe that he was single and colour-blind.

Dave looked across at Yvonne and said, 'Before we go in, what do we actually know about Frank Kohler?'

'No record. Not even a speeding ticket.' Yvonne had swung the door open and was getting out. 'He has a half-sister living with him, name of Irene Kohler. Apparently she goes to the history society meetings occasionally. Again, squeaky clean.' She looked across at Dave. 'These aren't the kind of people that we usually get called out to see, unless there's been an attempted burglary or something like that. They are certainly not the shady sorts that fill our days, are they?'

Dave glanced up at the high gables and leaded windows, then rang the bell. 'And this doesn't look like the sort of place to house a family of villains, does it?'

'How about a murderer?' asked Yvonne darkly.

'Pass. But perhaps we should keep an eye open for bottles of arsenic in the wine rack.'

There was the sound of an interior door closing, then through the coloured glass a shadowy figure could be seen approaching.

Frank Kohler stood to one side and the two police officers entered. 'I got your call, but Irene is out. She works in the Cancer Research charity shop some afternoons.'

Dave decided that the hint of accent was German.

'Can I get you a drink?'

'That would be very nice, sir,' said Dave, wanting to use every moment that the man was out of sight to get a good look round. 'Coffee, please.'

'Tea for me, if it's not too much trouble?' added Yvonne with a smile.

Kohler went to put the kettle on, and Dave took in the high ceiling with the deep ornate coving and central boss, the long casement windows with the expensive drapes, and the kind of furniture that had history attached to it, not a zero per cent finance agreement.

'Family money?' he whispered to Yvonne. 'Must be. You'd need more than the chief constable earns for all this.' Yvonne looked around and her eyes fell on a gilt-framed picture over the fireplace. 'Look at that! I'm no expert, but that looks pretty authentic to me.'

'You obviously have a discerning eye for quality, Constable.' Kohler appeared in the doorway. 'Because you're quite right. It's a Victorian artist, not wildly famous but quite collectable by lovers of the Idyllists.' He walked across to a winged armchair and sat, looking from one police officer to the other. 'So, how can I help?'

Dave began. 'You probably know that the airfield is cordoned off at present?'

'My neighbour rang to tell me. Is it something to do with the owner's death?'

'Not exactly. There has been a significant discovery at Flaxton Mere.'

The man looked perplexed. 'Oh? Like what?'

'We are not at liberty to say, sir. But it is being treated as a murder enquiry, and we can tell you that another secret chamber has been discovered.'

'Good God! But I've been doing historical research out there for years! Where did you find it?' He seemed genuinely surprised.

'Sorry, sir, I can't say exactly where at present.' Dave looked apologetic.

'Well, that place is full of surprises, isn't it?'

'Apparently, Mr Kohler. And as you are one of the few people who have a working knowledge of it, I'm afraid we need to ask you some questions.'

The man stood. 'Let me get the drinks.'

As he left the room, Dave followed him, making admiring comments about the house, and allowing Yvonne to take a closer look at the room.

'So, is it just you and your sister live here, sir?'

'Half-sister. We shared the same father. And yes, it is just us. I'm sure some would think it's a waste of such a big house but so long as we can afford to look after it, that's how it will remain. It's our family home.'

'And a very beautiful one, sir. I'm sure I'd feel the same.' Dave knew damn well he would, if he lived in a mansion like this. 'You've lived here all your life then?'

'Almost. Since I was a boy. My father was from Munich, but he had to leave Germany when the war began.' He paused, then added, 'Political reasons.'

'What did your father do for a living, sir? This house would not have come cheap, even all that time ago.'

'His family were certainly not poor, Officer. He left in considerable haste, but he did have enough time to arrange his finances. He was a master craftsman, a cabinetmaker. You will see the proof of his expertise throughout the house.'

They walked back to the sitting room, Dave talking loudly to alert Yvonne to their return. 'And your profession, sir?' Dave gingerly accepted the bone china cup and saucer, wishing it was a mug, something more suited to his chunky fingers.

'Antiques. I buy and sell. Most of my sales are through the internet or auctions.'

'And your interest in Flaxton Mere?'

'Via the history society. We were the first ones to discover that it had an interesting wartime history, one that had been buried until we began ferreting through the archives.' He frowned and stared directly at Dave. 'Am I some kind of suspect for whatever has happened?'

'We need the help of all the members of your group, not just yourself.'

The interview went on until Dave raised an eyebrow at Yvonne. They were getting nothing of use. They thanked Kohler and left.

In the car outside, Yvonne pulled a face and closed her notebook. 'Nothing much of value there, was there? Other than the Victorian Idyllist, that is. And the porcelain, *and* the furniture.'

'Nothing obvious. And he really seemed shocked to hear about the enquiry. Still, you never know. Where to next?'

'The Brewers. They live on the other side of the green, the house on the corner of the lane that goes out to the fen.'

* * *

Bill Brewer and his wife, Margaret, sat next to each other on a large, comfortless sofa. Their eyes were huge, and they often answered together, or split their sentences between them, making the interview seem disjointed and slightly frenetic.

'We've been going there for—'

'Fifteen years at least, maybe —'

'More like twenty. It's been our hobby, you see—'

'William's parents left hundreds of old photos—'

'Local stuff, all pertaining to this area—'

'Mostly wartime pictures.'

Dave was starting to feel slightly dizzy and decided that if they were the killers, they had most likely bored their victims to death.

The interview lasted about half an hour, and he and Yvonne came away with dazed expressions. If it wasn't so bloody serious, they would have laughed.

Dave pulled at his seatbelt, then saw Cat and Niall hurrying across the green towards them. He wound down his window. 'Anything interesting?'

Cat shrugged. 'Nothing too exciting, although that Andrew Friar bloke is well odd. His mother said he had a head injury years ago, and it affected his brain, so it's hard to tell if he's experiencing neurological problems or is just plain creepy.'

'I'd definitely settle for creepy. And that other chap, Selby . . .' Niall gave Dave and Yvonne an exasperated grin. 'Phew! He's a right pain in the arse. Plus he's mega pissed off that we've discovered a part of the airfield that he doesn't know about.'

'That's true,' added Cat. 'That seemed to bother him more than the fact that we were conducting a murder investigation.'

Dave narrowed his eyes. 'You don't think the anger was actually because we've discovered a part of the airfield that he *does* know about?'

'We wondered that. But on reflection we don't think so. He just seems pig-sick that after a couple of hours on the fen, a pair of flat-footed coppers unearthed something that years of historical investigation have missed.'

'Understandable, I suppose, but I'd definitely make a note of his reaction when you write up your report.'

'Certainly will, my friend.' Cat indicated back towards their vehicle. 'But it's time we were heading back to base, because our two trusty coppers here have a little job of their own to attend to tonight, out on Flaxton Mere.'

Niall nodded and threw Yvonne a knowing look. 'We sure have. See you at the nick.'

Dave watched them go. He silently wondered if the murders were the work of a complete unknown, a lone fen-lander who had walked that particular stretch of marshy water-world from his youth. A home-grown killer. As he drove back to base, he decided to ask the boss if maybe they should look closer at some of the old locals, the web-foots that have a particular love for their remote and eerie home-land. Dave shivered and decided there was nothing more dangerous than a faceless adversary.

CHAPTER TWENTY

Two hours later, Nikki and Joseph had returned to the comfortable house in Castor Fen village, and were sitting once again in Joshua Flower's study, surrounded by the same books and the same paintings, but opposite a different Flower.

Simon, like his brother, expressed total incredulity at their discovering another underground chamber. 'Frankly, Inspector, if anyone should know about it, it should be me. I'm the canary that they send down the pit to see if it's safe. This is an awesome discovery! Can you tell me where it is?'

Nikki looked at Joseph, then shrugged and nodded. One look at the concentration of uniforms out on the marsh would tell him the answer to that one anyway. 'Below one of the pillboxes on the marsh side of the airfield.'

He shook his head in amazement. 'Well.' He let out a low whistle. 'All I can think is that I've rarely paid much attention to the pillboxes. Once you've ascertained what they were protecting, and what their design and armament was that's it, really.' His expression changed to one of exasperation. 'Damn it! I really should have known! There's an escape route from the main bunker. It had a tunnel that has since been sealed, but it ran from the bunker to just outside the perimeter fence and directly to a pillbox, a specially designed one that was actually a concealed exit. They must have used the same camouflage, only the one you discovered was not an exit, but an entrance.' He let out an irritated growl. 'Why the hell didn't I make the connection?'

Nikki watched his reaction with interest. 'Mr Flower, the underground chamber was not purpose-built at the time of WWII. It has nothing whatsoever to do with the RAF. It's very old and apparently part of a monastery that stood on the site hundreds of years ago.'

The man's brow folded into furrows. 'Really? I'd have thought it was part of the war installation, but then again it shouldn't surprise me. If you recall, DS Easter, I showed your daughter Tamsin one of the monks' tunnels that led out to the marsh. If that tiny chapel could remain intact, then so could others.' He dropped his head, then lifted his eyes and looked hopefully at Nikki. 'Do you think I could see it?'

'It is a crime scene, Mr Flower. That's not possible.'

'I work crime scenes all the time, Detective. I'm with the fire service, remember? We often attend cases of suspected arson.'

'I'm sorry, but there are aspects of this case that we are not making public yet.' Nineteen of them, to be precise, thought Nikki. 'However, we may ask for your help later on.' She weighed him up, and knowing his history with the emergency services, decided to tell him a little more than they had the others. 'We suspect there is another way in, Simon, a "back door" so to speak, although so far we haven't found it.'

'So why do you think it exists?' His grey-blue eyes held a sharp intelligence.

'Let's say that the crypt contains items that would have been difficult to manoeuvre down steep steps.'

'Really?' He stared at her shrewdly.

Nikki could see that he was desperate to know what these *items* were, but no way was she going to tell him that.

'Well, I'd be glad to help, anytime. Up until tonight I believed that I knew more than anyone about that place. Now it seems I was wrong.' He bit anxiously on his lip. 'But even so, I'm more than willing to help you look for this alternative entrance. And I do have quite a bit of previous knowledge of the place to call upon.'

Nikki nodded. 'And we might be very grateful for that once our preliminary searches are complete. Meanwhile, when we called earlier we asked your brother to provide us with a potted history of RAF Flaxton Mere. Anything you can add would be much appreciated. As their "canary," you have probably trodden paths that the others have not.'

'I'll certainly give it some thought, Inspector. Will that be all?'

'For now, sir. Thank you.'

* * *

As night closed in, the mysterious lights of the Jack O'Lantern once again danced across the marshy ground of Flaxton Mere. And on the wind from the sea, terrible noises could be heard. Moans and wailing voices, screams and cries that could turn the unsuspecting traveller's blood to ice. Except that this time the show was being mounted courtesy of PC Niall Farrow and WPC Yvonne Collins.

It had taken an hour, with three uniformed constables and a dog, to locate the powerful lamp, the sound system and the automatic switch gear that activated it. Then having discovered the lamp, they traced the electrical lead down into a shaft, not unlike the one that poor Pike had taken a dive into. For some time they tramped down a long sloping passageway until they came to a carefully hidden door beneath the control tower. And that, to their amazement, led down a long, high tunnel to the back of the burial chamber.

By ten o'clock that evening, DI Nikki Galena had her "back door."

* * *

'Stuart!' Rory almost fell into the white-suited arms of his old university friend.

'Jesus Christ on a bike, Wilkinson! You look like shit!'

'You always did know how to make a guy feel special, Dr Bass.'

The forensic archaeologist put down his flight bag and did a 360 degree take on the chamber. 'When you said this trip would be worth my while, I had my doubts.' He frowned admonishingly at his friend. 'Especially when it came to leaving my beautiful, and now somewhat irate, bride in the middle of our honeymoon, but bloody hell, you weren't joking, were you?'

'It needs to be seen to be appreciated, doesn't it? Although I'm not too sure said lovely young bride would agree with me.'

Bass moved across to the second chamber and his eyes widened at the sight of the stone shelves stacked with coffins. 'Now that's what I call a library!'

'Slightly macabre genre of books in the collection, don't you think?'

'This is a jaw-dropping, gob-smacking marvel, Rory!' He turned back to his friend, his large brown eyes sparkling with excitement. 'How do we get a strong coffee around here? I need to kill the jetlag and hear the story before I start work.'

Rory would have liked just a little of his friend's energy. 'I'll get one of the lads to go to the late-night garage. They sell half-edible doughnuts too. I think I need a sugar hit, and I'm afraid I can't actually leave the scene for a bit. Sit down here,' he pointed to a wide stone step, 'and I'll explain.'

* * *

Stuart had begun work even before the doughnuts arrived.

'I think that if the police extend their search, they will find a store of some kind, stacked with plain coffins.' His large physique was surprisingly graceful. He moved from coffin to coffin, scaled the tower athletically, and with considerable elegance. 'Taking on board what you've told me about the original plans for this airfield, I would expect at least a hundred coffins stored somewhere.' He swung to the ground. 'Strangely enough, I've seen a similar thing once before.'

Rory found the energy to look mildly astonished.

'An underground fallout shelter was being stripped out prior to a massive rebuild. It was beneath some old government buildings. It dated back to the fifties or sixties and the Cold War, a time when the fear of a nuclear attack gave rise to all sorts of frightful ideas on how to prevent the rich and important from being vaporised. Well, sadly for the contractors, they found a grave. It turned out to be Roman, but it put a temporary hold on their excavations. Anyway, they had a coffin store too.'

'But I thought they used papier mâché and cardboard coffins during the war?'

'They did, but only because back in the 1930s it had been calculated that if the *Luftwaffe* launched what was called the "knock-out blow," it would be such a huge air attack that in the first three months they would require 60,000,000 square feet of coffin timber! I think by the time this place was getting up and running, the military had more faith in the RAF, and perhaps the wish for something a little more substantial than papier mâché to be buried in.'

'Would they have used local people to construct them?'

'Doubtful. This was a secret project, although the timber might have been sourced from a local merchant.'

'Something for our detectives to check out, I suppose.'

Stuart looked at Rory, his head slightly to one side. 'I know you are knackered beyond words, but something else is worrying you, isn't it?'

'Oh, did I forget to mention that the killer called by yesterday? We had a nice chat about this and that, then he left for a pee and I haven't seen him since.'

Stuart looked sideways at the pathologist. 'Right. Fine. Any chance of running that by me again? This time with a tad more information attached.'

Rory did his best to explain.

'You actually *spoke* to a mass murderer?'

'No, I actually spoke to a serial killer. Mass murderers kill randomly, like the Hungerford massacre.'

'Don't split hairs, Wilkinson. You know exactly what I mean.' Stuart's dark eyebrows almost met in the middle as he mock-frowned at Rory.

'Mm, perhaps I just don't like to think about it too deeply right now. As our main objective is to give our detectives some dates, like when matey-boy here began his life's work, I suppose we had better crack on. Have you got another hour left in you, or would you prefer to start afresh in the morning?'

'Lord! If you can keep going, O pasty-faced apparition, I'm bloody sure I can!'

CHAPTER TWENTY-ONE

Nikki was opening the morning meeting. 'There have been a few developments overnight, so listen up. One: we now have our alternative entrance into the underground chambers, so we know how all the mortuary equipment was brought in. And that is thanks to the ingenuity of PC Niall Farrow and WPC Yvonne Collins. Also thanks to them, we now know about a series of deterrents, or "people-scarers." Our killer has been keeping visitors away with a load of clever little tricks to repel the inquisitive and the unwelcome. The superstitious are treated to lights on the marsh, audio tapes of aircraft, war-time sirens and general carnage and destruction, and a light show that, seen from a distance, resembles flickering flames.'

'I *knew* that scenario was somehow familiar,' said Yvonne. 'An air raid was one of Miss Quinney's favourite complaints a while back. I should have remembered it was her that mentioned it.'

'But how's he done all that, ma'am?' asked a uniformed officer. 'Flaxton Mere is hardly a Pinewood set, is it?'

'He's had plenty of time. And he's smart. So far we have located two petrol-driven generators and some pretty hefty bat-tery-powered ghetto blaster-type sound systems with timers.' She stopped for a moment, considering some of these, then continued. 'Have you ever seen those up-market irrigation systems for watering lawns? The ones that disappear down into the turf so you can mow over them? Well, he's used that principle, but instead of sprays, he has hollow pipes that conduct sound. Yvonne and Niall tried them out, and depending on what you fancy sending through them, they are damned eerie.'

'Yes,' added Niall grimly. 'It's no wonder Pike nearly died of fright, and that the locals reckon the fen is haunted. It is, but not by ghosts.'

'It should be. There are enough bloody bodies underneath it!' Bob Tinker's half joke sounded hollow.

'Thank you for your input, PC Tinker. Our psychologist, Richard Foley, is studying the info we have, in order to give us an idea of what kind of person we are looking for. You will be updated as soon as that information is available.' She glanced at a sheaf of notes that lay on her desk. 'We have interviewed the history society members,' she frowned, 'but none of them leapt out as being first-class suspects. However, they all deserve careful scrutiny, as they are the ones closest to the airfield, and they are also pretty desperate to get a protection order on it.'

'What about the bloke who got topped, ma'am? Karl Shine? He knew the place. After all, he did own it. Perhaps someone knew what he was up to and got in first.'

'Not very likely. These killings began way before Shine's time.'

'What about the people who work from those hangars, ma'am? There is not a straight one among them.'

Nikki shook her head. 'Joseph has checked all of them. They only started renting when Shine bought into the airfield. Again, they are too recent.'

'So it looks like either an old-time local, or one of the history group,' said Dave.

'I agree, so dig deep with all of them. Forget the genteel exteriors and find me some dirt. I want to know everything about them and their families, both living and dead, going back at least two generations, okay?'

'Ma'am?' Cat looked up at her boss. 'What about suiting them up in forensics overalls and getting Professor Wilkinson to see if he recognises one of them? If he really did talk to the killer, something might give him away.'

'I've already put that to Rory. He's happy to give it a try, but the killer could disguise his voice or his general demeanour. He's too clever, and he's been getting away with murder for around two decades, so . . .' She looked at the young detective. 'Sorry to be negative, but think about it. The killer was wearing a mask, a scene suit, gloves and plastic shoe-protectors, all in poor light. I know Rory said he would know him if he saw him again, and in a one-to-one, unprepared situation some small gesture or intonation of speech just might give him away, but not in a line-up. And I've already shown him the photos of all the male members of the history society, and none of them were familiar to him. Poor Rory is exhausted. Frankly I don't think he'd recognise his own mother in poor light and a hooded suit, do you?' She looked around the room at the sea of serious faces. 'By the end of the day we should have something better to go on, some idea of a timescale and hopefully a profile of the killer. Meanwhile, I want all your energies directed towards tearing that history society apart. So, go to it.'

* * *

Tamsin sat on the other side of her father's desk. 'You haven't told her what Tug Owen said, have you?'

'How can I, Tam? She's run ragged with this investigation, and she still has her father's funeral next week to cope with.'

'Oh, I agree. I just wondered if you wanted me to keep on digging around to see where Eve might have disappeared to. Tug reckoned they parted on bad terms, but when he realised that he'd goofed, Nikki's father went looking for her. Okay, so he never found her, but with these wonderful inventions,' she indicated the computer, 'there's a good chance that I may be able to track down something about her.' She looked at him hopefully. 'And I can do that right here, on my own laptop.'

'Well, if Nikki hasn't given you anything special to do, you go ahead.'

'Dad, I have to ask this before I start. Knowing what you found in that crypt, and considering that Eve went missing after working at Flaxton Mere, do you think she might be one of the victims?'

Joseph moved closer to his daughter and whispered, 'I've thought of little else since talking with Tug. I'm going to ask the pathologist if they've found a woman of her possible age and description.'

'Then give him this.' Tamsin passed him a printout photo. 'I enhanced her image from the picture Nikki found in her father's book.'

Joseph stared at the printout of Eve. It was easy to see why Nikki's father had been attracted to her. Even without the bond of shared trauma, there was definitely something very attractive about her.

'You can see it too,' murmured Tamsin. 'Although I can't fathom what it is. Maybe she looks like one of those gorgeous actresses in old wartime films.'

Joseph folded the sheet and pushed it into his pocket. 'I'll go and see Rory as soon as, although with the workload, I'm not sure when that'll be.'

'Don't sweat it, Dad.' Tamsin returned to her laptop. 'There's plenty of time.'

Joseph felt his heart give a little lurch and he sincerely hoped there was.

'For you, sir.' Niall appeared with an armful of paperwork. He looked from Joseph to Tamsin and grinned. 'Have you joined the force too?'

Tamsin smiled at him. 'No fear. I'm under house arrest actually.'

Joseph gave his daughter a withering look, then turned to Niall. 'Can I ask a favour?' Without waiting for a reply, he said, 'If Tamsin needs to go out to the café or anything, would you tag along with her? Show her around?'

Niall nodded quickly. 'No problem, sir. Be my pleasure.'

Tamsin glowered at her father. 'I'm not a child! At home I walk the streets of Chicago at night without a bodyguard, so I hardly need one here.'

'Oh do you? I'll worry about *that* at a later date, but as Greenborough has a psychotic killer roaming its streets, I think it's one up on Chicago right now, thank you.'

'The sarge has a point. So humour us, yes?' Niall turned on a dazzling smile.

Tamsin shook her head in disgust, but didn't argue. Joseph noticed a wry smile hovering on her lips.

'By the way, Niall, that was a damn good job out on the marsh.' Joseph clapped him on the shoulder. 'Well done to you and your crew-mate. Finding that other entrance was a stroke of pure genius. And I'm sure it's helped to speed up the enquiry. Nice one.'

Niall glowed red, and managed to splutter that it was nothing, really.

After he had left, Joseph said, partly to himself and partly to his daughter, 'That lad has the makings of a damned good police officer. He has all the right instincts. He could go far, given the right breaks.'

Tamsin did not answer, but Joseph had noticed that her eyes had followed PC Niall Farrow all the way out of the room.

* * *

By late morning the undercroft had taken on a very different appearance. The SOCOs had removed every trace of evidence that had been left behind, and using the killer's own mortuary table and several portable units of their own, the two forensic scientists had set up a passable on-site field station. The two most recent victims had been moved directly to the mortuary, but all the others were being carefully examined in the makeshift underground laboratory.

Stuart Bass was as excited by this strange chamber of death as he had been about any archaeological dig that he could remember. And as the hours went by, the more elated he became.

'Looks like three distinct periods of usage, Rory.' He was swinging from the top of the tower and investigating a series of hooks embedded deep into the ceiling of the burial chapel. 'These were the original fittings for a simple block and tackle that allowed the monks to haul the coffins up to the higher tier. So we have the resting place of the holy order that built the monastery. Then it would seem from the later plain coffins, that the military used it for some purpose, probably storage. I'm damn sure they didn't embalm their dead and place them on display. The casualties of war would have been recorded and buried in a far corner of the airfield designated as a cemetery.'

'And now we have its last use. Someone's personal chapel of rest.'

'Last but one, Wilkinson. Right now, it's a field path lab.'

'Ah, yes. And I keep wondering what our killer thought about it, when he paid me that impromptu visit.'

'Well, you are probably not number one on his favourites list right now.'

'Hardly. Trampling all over his *sanctum sanctorum*.'

'Better keep looking over your shoulder then, my friend.' Bass was only half joking.

'I think the time has come to tell you that I didn't invite you here *entirely* for your valued academic brain. I actually required your muscular body to watch my back.'

'Well, if that's the case, we'd better order another camp bed, hadn't we?'

* * *

'If nothing else, ma'am, our songbird Pikey is singing like a good'un!' PC Bob Tinker had just returned from the hospital.

'I've turned everything over to the narcotics team. They are ecstatic over some of the info he's coughed up.'

'Anything to get off the hook, huh?' Nikki didn't like Pike, but then she didn't like anyone involved in the drug world.

'To be honest, I believe he's had enough of the street life, ma'am. Maybe the hoods didn't get to his gran, but that was only because of divine intervention. If she hadn't had that heart attack, God knows what they would have done to her. Several people saw a dark car out there the next day. It had to be them, and Pike is well shaken by the whole thing.'

'And do we know who "them" are?'

'A couple of lowlife goons who collect from bad debtors, but we aren't sure who they are in the pay of.'

'Then keep a very close eye on Pike.' Nikki's eyes narrowed. 'Those goons will be after him.' She paused. 'Has Pike been told about his friend Anson Taylor yet?'

'Did it myself, ma'am.' Bob Tinker drew in a breath. 'I know he's a right little scrote, but I did feel a bit sorry for him. He's still facing a possible amputation, his granny has died, and now his best mate, well, actually his *only* mate, has been snuffed. He's not having the best of times.'

'Then let's hope having to deal with serious trauma really does drag him onto the straight and narrow, shall we?'

As Tinker left, Joseph came through the door. 'Thought you should know that we've had a partial ID on the dark-haired victim from the crypt.'

Nikki looked up from her paperwork. 'Really? That was quick!'

Joseph pulled a face. 'Well, it's not much, but one of the engineers from the dodgy lock-ups recognised the photo of the dead man as one of Karl Shine's surveyors.'

'Do we know who they are yet? What company?'

'No. But as all their vehicles were unmarked, allegedly none of the men were communicative and they disappeared like the morning mist when we came on the scene, I'd say they were very unofficial, wouldn't you?'

'Mm, and there was no paperwork regarding surveyors at Shine's home.' Nikki leaned back in her chair. 'So what did our illegal surveyor do to get himself murdered, I wonder?' She frowned. 'Let's think about this. On the surface it looks as if our killer took out Karl Shine because he was planning on developing the airfield, doesn't it?'

'Yes, and maybe the surveyor discovered something that he wasn't meant to, then he told Shine, so the killer had to dispose of both?'

'But that's not right, is it? He certainly killed and lovingly embalmed the dark-haired man, but Karl was brutally murdered and left in his car to rot. Our killer takes great care of his victims. Shine was assassinated. Terminated professionally, and unless I'm way off track, this is a completely separate murder.'

'Oh lovely! Welcome to friendly Greenborough, home to countless murderers!' Joseph dropped his head into his hands and groaned loudly.

CHAPTER TWENTY-TWO

As the day wore on, Nikki found her thoughts returning again and again to the underground mortuary table. She shuddered every time she thought about it. Why couldn't they trace it? For heaven's sake, people didn't just go out and buy a relocatable mortuary, like they would a new dining-room table. They were highly specialised pieces of equipment, and with the internet they should have been able to easily pinpoint manufacturer, design, model, and supplier. But they'd found zilch.

Joseph joined her sometime after four o'clock, and flopped down onto a chair. 'We've got nothing new. We've scanned the backgrounds of all the possible suspects, and no one has the slightest connection with the funeral trade. And as Rory said, the art of embalming does not exactly feature next to model planes and embroidery in the craft and hobby magazines.'

'Rory also said the killer was a master professional, so maybe he's someone we haven't even spoken to yet.' Nikki closed the file that she was working on. 'Dave thinks it's some local man that we've overlooked. We've been so involved with the history society that maybe we're missing something.' She stared out through the office window. 'Where's Tamsin?'

'She declared that she couldn't last another ten minutes without a skinny latte, so Niall Farrow has taken her round to the Café des Amis.'

Nikki threw him a tired smile. 'I suspect a little bit of chemistry there, don't you?'

Joseph's face creased into a grin. 'Now wouldn't that be a turn up for the books? My Tamsin, associating with the enemy.' He looked concerned momentarily. 'And I can only guess what her mother Laura would think about that!'

'I think Tamsin's mellowing.'

'I'd like to think the same, but I'm scared to.'

'Hang on in there, my friend, I get the feeling that things will turn out well with you two. Just have patience.'

* * *

As Niall placed two white china cups on the table, Tamsin looked at him with interest. He was the kind of guy you couldn't help liking. But there was something more about him, something she found quite attractive. He seemed to be quite unaware that he was drop-dead gorgeous, and he had a fire of enthusiasm inside him. She recognised it from something that burned in her own soul. She always appreciated passion when she saw it. She just wasn't quite sure how anyone could be *passionate* about being a copper.

'You looked pretty pleased with yourself when my father said you'd done well.'

Niall grinned. 'It meant a lot.'

'Why?'

The young officer sat down opposite her. He looked surprised. 'Because your dad is something of a hero around here, Tamsin. To get an accolade from him is, well, a really cool thing to happen.'

Tamsin silently took what he had said on board, and stirred her coffee thoughtfully. 'Have you always wanted to be a policeman?'

'Never thought of anything else.' He gave Tamsin a long, thoughtful look, and she decided that he was debating whether to tell her more. After a while he said, 'When I was a lad, my dad was working a late shift at the factory and my elder brother had taken my sister down to the chippie to get our supper.' He stared into his coffee for a while, then went on. 'So I was on my own when the police arrived. I was eight years old, and my father had just been killed in an accident at work. Some machinery malfunctioned and . . .' He took a deep breath and left that part of the story untold. 'I never forgot how kind the police officers were, or how well they handled the situation and the care they took of us. From that day, I knew exactly what I would be when I left school.' His face broke into a grin. 'From day one I loved it. And when they finally teamed me up with Vonnie, I thought all my Christmases had come at once.'

'I like Yvonne. So is she a hero too?'

Niall leaned closer to Tamsin. 'Vonnie is a legend.' For the next few minutes he regaled her with stories of Yvonne's brilliant street policing career. '*And* she has the Queen's Commendation for Bravery, but you'll never hear that from her. She'd tell you she was just doing her job.' Niall shook his head. 'Thing is, though I love being a beat bobby, I want to get into CID. My goal is to get onto your dad's team. Apart from your father, DI Galena is top cop in my book.' He sipped his coffee, 'And most of the station would agree with me.'

'So what makes them different from other teams?' asked Tamsin.

Niall didn't hesitate. 'Respect, Tam. They've both earned respect from the men and women they work with. And that doesn't happen easily, believe me.'

Tamsin recalled the last time she had been in Greenborough, when another murder case had been hanging over Nikki's head. Tamsin had not really been around long enough, but even then she had picked up on some unspoken bond that the team had.

'Did you know that both the DI and your dad were offered promotion last year?'

Tamsin frowned. 'He never mentioned it. Why didn't they take it?'

'For the sake of the team. They decided that things were too good to mess with. Promotion would have meant big changes. See what I mean about loyalty?'

As they walked back to the station, Tamsin began to wonder if it was time to put the past behind her. She had seen her father only three times in the last three years, and she knew that he was a different man to the zealous soldier he had once been. She had never believed that leopards could change their spots, but from what she'd seen for herself, and from what she'd heard from people like Niall, maybe she had been wrong.

As the police station came into view, Tamsin decided that she wanted to forget about the times her father had left them to go kill people, and all the times that he had put his army career before their happiness, but she wasn't sure that she could. She would try — after all, that was why she was here, but . . .

'Before we go in . . .' Niall touched her arm lightly. 'Look, this is probably not the best time to ask, knowing that we are involved in the biggest and nastiest case any of us has ever seen, but would you fancy coming out for a drink with me later?'

Tamsin hoped that she looked calm and just a little indifferent. Niall was a cool guy, but she didn't want to lead him on. After all, she would be returning to the States in the not-too-distant future. Still, a drink wouldn't exactly hurt, now would it? 'If you like.'

Niall grinned at her. 'Great. Let me put your number into my phone.' He opened his phone and quickly punched in the numbers that she gave him. 'I'll ring you later, then you can pick up my details.' He opened the door for her and they went inside, talking easily together.

Back at her desk, Tamsin decided that perhaps it hadn't been such a bad idea to work with her father after all.

* * *

As night clouds moved slowly across the sky, the men and women working out on Flaxton Mere began to get jumpy. It was not a happy place in bright sunshine, but at night, even knowing that the ghostly lights and eerie noises had been man-made, it was miserable. Maybe it was made worse by the fact that the Mere had been used in such an evil way, that the sinister goings-on had been engineered by a psychotic killer. And the knowledge that he was still on the loose.

'She's out there again, Sarge. What can I do, apart from slapping her in a cell?'

Reg had seen a ghostly figure drifting around the airfield. After conquering a major attack of the horrors, he realised it was the sister of the dead dealer, Anson Taylor. He had tried to reason with her, but she had simply said that she couldn't rest and wanted to be close to where her brother had died.

'Get her home again, Reg. And tell her to see her doctor. She needs a sedative or something. Are there no relatives? She shouldn't be alone.'

'Just a father that she hates. And I know why. He knocked her mother around and abused her too, but when he started on her kid brother, Steph came to us.'

'Good for her. That took guts.' The sergeant shrugged his broad shoulders. 'Well, I've got no answers, Reg. Just get her home, I guess. It's all we can do.'

'Couldn't we let her stay for a bit, sir? Now we know it's not the Lady in White. And she's not doing any harm. I get the feeling she'll only keep coming back.'

'Then talk to her again, but if she stays, she's your responsibility, and make sure you take her with you when your shift is over, all right?'

Reg thanked his sergeant and walked off towards the pale, unkempt figure that sat on a grassy mound a little way from the pillbox. He sat down beside her, and together they stared at the floodlit structure. When he told her that she could stay until he went off duty, she placed an ice-cold hand on his, and croaked a pitiful 'thank you.' It made Reg wonder what the hell life was all about.

* * *

Nikki and Joseph sat in the tiny kitchen in Knot Cottage, sipped cold white wine and ate a bowl of tuna pasta that Joseph had quickly put together when they got home. It was after nine thirty, and as Nikki had forgotten to shop again, she was glad of the impromptu supper. 'What time is Tamsin due back?' she asked, wiping a slice of garlic bread around her empty dish.

'Niall said he'd have her back by ten. We all need our sleep.'

'Sleep doesn't come easy, knowing there's a killer out there.'

'Plus the timing stinks. You still have your father's funeral to worry about, and I've got Tamsin to stay with me for the first time since she was in school uniform.'

They talked for a while about the case, then Joseph took the dishes and placed them in the dishwasher. 'Are you alright in the farmhouse alone, Nikki?' He looked at her anxiously. 'I mean, I know you're as tough as old boots, but these are extraordinary times. Tam and I could come and stay over. I'd offer our hospitality here, but one loo, two bedrooms and three of us could be interesting.'

Nikki yawned. 'I'm fine, Joseph, but thanks. And if I spook myself at three in the morning, I promise that I'll make up the spare beds, okay?'

'Do that.' Joseph walked to the window and looked along the lane. Then he glanced at his watch. 'I'm beginning to wish I'd told them to leave this "date" until we were less stretched. Young people don't have much idea of time, do they?'

Nikki checked her own watch. 'It's only ten past. And at their age, I don't think I cared too much for curfews either.'

'If there wasn't a murderer loose, I'd agree.' He ran his hand through his hair, in a gesture Nikki had noticed that Tamsin had inherited.

'Niall's a sensible lad, and he worships you, so he's not going to blow it on his first date with the sergeant's daughter, now is he?'

'I guess not.' Joseph gave a short laugh. 'By the way, Tamsin asked me about our refusing promotion. It seems that Niall told her that we did it to hold the team together. I think it made something of an impression on her.'

Nikki smiled at him. 'Good.' Of course, turning down promotion wasn't entirely because of the work dynamic, and they both knew it. They had reached a watershed moment in their relationship, and they were scared, too scared to lose what they had, and too scared to change anything. And so they had drawn a line under any form of moving forward, personally and in the workplace. And here they were, a year on and still too scared to rock the boat.

Joseph settled back in his favourite chair and his smile faded. 'Nikki, I don't know about you but I'm having trouble getting my head around the sheer scale of this case. You read about prolific serial killers, but somehow they don't seem real, do they? And here we are in the middle of the Fens, with one of the worst cases this country has ever seen. Someone has *deliberately* taken all those lives, year after year. It's like some horrible, gruesome hobby that has existed alongside his "normal" life — whatever that is.'

'I know what you mean, it feels totally surreal. But it does happen. I was given a paper to read once about Victorian murderers, not just Jack the Ripper, but there was this woman Amelia Dyer, they called her the Angel Maker, and she murdered four hundred babies before they caught and hanged her. Now that totally scrambled my brain.'

'I've seen some terrible things, Nikki, in the military.' A shadow seemed to fall across his face. 'Things I never want to see again, but something like this is so . . .' Joseph fought for words, 'so devious, so . . .'

'Sick?'

'He's a predator, and he's been living among us, preying on innocent human beings and taking them to his own private house of horrors. If this were an episode of *Tales from the Crypt*, no one would believe it.'

'Well, he won't be taking any other poor souls down there, thank God.' Nikki yawned. 'Sorry, Joseph. I really should go, but I want to know that Tamsin is safe.'

'You go. You look all in. If you like, I'll ring you when she's home.'

Nikki stood up and pulled on her jacket. 'Maybe I should. I'm out on my feet and we need to be back at work at the crack of dawn.' She took her car keys from her pocket. 'Thanks for supper, Joseph. I appreciate it. And don't forget to ring me.'

The chilly night air brushed her face as she stepped outside, and to her relief, she saw headlight beams swinging round off the road. 'I guess we worried for nothing.'

A palpable wave of relief came from Joseph. 'Crisis averted.'

As Nikki drove out into the lane, Niall's Vauxhall swept past her. She caught sight of a smiling Tamsin giving her a friendly wave, and Nikki felt an acute pang of sadness.

Her Hannah should be doing that. Going out, having fun, meeting good-looking boys and getting told off by her mother for being late home. But she never would, not now.

As the dark outline of Cloud Cottage Farm rose up ahead of her, Nikki suddenly felt terribly alone.

CHAPTER TWENTY-THREE

Just after six in the morning, as Nikki was sleepily rinsing out her coffee mug, her phone rang. She picked it up, fully expecting it to be the station sergeant but Joseph's agitated voice jarred her into life. 'Say that again, and slower.'

'It's Tamsin. She went out for a morning run, and she hasn't come back.'

Nikki dropped the mug. 'I'm on my way over.'

Five minutes later she was sliding into a space between Joseph's station wagon and Tamsin's hire car. She jumped out and saw Joseph standing in the doorway.

'I didn't know she'd gone,' he stammered, his face contorted with worry. 'Sure, she has been going for an early morning run lately, but I didn't dream she'd go today. What the hell was she thinking?'

'Does she always do the same route?' Nikki gazed across at the remote marsh path but saw nothing moving.

'I think she does a circular run, along the sea-bank, then across the field path, down the road past your house, then back down the lane.'

Nikki bit on her lip. 'When do you think she went out?'

Joseph shook his head. 'When I showered, I guess, and that was over half an hour ago.'

'Surely her run would take longer than thirty minutes?' said Nikki hopefully.

'Twenty minutes max. And there's no one in sight, in any direction.' His voice was shaky. 'Oh, Nikki, I've got a very bad feeling about this.'

'Look, there's a good chance she's fallen, maybe twisted her ankle. The paths are full of ruts from the tractors.' She strode back to her car. 'You're fitter than me, you take the sea-bank. I'll drive along the road to the end of the far field, okay?'

As she slammed the car door, Joseph was already sprinting off along the rough track that led along the river bank to the marsh.

An hour later a squad car was touring slowly along the lanes of Cloud Fen, and several uniformed men and women in Wellington boots were scouring the footpaths that crisscrossed the area of marsh close to Knot Cottage.

Joseph and Nikki sat in the kitchen. Nikki heaped sugar into yet another cup of coffee.

'Her jog pants, sweatshirt and trainers have gone, and her day clothes are laid out on her bed, so there is no doubt of her intentions. Her phone has gone, but her house key and car keys are still here. I've rung her number a hundred times, but it's switched off.' Joseph got up and began to pace. 'And like most young people, her phone is her life support system, it's *never* switched off. She's been abducted, Nikki. There's no other explanation.'

Nikki passed him the drink and said, 'There's probably a dozen other explanations. We're just so aware of what has happened at Flaxton Mere that we can't think of anything else.'

'He's got her, I know it.'

Nikki looked at Joseph. She couldn't offer any more platitudes because, deep down, she thought he was right.

* * *

176

Rory moved uncomfortably in his sleeping bag. Across from him, half illuminated by the bluish glow of his laptop screen, he saw the hunched figure of Stuart Bass. He had been on his computer for most of the night. Rory sincerely hoped that he was emailing his forsaken bride, but frankly he doubted it. Most likely it was morbid research.

He turned away from the ghostly figure and decided that tonight they would go home, and sleep in proper beds with clean, fresh duvet covers that had been rinsed in meadow-sweet fabric conditioner and stored with lavender bags between them.

Rory sighed. It really comes to something when your dearest wish in the whole world is not for chilled Bollinger, but for a two-litre plastic bottle of fabric softener! He pulled the sleeping bag higher around his head. Just one more day down here with the army of forensic help that had accrued around them, and they should be able to have the nights at home.

He had barely slept, but even though he closed his eyes tightly, he was still horribly awake. For the first time since he saw the crypt, Rory had felt uneasy. He moved again, unable to find a soft spot on the canvas camp bed. It was probably sleep deprivation, but whatever, he felt disturbed and his thoughts were not comfortable ones. He kept seeing the figure of the bogus SOCO, and found it hard to believe that he had actually held a conversation with the curator of this museum of death.

Many times he had appeared in court as the expert witness. He had looked across at the accused and wondered about them. The drunk who had lashed out, gone too far, landed one too many punches, or the battered wife who'd been hospitalised once too often and had turned on her husband with a carving knife. Or maybe the battered husband who finally unleashed his hurt and shame and pushed his bully of a wife down the stairs. Murder was not usually served cold and alone, but came accompanied by steaming hot side-dishes of rage, passion or hatred. There were reasons. The deliberate taking of another life was never justified, but there *were* reasons. "I shot him because he broke into my house and threatened my family." "We fought because I found him in bed with my wife." "The baby wouldn't stop crying." He'd heard them all, but this killer was different. This killer was more like a collector, and the dead bodies his specimens, like beautiful butterflies.

Stuart Bass closed his laptop and the blue light was extinguished. 'Still awake?'

Rory raised himself on one elbow, and began to fight with the zip. 'Sadly.'

Stuart endeavoured to squeeze his large frame into his own bag. 'Thinking about your silent bedfellows? Or maybe the possible return of the murderous, axe-wielding SOCO? Ah well, sweet dreams.' He pulled on the zip, then groaned. 'Oh, bugger! What now?'

Two uniformed officers were approaching them, and from their purposeful stride, Rory guessed they were not going to offer to tuck him in.

'Professor Wilkinson! I'm sorry, sir, but we've had the order to evacuate.'

'What!' He fought to get out of the restricting bag. 'Is this some idea of a joke?'

'There's been a development, sir. You have to pack up immediately. Some HGVs are on their way to collect all your equipment and the remaining coffins.'

'Hell and bloody damnation! We are this far,' he held his thumb and forefinger a half inch apart, 'from finishing. What can be more important than nineteen bodies, for God's sake?'

The officer shrugged. 'Sorry, but DS Easter's daughter is missing, and if the worst case scenario is right and the killer has her, there is a high possibility that he will bring her here. That means you could be in danger as well.'

'In which case, better do as he says, mate.'

He felt Stuart's hand on his arm. Rory's heart sank. Stuart was right. They had no choice.

* * *

Dave thought Nikki had aged ten years overnight.

The news of Tamsin's disappearance had rocked the station, and when the DI called a meeting in the murder room, everyone turned up.

She began immediately. 'You've all heard what happened early this morning. I've just been told that one of the search parties has found signs of a scuffle.' She drew in a deep breath then added, 'And a piece of cloth was found in the mud. It had been soaked in chloroform.'

Dave let out a low whistle. 'That stuff is archaic!'

Nikki nodded. 'That's true, and I've spoken to the forensic team about it. It seems it's a very dangerous substance, much misrepresented in the whodunnits.' Her face looked haggard. 'It does work after several minutes, but it also causes convulsions and it can be lethal. He reckons that the point where the victim relaxes,' she swallowed, 'is not far from the moment of death, as it paralyses the heart muscles.'

Dave was heartily glad that Joseph was not in the room. For a moment all he could see was the bright face of Tamsin Easter. He dragged himself back to what the boss was saying with difficulty.

'I cannot stress enough how important it is to find Tamsin quickly, because there is another worrying fact about chloroform . . .' She paused. 'It can have a delayed effect. And in some cases, it can kill. So we need to get out there and find her. Now, this is how I suggest we tackle this.' She looked around the room. 'I want every member of the splinter group of the history society brought in. While we question them, I want all their houses and work premises searched. But I have no intention of holding any of these suspects for long.'

There was a low mutter of dissent, but she pressed on.

'Think about it! If they are connected in any way, they could lead us to Tamsin. Which is something they *can't* do if they are incarcerated in our custody suite. We keep them all under constant close surveillance. It's a hope, just a hope, but we have to follow it up. Now, apart from bringing in the suspects, our main search area will have to be the old airfield.

This time, however, we will not have our friendly guides with us.' She paused. 'This is not easy for any of us. Joseph is a valued colleague and we all feel deeply for him at this time, but I do ask you to stay focused.'

She looked into Niall Farrow's shocked face. 'Don't let your emotions take over. We have to find her, and fast. She is in grave danger. Go to it, and good luck.'

As the officers dispersed, Dave caught up with the DI. 'Guv, where's the sarge?'

'He's with the super. Being told to stand back and leave the investigation to us.'

'And will he, ma'am?'

'Would you?'

* * *

Frank Kohler and his sister, Simon Flower and the Brewers were being questioned in different interview rooms.

Nikki paced the murder room, cursing loudly to anyone who was within earshot.

'Where the hell are the others?'

Cat Cullen joined her. 'God knows where Marcus Selby is, but Andrew Friar has been picked up from a liquid lunch in a local bar. Pissed out of his brains — or appears to be. The officer who brought him in isn't too sure, so he's getting the FMO to check him out in case he's faking it.'

'And Joshua Flower?'

'His brother says he's gone on a ramble. Apparently it's nothing unusual. Joshua often goes out on the Fens, watching waterbirds and the like.'

'Very bloody convenient! ' Nikki almost spat the words out.

'We've got two officers at their house. They'll bring him in as soon as he comes back.'

'*If* he bloody well comes back.' Nikki's tirade suddenly evaporated. 'Cat, come with me. We need to speak to Simon Flower again.'

* * *

In a small windowless room, Simon Flower sat patiently, waiting to be seen. There was no lawyer present, and Simon had been told he was free to go at any point. He was purely assisting them with their enquiries.

Nikki slowly and concisely explained that Tamsin Easter had been abducted.

'My God! Tamsin?' His eyes widened and darted from one detective to the other. 'But that's absolutely terrible! How is DS Easter taking it?'

'Much as you'd expect,' said Nikki tersely.

The man sat shaking his head from side to side in apparent disbelief. Then he looked at Nikki and asked, 'Do you think this has anything to do with whatever has happened out at the airfield?'

Cat answered. 'We cannot rule it out, and because of your associations with Flaxton Mere, we need to know your whereabouts between five thirty and six thirty this morning.'

Simon looked astonished, then he shrugged. 'I was at home alone, probably showering or getting dressed around about then.' He paused. 'But I did ring work around six-ish. And they do log calls into the fire station.' He frowned. 'I was on standby to attend an industrial blaze out at Barley Gate, but I was stood down as another investigator was in the area. That's why I was at home when your officers called to search our house.'

'And your brother?' asked Nikki.

'As I said, out birdwatching. He often goes out before dawn.'

'It's now two o'clock, sir, and he's not returned. Aren't you worried?'

'Why? He's probably driven up the coast. My brother comes and goes. He's enjoying his freedom.'

'And he has no mobile phone?' asked Cat incredulously.

'He doesn't own one. He says they are anti-social.'

Nikki's eyes were hard. 'How convenient.'

Simon Flower sat back and stared at her. 'Ah no! You surely can't think Josh has anything to do with that lass disappearing? That's madness!'

'And what would you think if you were me?'

He sighed. 'I can see where you're coming from, DI Galena, but you don't know him. He'd never hurt a fly. He couldn't.'

'Well, we can't find him, Mr Flower. And our officers have checked all the places you said he likes to go, so where now?'

'I'm sorry, I have no idea.'

Nikki stood up and pushed her chair back. 'Then there's damn all else we can do. You had better get home, sir. And ring us the minute you hear anything or you clap eyes on your brother, understood?'

* * *

Dave drove Flower home, and checked on the surveillance car parked outside.

'Nothing happening. Quiet as the grave.'

Dave winced at the choice of words. 'We've put another car around the back, so keep your eyes peeled and we'll have the radios set on "talk-through." Let me know if anyone goes in or out. And if Professor Flower turns up, bring him in immediately.'

Dave had always believed that men should not show emotion, but as he drew into the station car park, he felt a lump in his throat as he thought about what Joseph Easter must be going through.

* * *

'Ma'am, we've picked up Marcus Selby.' Reg Jenkins entered the murder room. 'Been fishing. He arrived back well kitted out with equipment, and had a couple of fresh fish in his bag.'

'And Joshua Flower?'

The constable shook his head. 'Nothing, ma'am. We've notified all the local stations and circulated him as wanted, plus we've put out the details of his car.'

Nikki turned back to Cat Cullen, who sat staring at her notebook.

'Got something?'

'Not sure, ma'am. I've been going through some reports. Do you remember that the bodies from Flaxton Mere were sort of embalmed and herbs were used?'

Nikki nodded.

'Well, one of the beat bobbies had a word with the owner of that posh greengrocer on Lower Hill. He sells a lot of fresh "locally grown" herbs and he said that his supplier is one of our historians: Margaret Brewer.'

Nikki frowned, then said, 'A supplier, as in a herb-growing business? Did we know about this? Who interviewed them?'

'Me, ma'am,' Dave answered immediately. 'They never mentioned herb growing. They said they'd retired early and their hobby was the WWII airfield. But another thing about the Brewers — we're having trouble checking their background. In fact we draw blanks on practically everything they've told us.'

'Like what?'

'Employment, for one thing. The company that William Brewer said he worked for on a freelance basis seems to have disappeared. And we can't find a marriage certificate for them. I've been checking the registers and zero. Cat's taken over that one, guv,' said Dave. 'She likes paperchases.'

'Okay. Yvonne, time to practice your knowledge of botany, at the Brewers.'

Yvonne grimaced. 'I barely know my basil from my rosemary.'

'Good. Go check out their back garden, and without giving anything away, throw in some comment about the husband/wife thing to one of them, preferably her. Nothing heavy, just see how she reacts.' Nikki paused, 'And take Niall with you but keep an eye on the lad. I think he's got a soft spot for Tamsin Easter.'

Yvonne nodded, 'Of course, ma'am. And it's alright, I'd worked that one out for myself.'

'And what can I do?'

Nikki turned round the moment she heard Joseph's voice. 'You're with me, my friend. Either officially or unofficially, I don't care.'

'Thanks, Nikki. Luckily the super understands. He's told me all the things he's obliged to and asked me to keep a low profile, but I need to get out there.' He looked at Nikki imploringly. 'We need to find my girl. I *can't* get her back then lose her all over again. I just can't.'

'I know.' Nikki felt tears forming and bit them back. 'So let me fill you in on the morning's findings.'

When she had finished, Joseph nodded, then said, 'Joshua Flower. Has it occurred to you that he might be another victim?'

Nikki pulled a face. 'I can't say that I'd looked at it that way.'

'Worth considering?'

'Maybe.'

* * *

As the afternoon progressed, scores of uniformed officers continued the search for Tamsin Easter and Joshua Flower. They knocked on doors, picked their way through gardens and wasteland, stopped motorists and questioned numbers of vagrants and homeless people.

On Flaxton Mere, sombre-faced men, women and tracker dogs covered acres of marsh and farmland, hunting for anything that might lead them to the whereabouts of the missing girl and the history professor.

The airfield teemed with police officers. No one went below ground, and only the people working on emptying the crypt were allowed to leave. Overhead, a helicopter with a heat-seeking camera slowly circled the area.

Greenborough police station had become a giant magnet, attracting both the media and the general public, all demanding to be told the truth about Flaxton Mere. Finally the chief superintendent gave a statement. He kept it very much to a plea for help regarding the two missing persons, and chose to omit the full details of the horrific find beneath the airfield.

'Guv!' A young detective with strange, staring eyes and an uncanny knack of looking like a teenage drug addict stuck his spiky, gelled head around the murder room door. 'Sorry to interrupt, ma'am, but we've found Flower's car.'

Nikki, Joseph and Dave looked up sharply. 'Where?'

'A disused barn between the main road and the airfield. The chopper spotted it through a gaping hole in the roof.'

'And has anyone seen Flower?'

'No, ma'am, but we've increased the manpower down there. They've got all the entrances and exits well and truly covered. He hasn't gone onto the airfield.'

Nikki was not even mildly convinced of that. Joshua Flower knew that place better than any of them. If he wanted in, then she was certain he'd get in.

She looked at the odd, pale eyes and said, 'Okay, get forensics. I want that car brought back to the lab and stripped down to bare metal.'

'Already done, ma'am. They're on their way.' The young man left and Nikki turned to Dave. 'Are Yvonne and Niall back from the Brewers yet?'

'We're here, ma'am. Just got in.' Yvonne opened her notebook. 'Well, they certainly grow herbs, ma'am. Big time. They must have half an acre of them.'

'And how long have they been doing that?'

'Years. It started as a hobby that, well, grew. Thing is, they don't exactly sell them. They just ask for a small dona-tion to buy new seed and compost. It's not a business, it's just what they enjoy doing. Friends can walk in and help themselves, and businesses like the greengrocer pay what they think they're worth.' She leafed through her pad. 'I got her to give me a list of who she supplies, and I've found a familiar name, ma'am.' She looked at Nikki meaningfully. 'Professor Joshua Flower is a very good client.'

The DI stiffened. 'And why is that?'

Niall tilted his head on one side and added, 'She thinks he has a friend who makes something called potpourri? Reckons she's a local woman who makes dried flower arrangements and herb pillows for charity shops and church fetes.'

Nikki wasn't convinced. 'Check that out, guys, and what about their dodgy marital status? Anything on that?'

'As you say, ma'am, distinctly dodgy. Even though her old man wasn't there, Margaret Brewer clammed up tight.'

'Ma'am? Telephone, in your office,' Cat called out. 'Simon Flower for you.'

'I still haven't heard from Joshua.' Simon Flower sounded worried sick. 'I've phoned everyone I can think of, but no one has seen him. I didn't think too much of it at first, but now, well, I'm really concerned.'

Nikki wondered how much to tell him, then opted for the truth. 'We've found his car, Mr Flower, out near Flaxton Mere.'

There was a silence, and then she heard a long intake of breath. 'Well, I guess it shouldn't surprise us, should it? You know how much he loves it.'

'Yes, but he knows it's closed off because of our investigation, so why go there? To look for nesting waterfowl?' Her voice held a clear message.

'I . . . uh . . . I don't know.' His voice suddenly lost its strength. 'You think he's the one you're looking for, don't you? For whatever you found at the airfield, *and* for taking Tamsin.'

'We need to find him, Mr Flower, even if it's to eliminate him from our enquiries.'

'Can I help? I'm going stir crazy stuck here.'

'For now we need you to be there, in case he rings or finds his way home. I'm sorry, sir. We'll be in touch as soon as we hear anything.'

* * *

Superintendent Greg Woodhall gave Nikki a long, hard stare. 'This long-term dealer of death was already frightening the shit out of me, and now we have the daughter of one of our officers missing.' He leant forward in his chair. 'You've talked to this Professor Flower, Nikki. Do you think it's him?'

Nikki let out a loud sigh. 'Whatever I think, he knows more about that old airfield than any of the others. Plus his car has been found close by, and he's been purchasing massive amounts of herbs for years, and herbs were used extensively in the embalming process.' She paused. 'And he's missing.'

'Answer the question, Detective. Do you think it's him?'

Nikki bit her lip. Greg Woodhall had only been superintendent for a few months and she was used to Rick Bainbridge's way of working. But Nikki was too close to Joseph, and it was his daughter who was missing. She couldn't trust her own judgement. 'I really don't know, sir.'

'With all that evidence, Nikki, I should have thought you would be champing at the bit to get him into custody. Why the indecision? Was he so charming when you questioned him?'

Nikki looked miserable. 'No, sir, I wasn't charmed.' She thought back to the interview that she and Joseph had conducted in the Flowers' study. 'I admit he's fascinating to listen to, but after a while I found him patronising and I didn't like his tendency to talk *at* you, rather than to you. Joseph thought it was a university lecturer's habit, but I felt somehow belittled.'

'Academics can do that. Their knowledge can be pretty awe-inspiring. But don't forget, some of the most intelligent people can be totally without common sense, and that, I hope, is where we come into our own. Common sense, solid logic and basic observational skills will catch more villains than a university degree.' He looked at her. 'So, I ask again.'

'He might be a highly educated professor, but . . .' She paused, trying to recall the conversation. 'He was so *passionate* about RAF Flaxton Mere. Joseph saw how hard he tried to communicate his love of the place. Everyone seemed to look up to him. Without a doubt he is the leading light in the history society. If he is the killer, then surely he wouldn't be happy to have all and sundry traipsing around the perimeters of his secret crypt.'

Greg Woodhall peered at her over his glasses. 'Listen to yourself, Nikki, and try to think a little differently. Instead of passion, what about obsession? Consider him not as a leading light but as the dominant figure. And if he is the killer, what better way to show his superiority than to allow everyone else, including the impotent police force, to get within a hair's breadth of his underworld?' Greg's gaze never left Nikki's face. 'Think. When we talk about Joshua Flower, are we not describing a psychopath? And does that not strike you as just a little scary?'

Nikki closed her eyes and whispered, 'Oh, shit! But if that's the case, where does Tamsin fit into his plan?'

'The daughter of one of those who invaded and destroyed his life's work? Do you have to ask?'

CHAPTER TWENTY-FOUR

'Okay, Joseph. We are going to work on the premise that Joshua Flower is our man. I want every detail about the Flower family for three generations dredged up and pasted on the wall. Get the brother to help if you need to.' Nikki turned swiftly to Cat and Dave. 'You guys help Joseph, but first find out how the evacuation of the forensics team is coming along. I'm sure Flower is out there somewhere. He just won't be able to give it up. It's his Shangri-La.' Her face took on a grim resolve. 'If he is there, then I'm willing to bet that's where we will find Tamsin.'

* * *

Cat glared at her computer screen. 'C'mon! You lazy sod of a machine . . .' Then she gave a whoop of delight. 'I knew it! She's not his wife at all!'

'Got something?' A young detective constable called Pete Mitchell looked at her with raised eyebrows.

'Something, certainly, but I'm not sure what it means. The Brewers are not married. So why pretend they are?'

'Search me.' Pete leafed through a heap of papers. 'Cat, do us a favour? Help me tie this up. The sarge wanted it sorted, but now he's asked me to get to work on the Flower family tree.'

Cat stared at the folder. 'Ah, the dead surveyor from the underground chamber.'

'Yes. I went back to Flaxton Mere and the man who recognised him remembered hearing him talk to Karl Shine, and apparently he had a pronounced Irish accent. I've put out a few feelers with the *Garda* and the Northern Ireland guys. All the details are in the folder. Would you have time to follow them up for me?'

'No sweat, my friend. The Brewers' matrimonial status can wait. I'm on it.'

An hour later, a smiling Cat sauntered over to her colleague, placed the folder on his desk and grinned broadly. 'Mission accomplished, Pete. Meet Michael Finn from County Clare. His gorgeous good looks stirred up a lot of bad memories in the Emerald Isle. It seems your enquiries created something of a stir, as Mr Finn is well known to the authorities for an assortment of very nasty offences.' Cat raised her eyebrows. 'As in related to terrorism, plus robbery, unlawful violence and possession of firearms, to mention but a few. *And*,' she added with considerable emphasis, 'it appears he's something of a genius when it comes to building construction and land surveying. He has degrees coming out of every orifice. Now what on earth was he doing wandering around Flaxton Mere?'

The young detective leaned back in his chair and raised both hands. 'I haven't the foggiest, but the boss will be delighted that we have an ID. So, would you like to tell her, or shall I?'

* * *

In a corner of the murder room, PC Reg Jenkins sat and stared at his notebook. Something wasn't adding up.

'What's the problem?' Dave called across the room.

Reg slapped the side of his head and almost shouted, 'Wrong fish!'

'Pardon?'

Reg explained. 'Selby said he was fishing in the private lake down at Fenhouses, but he had two roach in his bag. Well, there aren't any roach in that lake, it's stocked with carp. I know, I fish there myself. I caught a smasher a few weeks back. I use luncheon meat for bait, and sometimes . . .'

Dave pulled a face. 'Thanks for the tip, Reg, but what are you actually saying?'

'That I'd like a butcher's in his freezer. Those fish didn't come out of that lake. In which case, where was Selby when Tamsin went missing?'

Nikki had caught the end of the conversation. 'Get out there now, Reg. And bring him straight back if you're not happy with what he tells you.'

* * *

'Damn and blast it! How can they say we're in danger! After my little tête-à-tête, security's been so tight you can't cough without filling in a request form signed by the chief constable. They could have let us finish up.' Rory watched as a group of policemen lifted the last coffin into the back of the wagon.

'Don't blame them, mate. One, there's a young girl missing, and two, you're far too precious to waste.' Stuart patted him affectionately on the shoulder.

'We could be losing valuable evidence.'

'At least they borrowed a refrigerated lorry for you to keep your bodies in until you need them.'

Rory grinned for the first time in hours. 'Oh yes, from the local supermarket! Pray that they emptied it first! Guess what *your* breakfast sausages have been stored with, Mrs Grimsdale!'

'That's more like the Rory I know and love!' The forensic archaeologist yawned. 'Shall we go?'

'As soon as the boys in blue have cleared out. I want to do one last check, just to make sure we haven't missed anything.'

* * *

'Run that past me again, Joseph.' Nikki gulped down a strong black coffee.

'It's Selby, ma'am. We've just heard from Castor Fen. He's done a runner.'

'Where was the car that we had watching him, for God's sake?'

'There's a side door. It led out to a wooded area between two properties. He must have slipped out that way.'

'Put out a call, Joseph. I want him found and deposited in our custody suite until we know what the hell is going on!'

* * *

Cat grabbed the printout from the paper tray and ran to the DI's office.

'Ma'am! The Flowers' ancestors. Joshua's father's family were master builders who, according to RAF documents, were involved in the original construction of the proposed super-station beneath RAF Flaxton Mere.'

Nikki rubbed at her temples and thought swiftly. 'Really! So when the war was over and the old airfield fell into disuse, Daddy takes sonny boy and shows him the secret bunkers, the underground rooms, and all that.'

'Looks that way, ma'am. But we still keep finding inconsistencies with that damn history society. I know the professor is our prime suspect, but we thought you should see this.' She placed some sheets of paper in front of Nikki. 'We're not sure if this means anything or not.'

Nikki scanned the printouts. 'Ah, Frank Kohler's father was not just a cabinetmaker but did a nice line in coffins too, and as he got out of Germany for political reasons, he might have used his talents to help our own war effort.' She puffed out her cheeks. 'Why did Kohler junior not just tell us?'

'Probably the same reasons that the Brewers lied about being married. Skeletons in the cupboard.'

'Yes, what is all this about the Brewers?'

'I'm absolutely certain it's incest. They're brother and sister. It shouldn't take much to prove it, but unless you say otherwise, I'll put it on the back-burner until we have our psycho banged up.'

'What a can of worms we've opened in that innocuous history society! But yes, that can wait.' She read on, then laid the papers on her desk. 'Anything more of interest from Professor Flower's past?'

'The psychologist has been through everything we managed to pull together on Joshua Flower, and he says the profile is pretty damning. There are several points that stand out — his inability to hold down a job for one thing.'

'Mm. He admitted to Yvonne that he couldn't settle for long.'

'He has no real friends, either.'

'Other than casual ones, birdwatchers and the anoraks in his club.'

Joseph entered the room and sat on the edge of her desk. 'We've just picked up his home computer. IT is checking the hard drive.'

'Good. How is the brother? He rang me this morning. He sounded grim.'

'Pretty shaken. He can't get his head around the fact that his brother may not be all he believed him to be. He offered to help us in any way he can, but I think he's told us everything he knows. Poor bloke. He feels a deep loyalty to his brother, and part of him is certain that we are going after the wrong man, but he can't deny the obvious. Joshua's disappeared, and if he did go off on some innocent walkabout, then his timing leaves much to be desired.'

'Excuse me, ma'am.' The detective with gelled hair and odd eyes peered around the door. 'Just heard from the SOCO that went out to Flower's car, ma'am. He's found a sack in the boot, full of herbs.'

Nikki nodded, half to herself, half to the others. 'Then that just about clinches it. Thank you. Tell pathology we'd appreciate a report as soon as they can.' Nikki's hand reached out to her ringing phone. 'Sir? What? Yes, of course, we're on our way.'

She almost threw the phone down and grabbed her coat from the back of her chair.

'Joseph! Get the car! We have to get to Flaxton Mere. They've found Joshua Flower.' Swiftly she turned to Cat. 'Stay here. Keep me posted on everything that comes in. We have far too many loose ends, and I need you to be my eyes and ears here in the hub.'

'Yes, ma'am. I'll keep you fully updated.' Cat looked worried and a little sad that she wasn't in with the action. 'You take care out there, guv.'

Nikki looked over her shoulder and said, 'Good God, woman, I've got about fifty officers with me! I'm safe as houses!' Yet she was touched by the warmth in the younger detective's voice.

* * *

Lights swept the fen. Shadows assumed fantastic shapes then disappeared, only to be replaced by others. The decaying ruin of the watchtower had taken on the appearance of a haunted abbey, and almost on cue, a mist began to roll in from the marsh.

Someone who had no official part in the manhunt sat hunched and low in a small hollow. Protected by a few scrubby bushes and a tangled pile of concrete debris and brambles, the figure was well hidden. 'Please,' the voice was a whisper, 'let me last long enough to see this through. So much is at stake. Please?' The last word drifted off on the night breeze and was lost in the mist.

* * *

'This way, ma'am. The super is here already. He's waiting for you.' A uniformed sergeant met their car. Nikki glanced around and saw that their own men had been joined by an ambulance, the crews of two fire appliances, plus an armed unit.

Superintendent Greg Woodhall and a uniformed chief inspector stood together in the entrance to the control tower like two granite statues.

Greg placed a hand on her shoulder. 'One of the search parties found a small storeroom that we'd missed. It seems to have housed dozens of boxes of dried herbs and lavender. When we found it, though, most of them had been emptied.'

'You'll see why in a minute.' The chief's words sounded ominous. 'The second thing the search team found was another small chapel. That's where we're going now.' He and Greg entered the building, beckoning for Nikki and Joseph to follow them.

The long corridor was filled with officers, yet it was eerily silent. They moved through a low, open door that led to a short tunnel. This opened out into a much older chamber. A cordon ribbon was tied across the opening. The chief inspector stopped. Inside, an arc lamp had been set up, its white light glaring against the pale stone of the walls. Nikki shaded her eyes and squinted. Then she gasped.

The chamber appeared to be as old as the burial crypt, although much smaller. Directly in front of her were two squat stone columns, supporting a semi-circular arch. In the centre was a raised stone platform.

Cushioned by a thick bed of herbs and dried wild flowers, lay Joshua Flower.

He was fully clothed, lying on his back, and both arms hung over the edge of the stone ledge. The slender fingers of both hands pointed gracefully downward, coated with blood from the deep lacerations in his wrists. Huge pools of it had formed around the base of the slab and spread out across the flagstones.

Nikki noted a pocket-knife, blade extended, lying just a few centimetres from the right hand.

'My God! Pre-Raphaelite or what?' Joseph breathed.

Nikki placed a hand on Joseph's shoulder. 'What now, sir?'

Greg Woodhall leaned against the wall and stared for a moment at his dust-covered shoes. 'This place is sealed. No one comes in. I want Rory Wilkinson *and* Richard Foley to see this scene exactly as it is. The search team had the presence of mind to disturb nothing, and I had the paramedic go in purely to officially verify what was patently obvious. Other than that, the place is untouched, and I want it to stay that way until the pathologist and the psychologist have seen it.' He paused. 'We should make an official identification.'

Joseph looked at the super. 'Surely we should wait until the body is back at the mortuary, sir? This is all rather gothic. The poor sod could have nightmares for years.'

'No. Bring him here.'

Nikki added, 'That's a bit tough, isn't it, sir?'

The superintendent gave a little shrug. 'I think his imagination would give him more sleepless nights than seeing what really happened. Think about it. They both lived and breathed this place. Sorry, but I think it's fitting that Simon Flower sees how his brother chose to end his life, don't you?'

Nikki wasn't too sure, but said, 'Shall I go and break the news, and bring him in?'

'Perhaps Joseph would do it, Inspector. I need you to hear what Foley has to say.' He waited until Joseph had left, then added, 'Frankly, I didn't want Joseph hearing the psychologist's profile of the madman who might just have abducted his daughter.'

* * *

Richard Foley, the criminal psychologist, stared thoughtfully into the chamber. Out in the main corridor, beneath lights now powered by one of the generators, both the chief inspector and the superintendent were pacing up and down.

'Where the hell is bloody Wilkinson?'

The officer Greg spoke to looked worried. 'We can't find him, sir. His team and their stuff have all been moved out, but the professor and his associate are nowhere to be seen.' He looked suitably abashed, adding, 'Mobiles don't work down here, and even the radios are iffy in some parts. But his car is still here, so we'll keep looking.'

'Dead right you will!' The chief inspector snorted impatiently, and beckoned Nikki forward down the narrow passage to talk to the profiler.

'First impressions, Doc?' Greg Woodhall had his hands pushed deep into his pockets and his shoulders were hunched forward.

Richard Foley stared at the scene before him. 'I've looked at every aspect of this case, and very little follows the textbook profile of a serial killer, until you look closer. Then there is a pattern, of sorts.' He looked away from the body. 'This is his last act: the finale.' He turned to Nikki and the chief inspector. 'It's not unusual for psychopathic killers to kill themselves when they know it's all over. It allows them to keep control over the situation, and not give in. Some like to be caught, they love the publicity and see it as a triumph. "Look, I've been killing for years and you never even knew. I'm so much smarter than you." It is all about power.' He looked back at the tableau. 'Yes, I think he would see this as a suitable end to his work. His special place has gone. The people that he killed and "cared for" have been taken away. There is absolutely nothing left for him.'

'What about Tamsin?' asked Nikki, very glad that Joseph was not here, listening to the psychologist's words.

Foley shrugged. 'If Flower took her, he will have had a reason. It would be perfectly logical to him, but, DI Galena, this man was insane. Hence we can't follow logical patterns of conjecture.' He rubbed at his temple. 'We mustn't forget that she is the daughter of a policeman, so it might have been a gesture to get back at the police for destroying his lair, or she was his swansong. His final kill.'

The thought of Tamsin lying dead in this nightmarish underworld turned Nikki's blood to ice. She nodded and went out for some fresh air.

'Guv?' Dave called from where he stood with a group of armed policemen. He spoke quickly to them, then headed in her direction. 'I just had a call from Cat. They've picked up

Selby. The fishing trip was a cover for a meeting with a journalist. He was on his way to Peterborough when we stopped him, to clinch an exclusive with one of the nationals. So we can forget him, he was just trying to cash in on the situation. And regarding Joshua Flower — another nail in his coffin, so to speak — we already knew that his father and grandfather were builders, but apparently years ago builders often played other roles in village society, and the Flowers doubled up as the local undertaker!'

Nikki groaned. 'Oh Sweet Jesus! He learnt everything at his father's knee.'

Dave nodded. 'So what happens now? We feel like a congregation where the wedding's been called off. No one's quite sure what to do.'

'We are going to have to take this place apart. The clock is ticking against finding Tamsin, but she has to be here somewhere.' She felt a pang of fear when she looked around at the size of the airfield. 'I'm waiting for the go-ahead from top brass, then we'll continue the search, so hold your positions until further orders.'

Dave returned to his team, and Nikki was left looking across at what had once been home to heroes — ace flyers and many other brave men. She looked up into the dark grey sky and muttered a rare prayer for the girl's safety.

* * *

As the car drove across the fen, bringing Simon Flower to be reunited with his brother, neither Nikki nor Joseph realised that a pair of sharp, glittering eyes were following their progress. The concealed hollow was no more visible in the moonlight than it had been before the moon rose.

A figure moved, painfully flexing stiff, aching shoulder blades, and looked back towards the control tower. There was a different atmosphere about the place and the men and women who waited there. On the breeze could be heard voices, the bark of nervous laughter. Something serious had occurred in those grey, disused buildings. It would soon be time to move.

CHAPTER TWENTY-FIVE

Simon Flower was grey, unshaven, and walked with his shoulders drooping forward and his head bowed.

In the long corridor, the superintendent took him to one side. 'You are here because I thought it best.' He looked deep into the other man's eyes. 'If I'm wrong, tell me. You don't have to go in.'

To Nikki and Joseph's surprise, Simon said, 'I need to see for myself, sir. I have a very vivid imagination and I don't want to spend my life speculating about the manner of his passing.'

'Good man.' Greg indicated for Nikki and Joseph to leave, and led Simon into the passageway. It was a few minutes before they appeared again. If Nikki thought he looked pale before, what he looked like now was beyond description.

'Can we get out of here?' His voice cracked with emotion. Nikki was more than happy to get him back to the surface.

The three of them leaned against the wall of the old watch office.

'I've seen it, but I can't believe what I saw. Joshua couldn't have done such terrible things.'

Nikki answered, her voice soft and full of compassion. 'We are *so* sorry, Simon, but there is evidence, and more is coming in every hour. And the worst thing is that Joseph's daughter has still not been found.' She touched his arm. 'I know this is a lot to ask after what you've just seen, but have you any idea where Joshua might have taken her?'

Simon shook his head and said nothing.

Joseph added, 'Have you got anyone to talk to, any other family or close friends?'

He remained silent.

'We do have counsellors, Simon. Victim support has specially trained bereavement officers. It will help to talk, you know.'

'I know, I know.' He gave a mirthless laugh. 'I'm with the fire service, aren't I? Not only have I offered just that advice to families who've lost loved ones, but I've been there before, when our mother died. It didn't help my brother and me then, and I don't think it'll help now. Thanks all the same.' He turned to Nikki and added apologetically, 'I'm sorry, I know you mean well, but no one, *no one*, could understand. How could they?'

Simon turned to Joseph. 'I'm sorry about your daughter, really I am, but I don't know how I can help. I thought I knew everything about this place, but my brother's knowledge . . .' He shrugged. 'It seems I'd barely scratched the surface. I'd help you if I could, really I would.'

His gaze wandered towards the door of the building below which his brother lay. 'DI Galena? You said the pathologist would be seeing Joshua soon? When I went down there to identify him, it such a shock that I couldn't stay. But now, do you think I could spend a few moments with him, before forensics take over?'

Nikki looked at Joseph before saying to Simon Flower, 'We really shouldn't. It's completely against protocol . . . Hey, you know about contamination.'

'Please.' There was a world of pain in that single word.

Joseph raised an eyebrow and shrugged.

Nikki grimaced. 'Look, since you're part of the emergency services and you do understand the score, I'll take you back down, but I'll need to stay in the background, okay?'

They walked back towards the old weather-beaten door. 'Just keep well outside the cordon.'

* * *

Dave walked over to some of his colleagues, realising too late that Dice, the fireman-cum-amateur-detective, was giving them the benefit of his extensive knowledge of serial murder.

'Davey-boy! My old mate! This is a good one, huh?'

Dave smiled weakly and nodded feebly. 'Sort of, Dice, sort of.' In order to deflect the man's impending disquisition, he said, 'Hey, Dice? How did you get your nickname?'

'Me? Yeah, well, it's all about risk, isn't it? Dice with death, and all that. Had my share of close shaves, I can tell you. Dangerous game, fire-fighting.'

'So you're a risk-taker, are you?'

'Only calculated ones.' Dice looked hurt. 'I'm a professional, not like Schizo. He was worse, made Rambo look like Bambi.'

'Who's Schizo?'

'I worked with him years back. I swear he didn't know the meaning of fear. I've seen him do things you would not believe.' Dice shook his head. 'Some of the guys thought he was some kind of superhero, others just wouldn't work with him.'

'And you?'

'I thought he was dangerous, and weird with it. Nothing fazed him. Burns cases that would turn the strongest stomach, they were nothing to him. Bodies trapped in burning cars and spitting like a hog roast, no problem.' He stopped suddenly and stared at Dave. 'But you must know all this?'

Dave frowned. 'I don't know what you mean.'

'He was here earlier. *You* know him. He caught a lungful of toxic fumes and got slung off the appliances, stuck out to grass as an investigator. The bloke you were just talking to, Simon Flower. He's Schizo.'

* * *

201

Dave moved away from the group, thinking about what he had just heard. Simon Flower certainly did not come across as some heroic Red Adair, or even as reckless or irresponsible. Dave bit at his thumbnail. Now why was this information troubling him? Slowly he walked back towards the entrance to the bunker, then stopped. This was hardly the right time to tackle the poor blighter about his career. Maybe it would be better if he offered to chauffeur Flower home again, then perhaps he could throw in a mention about the fire service . . . On the other hand, to hell with all that! He needed to tell the boss.

* * *

'Sir?' Nikki stood in the opening into the tunnel and looked hopefully at Greg. 'Don't quote the rule book at me, because I know this is unorthodox, but Simon wondered if he could have a moment with his brother before the pathologist arrives. I'll stay close by.'

'I don't see why not, since he's used to crime scenes. After all, we're stuck here until bloody Wilkinson gets here.' He frowned and took her to one side. 'But wouldn't he rather wait until later, when his brother's tidied up and ready for the chapel of rest?'

'He seems pretty adamant, sir. I think he's beating himself up about running out just now.'

'Oh well, as long as he knows that he must not cross the cordon.'

The superintendent stood back, and Nikki beckoned to the drooping figure of Simon Flower.

A moment later, Nikki returned and stationed herself at the end of the tunnel where she could keep a watchful eye on the grieving man. 'He knows not to approach the body, sir. He just wants to say goodbye.'

Greg nodded. 'Fair enough.' He stared at her solemnly. 'We've still no news on Tamsin Easter, and it's critical that we locate her soon. God knows what state she will be in.

202

That stuff he used on her sounds horribly unpredictable.' The superintendent let out a disbelieving sigh. 'It's not something that a modern young abductor would use, but you can just imagine that potty old professor and his bottle of poison can't you?'

Nikki agreed. 'It is all very *Dr Jekyll*.' She glanced down the tunnel towards the man who stood motionlessly in the opening to the chapel. She noticed that his shoulders shook slightly. She supposed that he was finding his last words to his dead brother very difficult indeed. She began to feel like a voyeur, and she lowered her eyes. 'When can we resume the search, sir?

'A massive sweep is being organised now, Nikki. We have all those guys upstairs, plus a search and rescue team that has just arrived from the Peak District.'

Nikki sighed. They couldn't do any more. She just hoped they would be in time.

'Greg! Nikki! A word, please.' The uniformed chief inspector was marching down the corridor with Dave hurrying along in his wake.

'Listen, is Simon Flower still here?'

'Yes, sir.' She glanced back down the passageway to the tall shadowy figure. 'He's with his brother. I was just about to go and get him.'

'Hold on.' He held up his hand. 'Dave was telling me that Simon Flower had something of a reputation during his fire-fighting career. Has he ever mentioned anything to you?'

'No, sir, what kind of reputation?'

'Two schools of thought, apparently — intrepid hero or foolhardy maniac.'

'*That* Simon Flower?' Nikki indicated towards the tunnel. 'Are you quite sure, Dave?'

Dave nodded. 'His tag was Schizo. And the fire chief has just confirmed it,' he added quickly.

'Fire service?' Nikki clamped her jaw together tightly, as a sickening cramp twisted her gut. 'Flower? Oh shit! Simon Flower!'

The corridor went silent and everyone looked at her. Her voice dropped to little more than an urgent murmur. 'The bogus SOCO? Rory Wilkinson said his identity card was official, but not one of ours. It could have been a fire service ID card! And the man told Rory his name was Sean Fowler, but you've seen the size of the print on our passes! It could easily have been Simon Flower! And in that poor light, who would have known?'

'Are you absolutely sure, Inspector?' the chief demanded.

Nikki closed her eyes. 'Yes! Oh God! I think we've been blaming the wrong brother! Simon Flower killed his brother Joshua, and made it look like suicide!'

'Right! Let's get him out of th—'

The chief's voice was cut off by a dull thud that echoed and reverberated through the corridor like a minor earthquake, throwing the group of officers to the stone floor.

Amid the groans, Dave managed to extricate himself from the tangle of arms and legs. 'Okay! Who's hurt?'

Nikki gasped out, 'Just winded, I hope. Dave, if you're not injured, take whoever's left standing and go find Simon Flower! Then we evacuate this hellhole!'

CHAPTER TWENTY-SIX

'Rory! This is madness.' Stuart Bass tried to force his considerable bulk through a gap between a stone pillar and a rotting wooden door frame.

'How come no one found this before? Half the force has been tramping around these tunnels for days, and we just stumble blindly into it! It beggars belief!'

'Rory! I mean it! We shouldn't be wandering around here. This place is a bloody labyrinth! No one knows where we are, and you've said it yourself, this part was undiscovered until you fell, arse over tip into the opening. The search commander is going to make mincemeat out of us if we don't get back. And for the last time, I can't get through this bloody gap!'

'You do whine, Stuart.' Rory shone a torch down the long, wide passage in front of him. 'This is awesome! You could drive a tank down here!'

'Probably the original idea, but sadly as I'm not built like a stick insect, I'll never see it, and I'm def—'

A dull, bone-jarring thud shook the ground.

'Christ! What the hell was that?' No longer wedged, Stuart pushed himself up from the floor and brushed a thick coating of dust from his jacket. 'Come on, Rory. I've had it. Enough is enough. Rory? Oh shit!'

The gap through which he had endeavoured to fit himself was no longer visible, and a great pile of loose rubble and timber had taken its place. He began to claw at the blockage, then stopped and smiled with relief. From the other side, he could hear a string of colourful curses. 'Glad to hear that you're not buried under this impromptu cairn, Wilkinson.'

'Likewise, Bass. But I think I'm a fraction too late in heeding your sage advice to get out of here. I'd need a JCB to get through this lot. Can you get back okay?'

Stuart looked around. 'Yes, the tunnel behind is undamaged. I'll go for help.'

'Okay, and meanwhile I'll check this place out. Maybe I can get out from this side.'

'For God's sake don't wander off, you prat! Just stay put! I'll be back before you know it.'

* * *

'Are you alright, Nikki? Let me help you up.' Joseph was kneeling by her side.

Nikki gasped her thanks and leaned heavily on her rescuer. The pain knifed through her chest as she breathed, but she was pretty sure it was nothing life-threatening. 'Jesus! That hurts!' She looked around her and saw Greg, blood dripping down his face, making his way toward her.

'You okay, Nikki? Joseph?'

'We'll live. You?'

'The same.'

'And everyone else, sir?'

'The chief's taken a bang on the head. He's out like a light. It looks like just cuts and bruises for the rest of us.' He wiped his bloodied forehead with the back of his hand. 'Are you sure you're fit to walk back to the surface? One of the men has gone up top to get a paramedic for the chief. Maybe they should check you out too?'

'I'm fine, sir. Just winded and maybe a cracked rib, but what the hell *was* that?'

'I dread to think.' Joseph's face was ashen. 'But we should get out of here as quickly as possible.'

'Not until Dave's back. Let's pray he managed to get hold of Flower.'

'I don't think he was that lucky.' Greg's face was grave as he looked along the dust-filled tunnel, to where Dave was limping back. Alone.

* * *

Flaxton Mere seemed to have been thrown into confusion, and the watcher on the fen took advantage of it. Dressed in dark clothing, there was little to differentiate this figure from the others, so it was easy to move unobtrusively through the undergrowth and slip into the now unguarded pillbox. In moments, the shadowy form had disappeared down the stone steps and into the darkness below.

* * *

'It looks as if two of the marsh tunnels have collapsed, sir! And part of the big storeroom has come down. One wall has completely caved in, and water is slowly making its way through.' A uniformed officer, caked in mud and slime, sat heavily on a low wall.

'Is the fire service down there?'

'Yeah, they are trying to staunch the flow by blocking it further back up the tunnel, but it's pretty useless. The force of the water is becoming too much for them.'

'Okay, well done, now get yourself back to your original team, constable. I want all units out from underground and accounted for.'

As the officer limped off, Nikki looked anxiously at Greg. 'If the tunnels are flooding, what about Tamsin? And Rory and his friend? They've been missing for hours. They might all be in serious trouble.' She coughed and winced.

'I know, but the fire service are pumping the water, and we'll get everyone back down there as soon as we've done a head count.'

'I'm not thinking about the tunnels, but the danger from Simon Flower. If he's holding them prisoner and they're not already dead, God alone knows what ideas he might have for them!'

Dave and Joseph joined them.

'Dave found something when he went after Flower,' said Joseph.

'When I got into the chamber, it was empty, apart from the body.'

'But there was only one doorway! What is he, bloody Houdini?' said Greg.

'Sir, everyone was so intent on preserving the scene, they *assumed* it was a dead end. There's a small opening behind one of those two columns, right behind the body. You can't see it from the front of the room. I saw footprints through Joshua Flower's blood and they disappeared behind the pillar.' Dave rubbed at his leg. 'There were some steep steps. I started to go down, but there was no one in sight so I thought I should get back up. A team of uniforms with an armed unit are down there now.'

'Then let's pray he leads them to Tamsin.' Joseph's voice cracked with emotion, and Nikki grasped his arm.

'Hang on in there, Joseph. We'll find her. I know we will.'

* * *

Stuart Bass reported to the superintendent exactly what had happened, and a group of men were sent to try to clear the blockage and rescue the pathologist. As Stuart had feared, Rory, who was not renowned for his patience, had not waited to be rescued.

'This is not going to be easy, Mr Bass.' One of the men stood with his hands on his hips. 'If we attempt to move that stone pillar, we could have the whole roof down, along with half the marsh.' He drew in a lingering breath. 'And as the obstruction is on the other side, it looks like we need specialist equipment to shore this up before we chip our way through.' He shrugged. 'I hate to say this, considering the circumstances, but I'm going to have to ask the fire department for help.'

* * *

'Attention, please! This area is being evacuated! Would all personnel and their vehicles move away from the buildings! Repeat, move away from the buildings! The RV point is now the hangar area near the main gate.'

Nikki, Joseph and the superintendent looked at each other.

'What's this all about? We still have Tamsin, and our idiot of a pathologist, along with a serial killer, down in the bowels of the earth. Why the hell are we pulling out?' Nikki felt her stomach churn with fear.

A uniformed inspector hurried towards them. 'We are evacuating for a very good reason, Superintendent Woodhall. The fire crews have found timers, charges and detonators. The collapse of the tunnels was not a natural disaster. Someone has invited half the North Sea into Flaxton Mere!'

Nikki swallowed hard. In her mind she saw Yvonne Collins' report of her conversation with Joshua Flower when they first checked out the pillboxes. *Simon Flower, ex Royal Engineers.* Her mouth went dry. She looked at Joseph, and saw his jaw had dropped in horror. He was whispering his daughter's name over and over.

Greg Woodhall clapped his hand on Joseph's shoulder. 'Hold on, man. We don't even know for sure that your girl is down there. And if she is, we'll do our damnedest to get her out, you know that.'

'If he can't have his sanctuary, then he's going to make damned sure no one does!' Joseph bit back an oath, then turned and walked away, leaving Nikki with the two other officers deciding on an emergency evacuation plan.

* * *

Joseph was on a knife-edge. It was like being back in the battlefield, but with Tamsin caught in the crossfire. He sat on a half demolished wall and tried to collect his thoughts.

'Sarge?' Dave Harris, Niall Farrow and a big athletic man that he had never seen before were hurrying towards him. 'Sarge, this is Stuart Bass, forensics, mate of our missing pathologist. Listen, sir,' Dave looked distraught, 'we've just heard the evacuation order and we know exactly what's at stake, but we are not going if there's a chance Tamsin and the prof are down there somewhere. We wanted you to know that we are going back underground to look for them.'

Joseph closed his eyes for a moment, then stared at the men. 'Apart from getting yourselves killed, you'll get the book thrown at you for this, you know that?'

'Absolutely, sir.' Niall's jaw was set. 'And I also know I couldn't live with myself if that maniac gets to Tamsin without me doing something about it.'

'Okay, count me in. If we ever get out alive we'll think of some excuse. Let's go.'

As the four men ran back towards the control tower, Stuart said, 'Damn you, Rory Wilkinson! I should be on a sun-drenched beach with the most beautiful woman in the world right now, not trying to save your spotty arse from some psycho!'

CHAPTER TWENTY-SEVEN

Someone had caught him off-balance and he was easily over-powered. This didn't surprise him. The nearest Rory ever came to physical exertion was a little light-hearted wrestling before a more intimate form of exercise.

Opposite him, lying on a heap of blankets was the unmoving form of a young woman. She had regained partial consciousness a couple of times, but she had been too sick and confused to tell him anything. He guessed she was Sergeant Easter's daughter, and he was desperately worried about her condition. The sickly-sweet odour in the small room must be chloroform, Rory thought. He knew all about that insidious substance.

She needed medical help, but Rory was certain she wasn't going to get it from the motionless figure with the strange, bright eyes that sat a little apart from them.

Rory had known from the moment that he entered the room that, for both their sakes, he had to find a way of staying alive long enough to allow the police to find them. He tried to remember everything he'd heard or read about serial killers, but understandably his thought processes were not functioning too well. At least he seemed to have a little time, as neither of them had been immediately dispatched. The silent man was obviously waiting for something.

They were in a small room, lit by a battery-powered lantern. Both men sat on wooden chairs. The only difference was that Rory's feet were secured to the chair legs, and his hands were bound tightly together with duct tape.

Rory shivered. He'd heard that killers were often egotists, believing themselves superior and above, or apart, from the law. Maybe he should try flattery? Rory also knew that the last thing he should do was beg for mercy, and at that moment, blubbering was the only thing he felt capable of.

Simon Flower broke the silence. 'They are leaving now.'

'Ah. We'll have the place to ourselves. Alone at last, as they say.'

Flower looked at the pathologist with interest. 'You can joke? Aren't you frightened?'

Rory swallowed and pulled tentatively at his restraints. 'Shit-scared, old son. Absolutely terror-stricken.'

'You certainly don't seem it.'

'Well, rumour has it that you are a crazed psycho, teetering on the brink of total madness, but if you'll forgive my saying so, you don't seem like that either.'

Flower frowned. 'I'm not sure how to take that.'

Rory did not answer. At that moment he was dearly wishing that he'd chosen psychology for a career. He held on to the thought that the police would not abandon them. He just had to try to stay alive long enough to give the boys in blue something to rescue. 'Call me psychic, but I *knew* we'd meet again. We have met before, haven't we?'

'Oh yes. And I had every intention of making that happen, Professor Wilkinson. After all, I couldn't leave without thanking you personally.'

'Ah. For desecrating your beautiful mausoleum, no doubt.'

Flower looked around the tiny shadowy cavern. 'It wasn't a mausoleum, Professor. It was a sanctuary.' He spoke softly.

'Why did you kill those people?' Rory immediately regretted his words. What the hell was he trying to do? Hasten their execution?

Flower shook his head. 'If you recall our conversation of the other day, you told me my sanctuary was a peaceful place, a place of beauty. So in my eyes, *you* never actually desecrated anything. You chose to work and sleep there, which was extraordinary. You respected it. When I said I wanted to thank you, I actually meant it.' He smiled coldly at Rory. 'And why did I kill those people?' He shrugged. 'Why does anyone do anything? Because they want to? Because they like it? Because they can?' He paused. 'In my case, I enjoyed taking their dirty, stinking bodies and making them whole again. I mended them, took away their addictions and their filthy habits. I nurtured and looked after them in a most professional manner, and finally gave them peace.' The handsome face suddenly became hard. 'You saw my work! Was I *ever* a butcher? And where exactly is the difference between you and me?'

'I've never seen better,' said Rory truthfully. 'Your methods of preserving the bodies were a perfect synergy of modern science and historically documented embalming techniques. Amazing. Simply amazing.'

Flower nodded. 'And your thoughts on the difference between us?'

'You took their lives before you gave them the benefit of your expertise. I only offer them my care and considerable virtuosity when they are already dead.'

'Very good, but you have to admit there's a fine line. Most "normal" people could never find it in them to do your job.'

Rory thought the "fine line" was actually a chasm, but decided he was probably wise not to argue the point. 'True. True.'

He glanced at Tamsin. She was still breathing.

Flower moved closer, and Rory could feel the man's breath in his face. 'What sort of lives did they have anyway? You must have noticed the kind of victims I chose? Vagrants, methies, junkies, runaways.' The eyes were glittering dangerously.

'I see. You chose the ones that wouldn't be missed.'

'Of course. But that's not the whole reason. It goes deeper than that. I took those filthy bodies and made them clean. I made them pure! I turned their stinking, tainted selves into something wholesome again!' Flower leapt from the chair, knocking it over and scaring Rory. 'But who cares anymore? It's over now, stolen from me by one man's greed. That miserable, avaricious glutton called Shine.'

Rory saw the man's hands begin to grip and release as he paced the room. 'He's dead now, Simon.'

'Which is a great pity. Because no matter how he died, I could have made it a thousand times worse for him.'

Rory watched the man's composure begin to show signs of unravelling, and he tried to redirect the conversation. 'Er, can I ask you something? As a professional, I have to say that the equipment you use is excellent.' Rory deliberately faltered. 'Oh, I guess it doesn't matter what I say now.' He sighed a little theatrically. 'You see, the police couldn't trace where it had come from. They still have no idea.'

'Mm . . . ?' Flower continued to pace around. 'Oh, that. It's American, shipped over via the continent. The quality was better than ours.'

'How on earth did you get it here?'

Flower stopped pacing and said, 'It was ostensibly for a university project for Joshua's college. I paid for it online. It was easy to fake the documents and forge a signature. I collected it from the docks myself, hired an HGV, and under cover of night, drove it directly into one of the derelict buildings and put it together at my leisure.'

Rory nodded sagely. He wondered if the man talked at such length to all his victims. He chanced another swift look at Tamsin and wondered if he dare mention her precarious condition.

Flower went to the door and listened for a while before picking up the fallen chair, sitting back down and tapping his foot on the stone floor.

Rory decided it was definitely not a good moment to refer to Tamsin's plight. He searched around in his addled and exhausted brain for some other topic of conversation to spin out the time. 'I know I'm being a pain with all these questions, but if you don't mind me asking . . . ?'

The man gave him a suspicious scowl. 'You're becoming a nuisance.'

Rory smiled and nodded. 'That's me. A right vexation to the spirit. But something is really bothering me.' He looked enquiringly at Flower.

'What now?'

'It's about the most recent ones, the last two, uh, visitors to your sanctuary. When I examined them I realised that they were quite different to your other . . .' He fought to find an alternative word for *victim*. '. . . your other works of art.'

Flower seemed to relax. 'Ah, you could tell, could you? That surprises me. But yes, neither of them were part of my plan. They just needed to be dealt with because of their actions.' He threw Rory a conspiratorial smile. 'Mind you, I must say it made a very pleasant change to deal with such wholesome bodies.'

'The dark one was certainly something of an Adonis.' Rory tried to sound casual as he fought back a wave of nausea.

'And the other one was spotless! Apart from that stupid, childish tattoo there was not a blemish on him. He even smelt good.' Flower sighed. 'Something of a waste really. He blundered into one of the old buildings just as I was opening one of my secret entrances, so,' he shrugged, 'I didn't have much choice.'

'And the other one? The one with black hair?'

Flower's frown creased into furrows. 'His death is that bastard Karl Shine's fault. He was checking the ground, with some very sophisticated high-tech equipment, dangerously close to my sanctuary and to my devices.'

'Devices?'

'My carefully planned *son et lumiere*. Sound and light to keep the curious away and the superstitious cowering in their beds.' He gave a little laugh. 'Funny how modern techniques used in the army for distraction purposes can be adapted to feed people's irrational fears of the unknown.' He shook his head. 'All wasted now.'

'You must have spent a lot of time here,' Rory said with what he hoped sounded like empathy.

'Every hour God gave me. Whenever I could, day or night. This is my spiritual home.' He suddenly let out a low growling noise, stood up and began pacing again.

Rory's shoulders drooped. He knew he'd pushed his luck about as far as it would go.

Flower continued to pace, then looked at his watch and flopped back down into his chair, chewing on the inside of his cheek.

After a few minutes, Rory chanced saying, 'We seem to be waiting for something.'

'Yes, we are.'

'And . . . ?'

Flower dropped his head into his hands. 'I'm so very tired. There's such a lot to do.' When he looked up, Rory saw hollow eyes and a pallor of skin more appropriate to his own dissecting table. 'I have opened the exits at the furthest point on the marsh. They are flooding as we speak,' he gave Rory another creepy, conspiratorial smile, 'but not as badly as our friends in the police and the fire service think. When I was here last I prepared a few diversions. I left them a few little *indications*, detonators and the like. I've also just brought down a storeroom wall, purely for effect.' He pointed to a small device, something like a TV remote, clipped to the waistband of his trousers. 'My time in the Royal Engineers was not for nothing.' He rubbed his eyes, 'Actually, I have about two hours, until the high tide comes in and then, with the aid of this little beauty, no one will ever try to put a housing estate on Flaxton Mere again.'

Flower stood up and walked towards the door. 'Not long now and we'll be able to go. But we need to tread very carefully, because of my rather clever *diversions*.'

'Go where?' Rory felt a frisson of fear, then a glimmer of hope. He had used the word "we."

'Back to my sanctuary, where else?'

The glimmer of hope died.

Rory knew that he would never be able to keep up the banter, even though their lives depended on it. He sagged forward, and although a terrible ennui was creeping insidiously through his mind, he desperately tried to keep going.

'And what about that lovely young woman over there?'

Flower's head tilted, with a quick, twitchy motion. 'Yes. Now there we have a problem. Some people don't react too well to my preferred form of sedative, and she was one of them. So, what to do?' The question hung in the air.

'I could take a look at her, if you like? I admit that my patients are usually beyond help, but I am still medically trained.'

'Nice one, my friend. But I don't think so.'

Rory's head felt as if it would explode. How long could he keep this up?

Opposite him, pacing slowly backwards and forwards, Flower seemed to be in some sort of trance. He was muttering the name "Joshua" as he walked.

'At least your end came in the place you loved,' he concluded.

Rory felt as if iced water had been thrown at him. 'Joshua is dead too?'

'Oh, he's dead! Very dead! But,' Flower straightened up with a jerk, 'you don't think that I . . . ?' He let out a staccato, barking laugh. 'He died by his own hand.' Flower sank onto the chair, slowly shaking his head. 'Joshua knew I had to be involved. He believed I'd done something terrible.'

Rory's head ached and it was becoming difficult to concentrate. He knew that he was being used as a sort of confessor. And Flower seemed to want to take his time with his story.

'In the end I told Joshua everything. Everything I'd done over the last twenty years, and how and why. And I told him of my plans to give Flaxton Mere back to the sea. But he never answered me . . .' The voice broke. 'He never said a word. He just hugged me and cried like a baby.' Flower drew in a deep, noisy breath. 'He told me he loved me, then he ran from the house, jumped into his car, and I never saw him again until an hour or so ago when the police brought me here. He's in the small crypt . . .' He stopped, mid-sentence, then stood abruptly and said, 'It's time to go. I have to attend to one or two small jobs.'

'And the girl? What about Tamsin?' asked Rory desperately.

Flower slowly turned. His expression was steely cold. 'I've lost everything. This place was my life. So I'm going to share a little of that hurt with the detective sergeant. Let's see how *he* feels about losing something rare, precious and beautiful.'

CHAPTER TWENTY-EIGHT

Dave frowned. 'This place is a bleeding rabbit warren. They could be anywhere, and didn't someone say half the North Sea might soon be making its way down the tunnels?'

Stuart Bass was unconvinced. 'I think that's a diversionary tactic to get us out. He's buying time.' He bit his lip. 'While Rory and I were working in the burial chamber, we talked about how tormented the killer must be to be separated from his holy of holies. Rory always said that he'd be unable to stay away.'

'I thought the same thing,' said Dave. 'And now there's nothing left. He's even taken care of his brother. What's the betting he goes back to his sanctuary to kill himself?'

'And my Tamsin, and Rory?' Joseph asked slowly.

Stuart shrugged. 'Where else would he take them?'

'Then I think we'd better get our arses down there!' Niall was hair-spring taut.

Stuart started to agree, then they heard the sound of policemen's boots running up the long corridor behind them.

The uniformed inspector raised his eyebrows when he saw them. 'Your superintendent said you should all be severely reprimanded and read the riot act for this, but unofficially you might welcome a bit of support. Is that right?' He smiled.

Dave grinned. 'You are so right, sir! Now, what do you think about this?' He told the inspector of their assumption.

The man looked grim. 'Okay, it's worth a shot. I'll radio the RV point and tell them to give us another unit as back-up. Now, show us where the hell in this labyrinth we're supposed to be going.'

It took about ten minutes to get back to the surface and reach the pillbox. Then Joseph and the three others, backed by the small armed unit, slipped silently down the stone steps and into the burial chamber.

The inspector spread his arms and the policemen moved, in pincer formation, around the big crypt. Joseph looked across at him and raised his hands, palms up, as if to say, "What now?"

'He'll be here.' The inspector raised his finger to his lips. The support team concealed themselves, and the chamber appeared to be empty.

Out on the fen, a team of armed police officers formed a cordon around the pillbox. Underground, hidden and silent, the inspector's team waited.

One of the generators was running and a few safety lights had been left on. Above the soft humming, Stuart could hear his own heart beating. It felt as though the whole chamber were reverberating with its steady thump.

Then there was another sound. Footsteps, and a shuffling, dragging noise. It was coming from a narrow corridor behind the stone altar which had supported the mortuary table.

When Stuart saw the figure of his friend hobbling into the chamber, it was all he could do not to cry out. Then he saw that Simon Flower was immediately behind Rory, tightly gripping his arm, and holding him close. Stuart gritted his teeth. There was no clear shot for the marksmen.

He watched the two men stand perfectly still, and gaze wordlessly around the chamber. From his hiding place in the shadows, he wondered if Flower would feel as he had, that the magic had gone.

Stuart heard a low, almost inhuman keening sound that seemed wrenched from the depths of the man's dark soul.

Flower flung his prisoner to the ground, and ran howling down the steps towards the crypt, and the empty shelves where his victims had been stored. He stood in the archway leading to the burial chamber and gazed at the desecration. He slowly turned back to his prisoner. The pathologist was clasped tightly in the arms of his friend.

Stuart shuddered as the killer took a step towards them. Then, to his relief, the man halted, as the barrels of six automatic rifles pointed at him.

'Simon Flower! Keep your hands where we can see them! Then get down on the floor! Now!'

Flower froze. His hands were held out and his eyes were wide with anger and confusion.

'Get on the floor!' Two of the armed officers were slowly approaching him.

Rory whispered, 'He has a radio device on him. He's going to bring this whole place down!'

Before Stuart could open his mouth to warn the marksmen, Flower began to bend forward, as if complying with the order, then Stuart saw his hand slowly reaching toward his waistband. As he yelled out, he realised that his was not the only voice screaming.

Still on his feet, but motionless as a statue, Flower remained crouched over. Then his hands reached desperately behind his back, trying to grasp at something.

Stuart's brain refused to compute. There had been no shots fired.

Then he saw Simon pitch forward, the thick, black handle of a knife protruding from an ever-widening dark stain on his back. He crashed onto the ancient flagstones, revealing a white faced, black-clad figure that had emerged from the shadows behind him.

She looked down at the motionless body, and said, 'For Anson.'

CHAPTER TWENTY-NINE

'Rory! Where is Tamsin? Is she here?' Joseph threw himself down next to the pathologist.

'Yes . . . yes . . .' Rory stuttered, the shock beginning to take hold. 'She's back down a long corridor through there.' He pointed to the back of the altar. 'She's in some kind of big storeroom. We'll have to hurry, she's very poorly.' Leaning heavily on Stuart Bass, he staggered to his feet. 'Joseph, we have to go very, very carefully. I think Flower might have booby-trapped the room.'

Joseph exhaled, then drew in a long deep breath. He'd been in this sort of situation more times than he liked to count, but now his daughter was the one under threat.

'Are you strong enough to guide me?' he asked Rory.

'As long as Bass here continues to be support staff.' He looked anxiously towards Stuart.

'Let's go.'

'I'm coming too.' Niall Farrow moved quickly forward, but Joseph grasped his arm and held him back.

'Not this time, Niall. You're keen, dedicated and full of all the right things, but once Rory shows me where Tamsin is, I have to go in alone. This is no place for policemen or pathologists. It's a job for a skilled soldier.'

Niall was about to protest, but saw Joseph's face and backed off. 'Just get her out of there, Sarge.'

Joseph squeezed the young man's shoulder. 'I will. You can rely on that.' He turned to Rory and Stuart. 'Ready?'

'Ready.'

As Joseph moved down the tunnel, memories of his years in the army flooded back. Then he thought of his daughter. The sounds of war — the gunfire, and the roar of engines — faded and his daughter's voice filled his ears: "There's plenty of time."

Joseph increased his pace. Yes, there damned well would be plenty of time.

Finally he heard Rory say, 'Slow up. This is where I believe he started to place some sort of traps. Tamsin is in that room to the right, about twenty yards further on.'

'Okay. Now, you and Stuart get back. There's no telling what might happen. Get yourselves to safety, and tell PC Farrow to make sure that absolutely no one comes down this passage, understand? No one.'

As the two men made their way back, Joseph surveyed the passage ahead of him.

He could not move forward until the way was clear. He squatted down on his haunches.

It seemed an eternity before he spotted the first wire. Indirectly it was Simon Flower that made the discovery possible. He had left battery-powered lanterns at points along the underground tunnel, and although the light was patchy, Joseph's sharp, well-trained eye caught a tiny glint of metal wire.

He waited until the sounds of the retreating men had faded and then he sat a little longer, calming his racing mind. Then he began a careful evaluation of the situation.

'I naturally assumed that your request for privacy did not refer to me?'

Joseph swallowed hard. He hadn't heard Nikki until she was close to his shoulder.

223

'It damn well did. Now get back up that tunnel, and stay there.'

'Bollocks. Now, what exactly are we dealing with?'

Nikki's voice gave him enormous encouragement and left him weak with fear at the same time. 'You're not going to go, are you?'

Nikki sounded almost scornful. 'You need to ask?'

Joseph exhaled. 'Okay, this is what we have. There are trip-wires at intervals between us and the room where Tamsin is. I suggest they are little more than fireworks, something that would give a warning blast to scare us, but not bring down the roof.' He bit hard on his lip. 'I'm pretty sure he wanted me to find my daughter before he killed me. As I see it, I've got two choices. I either cut the wires and risk setting it off, or I deliberately trigger it. It will take far too long to disarm the damn things.' He turned and looked at Nikki. 'Back off a bit and protect yourself as best you can. I'm going to check them out.'

After a few minutes he returned to where Nikki was crouching low on the floor.

'It's safe. He must have set them up in a hurry. They were simple trip-wires to small detonators, so I've disconnected them. Now, just walk behind me and keep to the centre.' He pointed down the passage to the aperture leading into the room. 'Rory says that Tamsin is on the floor against the far wall. I'm assuming there will be other devices between us and her.' He stopped abruptly. 'Now, Nikki, forget that it's my daughter in there. We can't let emotion get in the way. This is a puzzle to be solved, nothing more.' He looked at her anxiously. 'Can you do that?'

'I used to do it every time I visited Hannah. I'm a pro. Just tell me what you want me to do.'

'Right. Follow me, then wait in the doorway, just in case anyone else thinks my order did not apply to them. I'll check out the entrance, and if I feel it's safe, you follow my instructions to the letter.'

For once in her life Nikki did not argue. She walked softly behind him, then placed herself in the middle of the doorway and stood still.

Joseph knew what to look for. 'At least he's used old methods. If he'd had more time, I'm willing to bet he would have used laser beams.' He moved slowly into the room, murmuring as he went. 'Possible pressure pad beneath this uneven stony area.' He stepped carefully around the broken flooring. 'Shit, this feels so familiar. Only back then, I had a bomb disposal squad behind me and a unit of armed operatives.'

'You've got all you need, Joseph,' said Nikki softly. 'Your expertise, your instincts, your gut reaction.' She paused. 'And someone who believes in you.'

'Dad?'

Joseph froze. Tamsin was turning towards him, her eyes unfocused and her body uncoordinated and floppy. 'Stay still, sweetheart! I'm coming to get you. Just stay perfectly still.'

The girl mumbled something, then reached out towards him and tried to get up. 'I feel sick.'

'Don't worry about it, Tam. You're going to be fine.' Nikki's voice was calm and commanding. 'Now listen to me. You must keep perfectly still and do everything your father tells you. Understand?'

Tamsin sighed and lay back down.

'I can't afford for her to try to get to me.' For the first time, Joseph sounded agitated.

'Breathe! And calm down, Joseph. She's fine. Just do what you were doing. I'll worry about Tamsin for you.'

It seemed to Joseph that it took hours to reach her. In fact it was only four long minutes. In those minutes, Nikki had constantly calmed and cajoled, and he had crept and sweated his way across the room.

And now he had to make the journey back through the shadows, and he had to do it carrying his half-delirious daughter, all five feet eight inches of her.

'Joseph! Hold it. Don't start back yet,' Nikki called out. He saw her turn and move out of his line of vision. Dave's voice spoke urgently in the darkness, then she returned to her position in the doorway. 'Okay. Whenever you're ready, my friend. It's time to go home.'

'That's Dave out there. What does he want?'

'Time for that later. Just get your girl out of this bloody Hades. The chopper is up there on standby, with the paramedics and an emergency doctor. She'll be in hospital in no time — if you just get your sodding finger out, Sergeant!'

That flash of the old Nikki made everything clear. He knew the way forward now.

Joseph took a deep breath, whispered, "I love you" to his daughter, and purposefully retraced his footsteps through the minefield. He didn't know that water was beginning to flood the tunnels.

* * *

As Joseph made his way to safety, Rory sat wrapped in a thermal blanket in the superintendent's office in Greenborough police station, and tried to recall everything that the murderer had told him. Shock was making him shiver, but he doggedly answered the questions.

'And he denied killing his brother?' The superintendent looked incredulous.

'Emphatically. In fact, I would swear that he didn't. I think Joshua tried to take the blame, to protect Simon and give him a chance to get away.'

'Even after Simon had admitted what he had done?'

'Definitely. There is some deep history there, and I'm sure you guys will dig it up. I suggest Joshua knew perfectly well what had sent Simon off on a killing spree lasting two decades,' said Rory. 'You've told me how Joshua was found, and I think he staged the whole theatrical shebang to confuse you.' He drew the blanket closer around him. 'Even down to the poorly-hidden car and the herbs in the boot. Everything.'

Greg Woodhall leaned back in his chair. 'Maybe you're right.'

Rory accepted a mug of tea from Yvonne Collins, and held it in both hands, savouring the warmth. 'What will happen to that poor woman, Stephanie Taylor?'

'She'll be sent for psychiatric assessment. But there's not a jury in this land that would put her in jail for what she did — or I sincerely hope not,' said Greg vehemently.

'How did she know where he'd be? How did she get inside?'

'Easy,' answered Yvonne. 'She's been hanging around the fen since before we found her brother. Reg kept taking her home, but in the end he gave up and let her wander. He felt sorry for her so he talked to her quite a lot, perhaps a bit too much. Anyway, she got it into her head that the killer would come back to his killing grounds, and she was right.'

Greg nodded. 'And you know the chaos when Flower first brought down those tunnels. She was dressed in dark clothing, so she mingled with all the other helpers and walked straight in!'

'Revenge served cold,' murmured Rory.

CHAPTER THIRTY

'For the umpteenth time, Tam, he'll be along when he's finished his shift.' Joseph shook his head and looked with great affection at his daughter. 'And I have a few things to sort out this evening, so you will have Niall Farrow all to yourself.'

Tamsin shifted around in the hospital bed and tried to get comfortable. 'You did bring in my make-up bag, Dad? And my hair straighteners?'

Joseph nodded. 'And the other twenty-plus things that you just can't live without.'

'God, I look a mess.'

'You look beautiful. You always look beautiful.'

Tamsin pulled a face. 'Bullshit! I'm a mess, and you know it.'

Joseph smiled down at her. Tamsin had been incredibly lucky. She had been carefully monitored for three days, and now the doctors were pretty sure that there would be no delayed effects from the chloroform. In a couple of days' time, if she continued to improve, she could go home.

And right now home meant Knot Cottage. Tam was quite happy with that. She had Skyped her mother and reassured her that Joseph hadn't tried to either kidnap or murder her. In fact he had saved her life, and she had decided to stay on for a while. She had told Laura that she wanted to be fully recovered before she flew, but Joseph knew there was more to it than that. Even through her hazy, drug-induced stupor, she had known it was her dad who had walked the line to carry her to safety.

There had been a major shift in Tamsin's attitude towards him, and now they had something to build on. There was a kind of irony about what had happened. After all, the one thing Tamsin hated most about him had been the very thing that saved her. His skill as a soldier had allowed him to carry his daughter through a minefield, and survive.

He gave a little smile of amazement as he placed her things in her locker. For the first time in years, Joseph Easter actually felt good about himself.

* * *

Nikki sat in front of Greg Woodhall's desk and leafed through a pile of reports.

'These pretty well explain most of it.' She rubbed her tired eyes.

'It's still hard to believe that Joshua would protect his murdering psycho brother.' Greg leaned forward, elbows on his desk and his chin resting in his hands.

Nikki grimaced. 'I think Joshua felt he'd failed his little brother years ago.' She sat back, closed the folders and sighed. 'When I rang you to tell you about the family being under-takers, I also had Cat tracking down old medical reports on the mother's death. I'd already ascertained that the father died of a heart attack, but the mother died of uterine cancer when Simon was thirteen. He took it very badly indeed. He worshipped her.'

'But thousands of kids lose their adored parents and okay, they may suffer terribly, but they don't become killers.'

'Possibly they didn't witness their mother being beaten and raped by some rootless tramp she had tried to help.'

'Oh shit!' Greg's head fell forward.

'The cancer set in shortly after. Simon swore the tramp had killed her.' Nikki shook her head. 'The psychologist believes that young Simon could not come to terms with the atrocious assault on his mother, so he started killing vagrants and doing his best to make them into something clean and respectable, thereby giving his mother back her dignity. Later, it became an obsession. He liked killing and dealing with the bodies.'

'Surely he must have had something in his make-up to make him take that path?'

'Doc Foley said the same, sir. His mother's death was the trigger. He always had the propensity to kill.'

'Hence, I suppose, his ability to deal so casually with all the horrific things he saw in the army, and as a firefighter,' Greg whispered almost to himself. 'Schizo.'

Nikki opened up another report. 'It says here that even as a youngster, Simon helped his father look after the bodies. Showed quite an aptitude apparently. His father had high hopes that he would take over the business. He was very intelligent, but even at school he had what one teacher described as "a morbid and almost obsessive interest in death."'

'Shame no one ever looked closer at that boy. Could have saved a lot of lives.' Greg drew in a long breath and leaned back in his chair. 'By the way, before I forget, I've had a memo from the Met. They've found a close link between our dead Irishman, Michael Finn, and one of their nastiest villains, a man named Freddie Carver. Now Carver has recently done a very hasty bunk from our shores, and apart from waving flags in the streets by way of celebration, they have uncovered intelligence that said he was preparing for a very big job in the City. Now he has pulled the plug and legged it.'

Nikki frowned, 'And what does that mean exactly?'

'The Met reckon Michael Finn was the king-pin for the proposed heist. Without him, Carver was scuppered.' Greg gave a smug smile. 'Back in the day, Carver used to be a bosom buddy of another family of villains called Shire. Ring any bells?'

'We wondered if Karl Shine's real name was Daniel Shire.' Nikki exhaled. 'Of course! Those shady surveyors were Freddie Carver's men. Karl went to an old family friend for help, and managed to get his right-hand man topped!'

'No wonder Shine's murder looked like a professional hit, because that's exactly what it was. Family friend or not, Karl Shine managed to shut down one of the smoke's biggest criminals, and he paid with his life.'

'So that's something else we can cross off our To Do list, and with all I've got on my plate, I'm eternally grateful.'

'Oh Lord, Nikki! It's your father's funeral the day after tomorrow, isn't it?'

Nikki placed the folders on his desk. 'Yes, sir. I'm taking the next couple of days off. She shrugged. 'Then I guess it'll be back to business as usual.'

'I suppose you haven't considered something as ridiculous as a holiday, have you? It's what most normal people would do after the kind of ordeal you've just undergone.'

Nikki stood up and made for the door. She turned and threw her boss a withering look. 'Sorry to disappoint you, sir, but I don't do holidays. And there is one particular criminal I still haven't laid my hands on.'

CHAPTER THIRTY-ONE

At least it was a sunny afternoon, and the grounds at the crematorium looked green and lush, with well-kept beds of yellow daffodils lining the drive.

Joseph had been surprised to see how many work colleagues had turned up to support Nikki.

As the final music played and they all filed out of the chapel, he saw Nikki standing alone by the door. She looked as smartly dressed as he'd ever seen her, and her bearing said she was totally in control. Although her lips smiled as she began to shake hands with the stream of mourners, he felt a wave of intense loneliness emanate from her.

Without a word he eased past the vicar and stood beside her. Her tired smile said it all.

'Almost over,' he whispered, touching her arm lightly. 'And you were brilliant.'

'I didn't feel it.' She looked at him with relief in her eyes. 'But at least I didn't crumple in front of everyone.'

It took some while for the chapel to empty, and then they made their way out to the area set aside for the flowers. Even though Frank had requested donations to charity, Nikki had decided that she couldn't cope with seeing a plain coffin, and had ordered a single tribute, a beautiful spray of pure white lilies and ice-white roses that cascaded along the full length of the coffin.

As soon as they were outside, Joseph left Nikki greeting distant friends and relatives and accepting condolences from strangers, and went to talk to Greg Woodhall.

'No Tamsin with you?' asked the superintendent.

'She begged me to let her come, sir, but I had to pull rank. She really isn't strong enough yet to cope with something like this. That damned stuff really messed up her system.'

'Thank the Lord, you reached her when you did, Joseph.' Greg looked back towards the tall chimney of the crematorium and shivered. 'The alternative doesn't bear thinking about.'

Joseph nodded grimly. 'Luckily she doesn't remember too much of her ordeal, but in a fuzzy kind of way she does recall that it was Nikki who stopped her from crawling across that booby-trapped room. And for that, she's one grateful young woman, I can tell you!'

'I'm sure she is.' Greg looked around at the familiar faces. 'Good to see such an excellent turnout from our guys, and as funerals go, it really was a lovely service, although I don't know how Nikki managed to read that poem.'

Joseph nodded. He still got goose-bumps when he thought about it. He'd told her not to put herself through it, to let someone else read, but Nikki had insisted. As soon as she began he had known it had been the right thing to do. He understood that it was something she had needed to do for her father.

Joseph looked around the crowded area and tried to spot the man Nikki had pointed out before the service as being Frank's old friend, Tug Owen. Then he noticed a lone figure walking away from the others in the direction of the car park. 'Excuse me, sir. There's someone over there that I really need to have a word with.'

Joseph left the superintendent and hurried after Tug. 'Mr Blake-Owen?'

'Ah, it seems that my carefully planned escape has been foiled.' The older man turned around and gave Joseph a weary smile. 'DS Joseph Easter, I presume?' He held out a hand and his grip was surprisingly strong. 'Call me Tug.'

'I just wanted you to know that I haven't told Nikki anything about what we talked about. I think it should come directly from you.' He looked at the old airman and decided to trust him. 'Nikki needs to know absolutely everything. Her father died before he could tell her something that was very important to him, and now that very thing is vitally important to Nikki. She deserves the truth, Tug, whatever that might be.' Joseph looked at the doctor earnestly. 'Look, the last place Eve was seen was at Flaxton Mere, and nineteen bodies were found interred there. I thought that she could have been one of the victims, but our pathologist has confirmed that no one brought out from that underground crypt resembled Eve. And that leads me to believe that she's still alive.'

'She is.'

It was a woman's voice.

In his haste to talk to him before he drove off, Joseph hadn't noticed that Tug's car was not empty. As he turned, the door opened and a tall, upright woman stepped out.

The black-clad figure stared at him, and Joseph stifled a gasp. She was much older, but there was no mistaking the woman in the photograph.

'Joseph, I'd like you to meet Eve Anderson.' Tug's voice held the slightest tremor. 'Eve, this is Joseph Easter, a close friend of Frank's girl, Nikki.'

Joseph numbly took her outstretched hand, and in an instant understood why Frank had been so desperate for Nikki to find her. 'It's a pleasure to finally meet you,' he stammered.

He was looking into Nikki's eyes and seeing the same quizzical upturn of Nikki's lips. But these eyes were not smiling. They were the eyes of someone bereaved, someone who has lost her soulmate.

'Did you . . . ? Were . . . were you in the chapel for the service?' Joseph managed to ask.

'No. I stayed outside. I had no right to be here.' The voice was deep and well-spoken.

'I think,' said Joseph slowly, 'that you had *every* right to be here.'

'More than most,' added Tug Owen. Then he turned to Joseph. 'And I agree that Nikki needs to be told, although not by me. It should come from Eve.'

'But not today,' the woman said firmly. 'Nikki has enough to deal with, and I have no wish to intrude or cause her any further distress.' She smiled at Joseph. 'Let Nikki say goodbye to her father. Let her grieve. Then,' she paused, 'if she'll agree to see me, I promise that I'll explain everything.'

Joseph took a deep breath and held it. He looked into those eyes that were so familiar, and knew instantly that Frank Reed had never had a "first wife" and there had never been a "tragic accident." He asked, 'Do you really mean *everything*?'

'Everything,' she replied, giving him a direct and knowing stare. She opened the car door and began to get back in.

Joseph stepped forward and held onto it, preventing her from closing it. 'I'm sorry, Ms Anderson, but the problem is you really don't know DI Nikki Galena. She's not your average woman, and she doesn't *do* unsolved cases, of *any* kind. And more than that, if she finds out that I've been standing here talking to her mother, and then let you drive away again, she'll personally see me hung, drawn and quartered! Come back with us now. Please?'

'I can't. This is not the right time.'

'I think it's the perfect time.' Joseph tilted his head to one side. 'Look, I'm under no illusion that this will be easy for either of you, but I'll guarantee there's no one Nikki would rather meet. Today, or any other day.' His smile broadened.

The woman shook her head. 'Alright, although this is not what I had planned.'

Joseph said, 'We need to go now before you change your mind. After everything that's happened recently, I really don't think I'm up to facing the wrath of Nikki Galena.'

THE END

The Last Flight

The angels have wept that one of their own
should be kept from the skies for so long.
Now their gain is our loss that you're finally free,
to go back to the place you belong.

The heavens are yours to play with again,
to fly and to dive and to soar,
And now you have wings of your own to use
and no need for an engine's roar.

Sadness, you said, was returning to earth
while your soul still glided above,
Now freedom is yours to fly for all time
And know that you do it with love.

For although my heart is now cleft in two
because your face I no longer can see,
the thought of you soaring through Cerulean blue,
brings solace and comfort to me.

Now starlight, and sunlight, and crystal clear air
will not allow me to mourn,
as you speed your way to eternity,
through diamond night to golden dawn.

Poem written by Nikki Galena
For her father,
Wing Commander Frank Reed DFC AFC RAF

AUTHOR'S NOTE ON THE LOCATIONS

I am fiercely proud of my adopted home of Bomber County and have always had an interest in the WWII airfields. Part of Lincolnshire's heritage is its involvement with the RAF in the last war and I very much wanted to incorporate one of these fascinating places into a Nikki Galena novel. And so I do hope the reader will forgive me for taking literary liberties with the topography of the area. I am aware that there are very few underground structures here due to being reclaimed land, but I have 'moved' RAF Flaxton Mere closer to the marsh for the sake of the story.

THE JOFFE BOOKS STORY

We began in 2014 when Jasper agreed to publish his mum's much-rejected romance novel and it became a bestseller.

Since then we've grown into the largest independent publisher in the UK. We're extremely proud to publish some of the very best writers in the world, including Joy Ellis, Faith Martin, Caro Ramsay, Helen Forrester, Simon Brett and Robert Goddard. Everyone at Joffe Books loves reading and we never forget that it all begins with the magic of an author telling a story.

We are proud to publish talented first-time authors, as well as established writers whose books we love introducing to a new generation of readers.

We won Trade Publisher of the Year at the Independent Publishing Awards in 2023. We have been shortlisted for Independent Publisher of the Year at the British Book Awards for the last four years, and were shortlisted for the Diversity and Inclusivity Award at the 2022 Independent Publishing Awards. In 2023 we were shortlisted for Publisher of the Year at the RNA Industry Awards.

We built this company with your help, and we love to hear from you, so please email us about absolutely anything bookish at feedback@joffebooks.com

If you want to receive free books every Friday and hear about all our new releases, join our mailing list: www.joffebooks.com/contact

And when you tell your friends about us, just remember: it's pronounced Joffe as in coffee or toffee!